THE INVISIBLE MAN

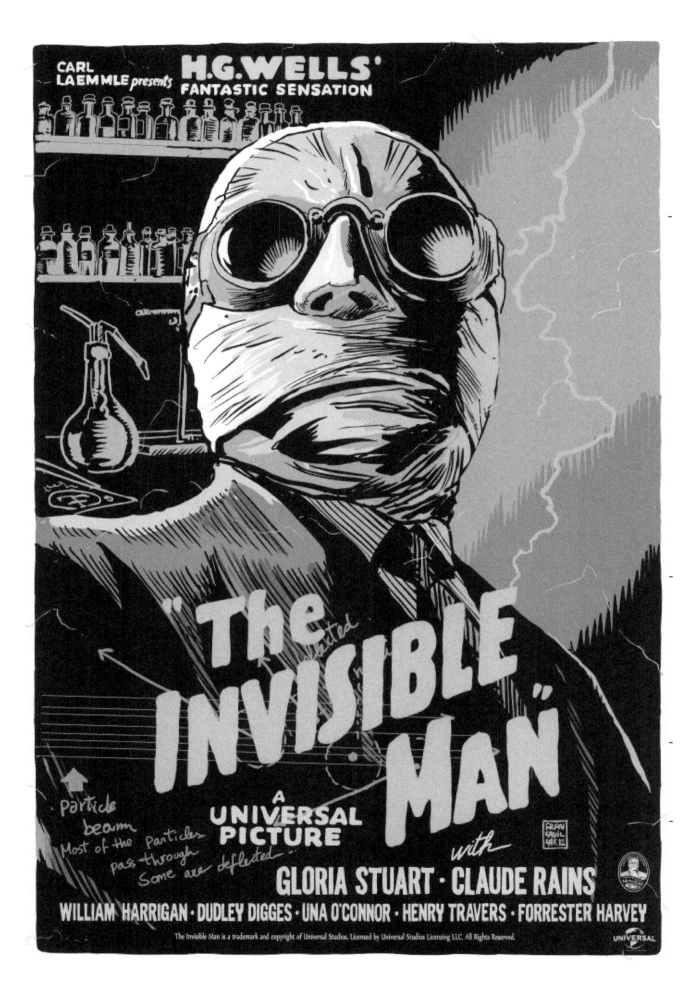

THE INVISIBLE MAN

Edited By
Philip J. Riley

Production Background
By
Gregory Wm. Mank

UNIVERSAL FILM SCRIPT SERIES
VOLUME 17
MagicImage Filmbooks is an imprint of
BearManor Media

BearManor Media
P.O. Box 1129
Duncan, OK 73534-1129

Phone: 580-252-3547
Fax: 814-690-1559

Editor-in-Chief - Philip J. Riley

The script *The Invisible Man* by R. C. Sherriff is reproduced from the original document.

Photographs are from the collection of William Forsche, Gregory Mank and the Editor.

Production Background ©2013 Gregory Wm. Mank

Pressbook courtesy the Ronald V. Borst Collection

Acknowledgements: Dr. James T. Couglin, G.D. Hamann, Doug Norwine, Gary Don Rhodes

First Edition

The purpose of this series is the preservation of the art of writing for the screen. Rare books have long been a source of enjoyment and an investment for the serious collector, and even in limited editions there are thousands printed. Scripts, however, numbered only 50 at the most. In the history of American Literature, the screenwriter was being lost in time. It is my hope that my efforts bring about a renewed history and preservation of a great American Literary form, "The Screenplay", by preserving them for study by future generations.

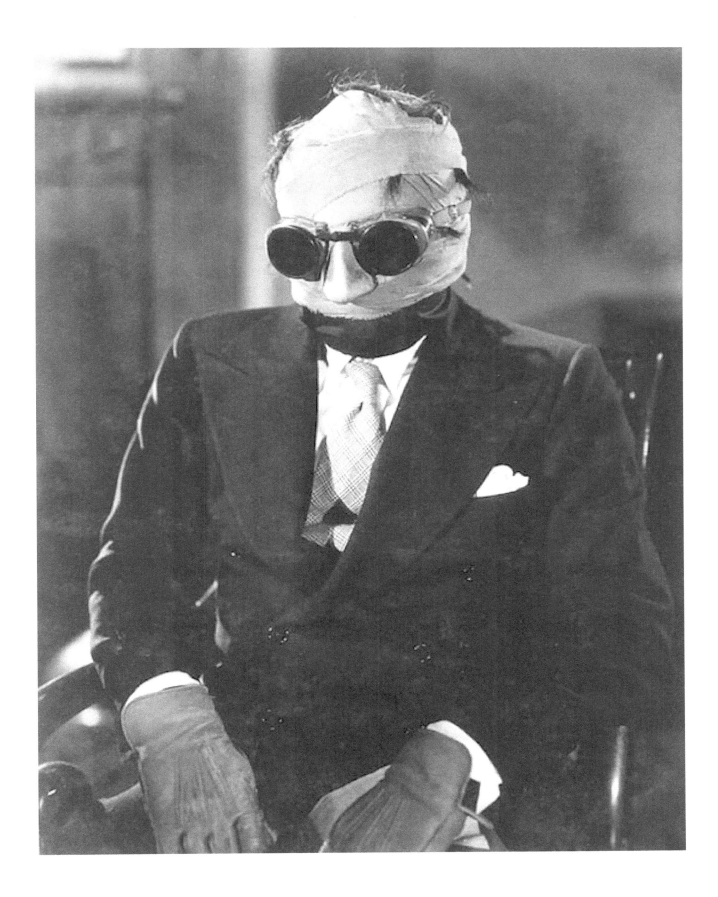

An Interview with Jessica Rains
By
Gregory William Mank

Jessica Rains on one of her very rare visits to a movie set: with Merle Oberon, her father, and her mother Frances on THIS LOVE OF OURS (Universal, 1945).

The only child of Claude Rains, Jessica Rains has an impressive list of film credits — *The Sting* (1973), *Sleeper* (1973), *Islands in the Stream* (1977), and *Honky Tonk Freeway* (1981) among others. She's also acted in many TV movies, including *A Sumer Without Boys* (1973), *Sarah T – Portrait of a Teenage Alcoholic* (1975), and *Ziegfeld: The Man and His Women* (1979), as well as appearing on such shows as *Medical Center*, *Family*, *Quincy M.E*, *Lou Grant*, and *Trapper John, M.D.*

Jessica collaborated with David J. Skal on the book *An Actor's Voice: Claude Rains* (The University of Kentucky Press, 2008). This interview took place on August 29, 2012.

Q. *So...Where and when did you first see* The Invisible Man?

A. It was a funky little theatre in Downingtown, Pennsylvania...I'm guessing I was about ten, so it was around 1948. I didn't really know very much about what my father did — we lived on a farm in Chester County, and to me, he was a farmer. I knew that he made films because he took me to the set, but only about twice in his life. Once it was because Bette Davis was making a pass at him, and he figured if he showed up with his wife and daughter, maybe she'd leave him alone. (At least that was *his* story!)

So, it was in the fall or winter, and he said to me, "Put on your hat and put on your coat, we're going out." And so I did, and we went up to Downingtown, and he was all muffled up. He had on a homburg, which he wore all the time when he left the farm, and he had a scarf wrapped around his nose and face. It was very cold, but also, I think he was probably trying to disguise himself.

He went up to the box office and he said, "I'll have two tickets, please." The theatre was a very little hometown theatre, and the guy who was at the box office was the man who owned the theatre, and the man who showed you to your seats, and the whole thing — and he recognized my father's voice.

And he said, "Oh no, no, Mr. Rains. I don't want you to pay. You must come in and be my guest!"

And my father said, "No, no, I must pay, I'm just like everyone else..."

Well, I don't remember what the outcome was, but I'm guessing that my father gave in graciously, and we went in for nothing. We sat in the back. And through the whole movie, (*laughing*), he was telling me, in a loud voice, how they had done the Special Effects.

"And this is the part where they had to make a mask of my face! So they put a straw in my nose, and covered my face with Plaster of Paris..!"

And of course, nobody was looking at the movie! (laughing) The voice was obvious, and everybody turned around to hear what he was saying! I'm sure I was very embarrassed, because I was ten or whatever... so that's basically the story.

Q. *Do you think he purposefully wanted the attention?*

A. No...I think he just wanted me to understand what he was doing. The same thing happened years later...he took me to see *Streetcar Named Desire*, the play. And (laughing) when a certain scene was about to happen, he turned to me and in a loud voice, said, "This is the *rape* scene!"

It was interesting: He did not go to see his own films. He did take me to see *The Invisible Man*, but he told me that at the very beginning, when he went to see the "rushes", or "dailies," the work from the day before, and he sat in the screening room, he just couldn't bear to see himself. Too upsetting. So he pretty much never saw films that he had done.

It's difficult — have you ever seen yourself on the big screen? It's very hard. The first film that I ever I did was *Kotch*, with Walter Matthau. I played his psychologist. And when my scenes came on, I was practically under the chair. I was so horrified, because your face is so *big*! (laughing) And everything's so *big*!

Q. *Talk a bit about the farm in Chester County.*

A. Apparently in England at that time, the most important thing to own was land. So when my father became solvent, so to speak, that's what he did — he bought land. The farm was about 600 acres, and it was gorgeous. He farmed it, he was out on his tractor, he was in his vegetable garden — and nobody else went into that vegetable garden! I had chores, and my mother made butter in a churn. We had 35 head of steer, eight to ten cows, which were milked every day, twice a day, and we had had chickens, which I fed and took care of. And we had crops ... acres and acres of crops.

We also had a little pond that he built for my mother and me — a spring fed it and it was totally natural. My mother and I spent a lot of time there; my father didn't know how to swim, having come from a poor family in London, who never went to the beach.

So we lived on the farm, and then when he made a film — generally twice a year, because he was under contract to Warner Brothers, and that's what his deal was — we packed up and went to live in Brentwood, California. We stayed there for however long it took to make the film, two months or whatever it was, and then we went home to Chester County. He only wanted to be on the farm.

A funny thing...My father got together with some neighboring farmers, and they went to the power company to have the high tension wires buried, because he

didn't like the way they looked! I don't know what's going on there now, I suspect that's all over and there's probably telephone and light wires everywhere. But when we were there, they were buried.

Q. *You would have been about five when your Father starred in* Phantom of the Opera *(1943) for Universal.*

A. We were out here, living in Brentwood, and my two best friends were Jan Dekker, who was the daughter of the actor Albert Dekker, and Mary Rowland Haight, who was the daughter of the producer George Haight. For Halloween we went out Trick-or-Treating. My mother drove the station wagon and my father went to Universal and borrowed the *Phantom of the Opera* cape. I don't know if he had the mask, I don't think so, but he had the cape, and I think the Phantom hat. Jan, Mary Rowland I were dressed as little gremlins. We only went to people's houses that we knew. When they answered the door, my Father recited some poem about All Hallow's Eve, then he would open up his cape — and we would jump out and do the Trick-or-Treat number. He had a good sense of humor!

Q. *I imagine you hear a lot about your Father from the fans.*

A. Something going on now, with *The Invisible Man* coming out on Blu-Ray...There's a whole big discussion going on about whether in the last scene in *The Invisible Man*, that was my father, or whether it was a dummy. Now why they would use a dummy is beyond me — I mean, it's kind of ludicrous — why would they bother?

Another thing...They're debating now about whether or not my father wore a wig, because he had all that hair. That's also ludicrous. I can tell you that for a fact — that was his real hair!

And there was this other Internet site — oh, God (laughing) — of women sexually attracted to my father. One of them was writing a romance novel about her life with him. It's just crazy what people can do in their spare time!

Q. *So you never saw your father as the "babe magnet" that some of his fans insist he was?*

A. Never! I'm not saying it wasn't true. But he was very, very devoted to my mother, and she was with him all the time. He was a "magnet" in the sense that women thought he was attractive, but I never saw him carrying on with anybody, or flirting with anybody, other than a twinkle in his eye.

Q. As for Bette Davis...?

A. Well, she was wild...and they were very good friends. Whenever she had problems with a husband, which was fairly often, she would come and stay on the farm. I remember once she came and Gary Merrill had beaten her up or something...I wasn't told very much about it. But she certainly was there...hiding.

Q. *Your Mom and Dad were married for over 20 years?*

A. Yes. They divorced in 1956, and he was married twice after that. When he died in 1967, he was a widower.

Q. *What are your personal favorites of your father's films?*

A. *Deception*. And when it came out, I loved *Caesar and Cleopatra*, but I saw it recently on television, and it seemed kind of odd and mannered to me. *Casablanca's* wonderful, but that's *everybody's* favorite movie!

Q. *Universal's done great restoration work on* The Invisible Man — *too bad you can't watch it again with your father telling his stories.*

A. The Academy called and asked me to introduce it at its showing. It looks terrific. They did a great job!

***

Variety Says:

NEW YORK: Roxy Theatre: "Doing smash business...Will end the week with $42,000 or better." (Note: It smashed the Roxy record and was held for a second smash week.)

CHICAGO: Palace Theatre: "Rides into top average money of the town at whizzing $27,000." (Note: Balaban & Katz put it into the McVickers AFTER the Palace run!)

PITTSBURGH: Warner Theatre: "Gave house best opening in months, should breast tape at $7,300, fine."

The Invisible Man
Production History
By
Gregory William Mank

The Universal Pictures family at the Breakfast Club, Los Angeles, March,1932. Carl Laemmle, Sr. stands front row center. The top row includes Boris Karloff, John Boles, James Whale, Bela Lugosi and Raymond Massey. Karl Freund kneels to the right of Laemmle. Also among the crowd are Tom Mix, Lew Ayres, and Mickey Rooney

"Even the moon's frightened of me – frightened to death! The whole world's frightened to death!"
— Claude Rains as *The Invisible Man*, 1933

June, 1933. A mysterious actor reports to Universal City, California.

It's his first starring role in a film – indeed, it's his first film at all, aside from a supporting part in the 1920 British feature *Build Thy House*. The Napoleonic player arrives in Hollywood with a bantam rooster flamboyance that belies his fear, insecurity, and haunted past. He's conquered a Cockney accent and severe lisp that had originally seemed to doom him to life as a mere call-boy at London's His Majesty's Theatre. High-heeled shoes add inches to his 5'6" height. His smoky voice is the result of a gassing at World War I's Vimy Ridge — a trauma that has also left him nearly blind in his right eye. The handicap so hurts the vanity of this very proud

man that, 30 years after his death, one of his six ex-wives, recalling his sensitivity, will implore a biographer not to report it.

He's won acclaim on the London and New York stage, where he has become the top character star of the illustrious Theatre Guild. Yet he's earned so little money that he's afraid to leave his apartment, fearful the phone will ring with a job offer and he'll miss it. He's been through three marriages, all of them emotionally devastating. Considering abandoning the theatre, he's recently bought a farm in New Jersey.

The actor was putting a new roof on a shack when the surprise call came from Hollywood.

So here he is at Universal, the personal choice of James Whale, the "Ace" director of *Frankenstein*, to play "The Invisible One" in H.G. Wells' *The Invisible Man*. He reports for life masks, nailed into plaster casts from which only his head emerges. Makeup men throw plaster at him so it sticks to his face. They put straws up his nose for him to breathe. He becomes claustrophobic and — reminded of his nightmarish recovery in an army hospital — shrieks in protest. The Universal work force curiously watches the bandaged-faced actor report to the soundstage in costume, looking like a goggled mummy, wearing a false nose, so desperate to preserve some dignity that the "mummy" goes to and from the stage wearing his homburg hat at a jaunty angle. In his big scene with his leading lady, the beautifully blonde Gloria Stuart, he has to stand on a box — even though he still wears his high-heeled shoes, and Gloria has slipped hers off. Humiliated, intimidated, he retaliates by ruthlessly upstaging her, only to have the director

and actress call him on it.

The Special Effects work proves especially agonizing. He wears black tights and a diver's helmet with air pipes, evoking some horrid deep sea diver mutant as he acts against a black background, the air rushing through the pipes and into the helmet so he can barely hear his co-workers, sweating profusely on the hot stage in the California summer heat. Frantic, frazzled, losing weight, nearly dehydrated, he finally faints.

The press, amused by the freakish nature of his role, mocks him. His director, aware of his ego, taunts him.

Yes, the moon is "frightened to death" — and so is Claude Rains as he plays the title role in *The Invisible Man*.

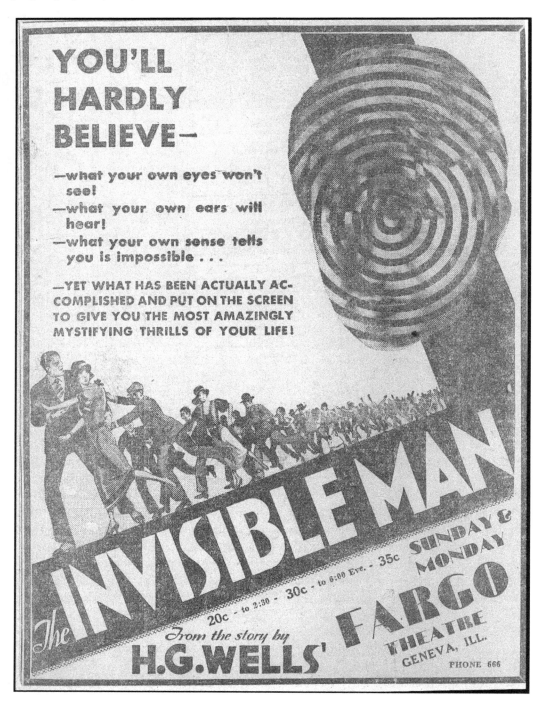

Part I.
The Ace

Claude Rains dines with director James Whale

The whole place is so marvelously SHAM that I now believe that Buckingham Palace is made of plaster of Paris, the King and Queen were never really married, the Prince of Wales is really Peter Pan, and the secret of Journey's End *is that it has never begun...*

James Whale, describing Hollywood in a letter to a friend, June 16, 1929.

Monday, August 24, 1931. Frankenstein begins shooting at Universal. Directing the film: Foxy, 42-year-old former London director/actor/scenic designer/cartoonist/Tango dancer James Whale.

Playing Henry Frankenstein is gaunt, 31-year old, alcoholic British star Colin Clive. Portraying the Monster is a sad-eyed, 43-year old English exile named Boris Karloff. Whale directs Clive's daring blasphemer to be so dynamic and Karloff's soulless Monster to be so pitiful that the horror film becomes almost subversive.

Monday, September 21: H.G. Wells, author of such works as *The Invisible Man, The Island of Dr. Moreau,* and *The War of the Worlds,* celebrates his 65th birthday. That evening: Claude Rains opens at New York's Guild Theatre in *He,* starring as an elevator man who fancies him self to be Napoleon.

Tuesday, September 22: As *Frankenstein* continues shooting, Universal pays $10,000 for the rights to H.G. Wells' *The Invisible Man.* The plot of Wells' 1897 novel concerns Griffin, an albino scientist, who bitterly lashes back at a prejudiced world via the power of drug-induced invisibility. Wells, wary of what Hollywood might do to his work, demands script approval.

It's a wise move. Universal will also buy the rights to the 1931 novel *The Murderer Invisible,* by 29-year old Massachusetts-born Philip Wylie — whose novel *Gladiator* (1930) will be the inspiration for Action Comics' *Superman* (1938). As Wells' Griffin of *The Invisible Man* wants to become invisible because he's an albino, Wylie's William Carpenter of *The Murderer Invisible* wants to be invisible because he's monstrous in size and appearance. It's easy to dismiss Wylie at this time as a Wells-wanna-be, but his book is both imaginative (Wylie's Invisible Man, in the half-way stage between corporeal being and Invisible Man, becomes a horrific skeleton), and exciting (a lynch mob pursues the skeleton). Indeed, writers tackling the screenplay will differ as to which book offers the best cinema potential.

Whatever the script, Universal has only one director in mind: James Whale.

Indeed, "Jimmy" Whale has become rather a power figure at the crazy kingdom known as Universal, nestled under the San Fernando Valley mountains with its zoo, lakes, and such back lot artifacts as the cathedral from the late Lon Chaney's *The Hunchback of Notre Dame.* Universal's 23-year old General Manager Carl Laemmle, Jr., son of the studio's founder Carl Laemmle, Sr., has great faith in Whale, who came to Universal after directing R.C. Sherriff's play *Journey's End* in London and New York, "ghost-directing" Howard Hughes' epic *Hell's Angels,* and directing Tiffany Studio's acclaimed 1930 film version of *Journey's End.* "Junior" also believes in horror films — *Dracula,* which opened February 12, starring Bela Lugosi and directed by Tod Browning, has been the studio's super hit of 1931.

Junior Laemmle hopes that James Whale — and horror films - will save Universal.

Friday, December 4: Frankenstein opens at the RKO-Mayfair Theatre in New York City. It will shatter box office records all over the country. Boris Karloff is a sensation.

Tuesday, December 29: The *Los Angeles Record* reports:

Boris Karloff is one of the few new stars of the year. It was after the thrills and chills which he contributed to Frankenstein *that Universal put him under five-year contract...Karloff's next at Universal will be* The Invisible

"JIMMY"   James Whale

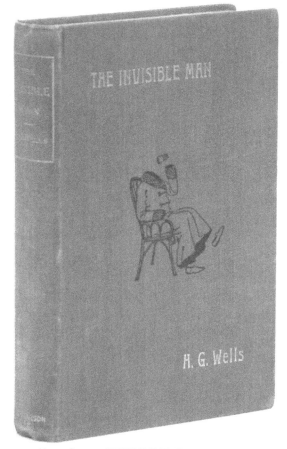

First edition of THE INVISIBLE MAN 1897

Man...*It will be started as soon as he comes back from a vacation in San Francisco, and after he does his part at Paramount in* The Miracle Man. *Probably about a month from now.*

Thursday, January 28, 1932: A month goes by, Karloff finishes *The Miracle Man* – but *The Invisible Man* does not start shooting. Instead, Universal begins *Night World* this week, boasting the studio's three top attractions: Lew Ayres, who'd starred in *All Quiet on the Western Front*, Universal's triumphant 1930 Best Picture Academy Award winner; Mae Clarke, who'd starred as the pitiful streetwalker Myra in Whale's first Universal film, *Waterloo Bridge*, and who'd been leading lady of *Frankenstein*; and Boris Karloff. The last plays "Happy" MacDonald, teeth-flashing nightclub owner, gunned down with a "Happy" smile.

The studio's obviously keeping Boris busy while *The Invisible Man*, or some other new horror opus, evolves. Meanwhile, James Whale has abandoned *The Invisible Man.* He's wary of becoming known as a "horror" director. He's cavalier about Karloff, whom he treated sadistically during the shoot of *Frankenstein*, (e.g., forcing him to carry Colin Clive over his shoulder up the hill to the windmill in the climax, chased by the torch-bearing villagers and bloodhounds, shooting all night, take after take). And he prefers to devote himself to preparing *The Road Back*, Remarque's sequel to *All Quiet on the Western Front.*

The Invisible Man has a star, but no script and no director.

KARLOFF in "THE BRIDE OF FRANKENSTEIN"– A Universal Picture   PRINTED IN U S A

Boris Karloff (Above)

Crowds waiting to see the premiere of Frankenstein (Below)

Part II.
The Invisible Octopus: Early Drafts and Directors

"You don't understand," he said, "who I am or what I am. I'll show you — by Heaven! I'll show you." Then he put his open palm over his face and withdrew it. The center of his face became a black cavity. "Here," he said. He stepped forward and handed Mrs. Hall something which she, staring at his metamorphosed face, accepted automatically. Then, when she saw what it was, she screamed loudly, and staggered back. The nose — it was the stranger's nose! Pink and shining ..."

From H. G. Wells' *The Invisible Man.*

Wednesday, February 10: Universal's *Murders in the Rue Morgue,* opens at New York's RKO-Mayfair. Poe's story gives way to a crazy sex romp, wherein Bela Lugosi's mad Dr. Mirakle hopes to mate his gorilla with a Parisian ingénue (Sidney Fox). The director is Robert Florey, and *Murders...*is his consolation prize after losing *Frankenstein* (which Florey had adapted, directing the legendary long-lost test with Lugosi as the Monster) to a usurping James Whale. Meanwhile, Florey has received another consolation prize: he's replaced Whale as the director of *The Invisible Man.*

Thursday, March 3: James Whale's new Universal film, *The Impatient Maiden,* starring Lew Ayres and Mae Clarke, (and which he completed December 29), opens in New York. While *Frankenstein* had set an all-time first week record at the RKO-Mayfair with $53,800, *The Impatient Maiden* sets a record low — $11,000.

Saturday, April 9: Robert Florey dates his draft of *The Invisible Man,* co-written with Garrett Fort (who contributed to the scripts for *Dracula* and *Frankenstein*). They've based their screenplay mainly on Philip Wylie's novel, including an invisible octopus, invisible rats, and the blowing up of Grand Central Station. Junior Laemmle bounces Florey's adaptation and Florey soon departs Universal.

Monday, April 18: James Whale, after the dud reception to *The Impatient Maiden,* returns to Universal horror this week — directing *The Old Dark House,* an elegant Gothic comedy based on J.B. Priestley's novel *Benighted.* Karloff stars as the mad, bearded, broken-nosed butler, Morgan. Also in the stellar cast: Charles Laughton, Gloria Stuart, Melvyn Douglas, Ernest Thesiger, Eva Moore, Raymond Massey, and Lilian Bond. In a joke typical of Whale's peculiar humor, he casts Elspeth

Dudgeon — an actress, billed here as "John Dudgeon" — as the 102-year old madman upstairs, wearing chin whiskers.

Thursday, April 21: Universal's *The Cohens and Kellys in Hollywood* opens at Broadway's RKO-Mayfair. The film features cameos from Universal attractions Lew Ayres, Sidney Fox, Tom Mix, Genevieve Tobin and Boris Karloff. Audiences don't care. The movie breaks the first-week low set by *The Impatient Maiden* — $7,600. The studio needs a horror hit.

Monday, June 6: John L. Balderston, playwright of the fantasy *Berkeley Square* and whose name has appeared on the credits of *Dracula* and *Frankenstein* (and will appear on such classics as *The Mummy*, *Bride of Frankenstein*, and *Mad Love*), submits a screenplay for *The Invisible Man* in collaboration with the film's director *du jour*, Cyril Gardner. It's Balderston's *third* stab at a script, and is also based primarily on the Wylie novel. How Universal expects these versions to win script approval from H.G. Wells is a mystery.

Summer, 1932: Universal writers John Huston (long before *The Maltese Falcon* and *The Treasure of the Sierra Madre*) and studio scenario editor Richard Schayer make attempts at new treatments for *The Invisible Man*. Any work that gets as far as Wells is summarily rejected.

Monday, July 18: The *Los Angeles Illustrated Daily News* publishes a profile of Karloff, writing that as Franken-stein's Monster, "he presented perhaps the strangest, most repellant character in the history of the screen. " The story continues:

All of Karloff's ingenuity in makeup will be called into play for his next picture, adapted from H.G. Wells' story, The Invisible Man, *for in many scenes his features must actually be invisible.*

The actor is carrying on experiments in secret, determined to make this characterization the most remarkable of his career.

Karloff would have been the first to say that the true makeup "ingenuity" actually comes from Jack P. Pierce. Also, whatever "experiments" conducted would be vague, as *The Invisible Man* still has no script — despite the coming and going of six writers and three directors.

Saturday, August 6: With no horror project ready, Universal loans Karloff to MGM, where shooting begins today on *The Mask of Fu Manchu*. Karloff, of course, is Fu, with evil daughter Fah Lo See (Myrna Loy) and a bevy of resplendent torture devices — including a seesaw that dips its victim into a crocodile pool.

September: The first installment of *When Worlds Collide*, by *The Murderer Invisible*'s Philip Wylie and co-authored with Edwin Balmer, appears in *Blue Book* magazine. The science fiction novel will be published in 1933.

Thursday, September 8: The play *The Man Who Reclaimed his Head*, by Jean Bart, opens at Broadway's Broadhurst Theatre. Claude Rains stars as Paul Verin, "a brilliant monstrosity," a deformed, asthmatic writer who kills an evil publisher for cheating him of his wife (Jean Arthur) and ideals — and then carries about the publisher's severed head in a valise. The *New York Times* reports, "Claude Rains has acted it with a Lon Chaney makeup and a panting of steam..."

Monday, October 17: In a dazzling bit of versatility, Claude Rains follows his grotesque portrayal of *The Man Who Reclaimed his Head* as the Chinese farmer Wang Lung in Pearl Buck's *The Good Earth* at Broadway's Guild Theatre.

Thursday, October 27: *The Old Dark House* opens at Broadway's Rialto Theatre as a Halloween attraction. Business is good if not exceptional: the first week's take is $24,500.

November: James Whale is once again director of *The Invisible Man* as Universal, facing a money crisis, cancels *The Road Back*. Meanwhile, Preston Sturges, later Paramount's great director/writer/satirist who'd win an Oscar for his script for *The Great McGinty* (1940), is writing a new script for *The Invisible Man*. The plot: a Russian chemist makes a madman invisible to wreak vengeance on the Bolsheviks who destroyed his family. Set to portray the invisible maniac: Karloff. After eight weeks' work, Sturges hands in his screenplay. Universal fires him the next day.

Saturday, November 5: Louella O. Parsons reports in the Los Angeles *Examiner*:

Young Carl Laemmle, rested from his two weeks' vacation in Palm Springs, returns with great ideas for Boris Karloff. Call him KARLOFF. Imitating the one and only Garbo, he has dropped his first name ...

The surname only billing is actually Universal's idea, not Karloff's; at any rate, Louella also notes that Universal has a new horror project for KARLOFF entitled *The Wizard*, an "original" by Ted Fithian, to be adapted by John Huston and directed by E.A. Dupont, director of the German classic *Variety* (1925). It will likely enter production in early 1933.

"James Whale starts *The Invisible Man* with Karloff in three weeks," writes Ms. Parsons.

James Whale vows to put all things right with *The Invisible Man*. Indeed, he announces that he will not only direct — he will also personally write the treatment!

Part III.
"Horror and Consternation in the Bedroom!"
James Whale's Treatment for *The Invisible Man*

...we lead up to the slow unwinding of his bandages, revealing for the first time in his features a horror so fantastic, so unbelievably hideous, that although he deals with the devil himself, we sympathize with his desire to become invisible...

From James Whale's *The Invisible Man* scenario.

James Whale's treatment for *The Invisible Man* is high Gothic — a wildly baroque tale that might have become Universal's most bizarre and truly disturbing horror show. A summary of Whale's work, which survives in the Universal Archives:

As "an important personage lies dying in a magnificent bedchamber," an old, crazed servant breaks his way through the gaggle of "priests, doctors and relatives" and vows he knows a miracle-worker who can cure the dying man:

...the servant is brought to the foot of the bed, in much the same manner as an early martyr, surrounded by priests...The servant tells his tale. He doesn't know who he is, but a strange, tall, thin man whose face no one has ever seen tends all the poor of the village, and refuses payment. He is surrounded by mystery. They think he is expiating some dreadful sin, and the villagers call him the Invisible Man. Horror and consternation in the bed chamber!

The "important personage" is, in fact, being starved or poisoned; nevertheless, the servant wins permission to summon "the Invisible Man." He leaves the house and goes to a lonely spot on the village outskirts, hopping over a wall "into a queer bleak churchyard with gleaming crosses, and grim ghostly monuments." He goes to "a monument, somewhat like an upturned sarcophagus, tall and grim, an exquisitely carved angel's head with spreading wings at the top." The servant knocks on the sarcophagus and a voice and rumblings arise from the earth:

CAMERA FOCUSES on the angel's beautiful face, which slowly hinges outward, revealing a dim, vague, but horrid shape in the aperture, framed on either side by the two delicate angel's wings. The face in the aperture is very startling. It is wrapped entirely in bandages, rather like a mummy, and wears a pair of heavy dark glasses. It moves and speaks:

"Well, William, what is it?"

Whereupon the servant begs him to come and see his master, adding, it is a matter of life and death. The voice, which is very beautiful, sardonically replies:

"It is always a matter of life and death. Come in."

We now have the thrill of introducing a mysterious BEING of the Dracula and Frankenstein order, but with the difference of meeting what is obviously a delightful person behind that cryptic makeup.

The Invisible Man lives below amidst coffins; we learn he's "miraculously" cured the servant's wife and child, and now he agrees to cure the servant's master. He enters the bedroom, ("The firelight is flickering with ghostly effect") and gives the man (who's been blindfolded) a mix of medicines. Indeed, the Invisible Man saves him.

Now Whale writes:

However, something dramatic must happen to the Invisible Man, and our story must develop. It might be that the daughter, who has remained concealed in the room, rushes forward dramatically, and tearing off the stranger's cloak and hat, demands to know who he is.

It is child's play to snatch a tense moment here, as the gruesome face savagely turns upon her and looks into the CAMERA.

In a weirdly tender scene, the girl might here discover her lover, who had mysteriously disappeared, because of a horrible disfigurement to his face during scientific experiments for the good of the poor sick. After a heartbreaking scene she enters the most exclusive order of nuns in a convent, and banishes herself from the world. The stranger returns to his tomb, and in an agony of spirit, wrestles with God.

Whale writes the prayer "is terrible in its intensity," with "music which has accompanied the entire picture in grand opera manner:"

O THOU WHO ART INVISIBLE
And to whom nothing is unseen
Who carest for the sick and fatherless,
Who created the earth and all that is upon
It, to whom there is no mystery in man or
Beast: THOU who gavest and takest away, hear
The prayer of thy servant, and remove from
The eyes of mortal man the harmful sight of
This frightful face, that I may be allowed to do
Thy will unseen....

After the prayer, and presumably many experiments, he removes the bandages, and we see his face with its "horror so fantastic." He indeed succeeds in making himself invisible. However:

With the old servant as an accomplice, and with all the arts of Camera and mystery trickery, the stupendous achievement is complete, but our horror grows as we discover that during the transition the mind has completely changed, and now has only a longing to kill those very people he had healed and befriended. His first victim is the poor, crazed servant and we FADE OUT on the delightful spectacle of his being slowly strangled to death by invisible hands. As a crowning piece of horror and before the death rattle of the victim announces his demise, the stranger's horrible face, which now has the added terror of a murderous mind, becomes visible in the victim's last fleeting moment from this beautiful world. Having been suspended in air the victim falls dead on the floor, with a face frozen in horror.

And so the reign of terror begins, as the Invisible Man plans and executes "a short series of diabolical murders." Corpses mount on a funeral pyre. In a terrifically melodramatic and blasphemous climax, the Invisible Man plans to kill his former lover:

Meanwhile the lovelady is about to take her final vows to enter the most exclusive order of Sisterhood. In this scene which offers scope for magnificent production, the splendor of the ceremony of consecration could be searched for impressive details.

Knowing the Invisible Man is on her track, we could build suspense by having the most elaborate presentation. The acolytes could trim the altar, priests, processing back and forth with all the ritual stressed. The procession of nuns with swing censors, the novices prostrate in white on the steps of the altar. The clanging of the bells, and the peal of the organ. The CAMERA, which is now on the face of the holy bride, exquisitely sad, and spiritually beautiful PANS swiftly across the Cathedral to a door, which slowly opens. A knife stealthily creeping towards the altar, accompanied by the soft footfalls of naked feet. The knife furtively passes in and out of pillars, and eventually comes to a stop, setting high up in the great carved chair of the Bishop.

We cut several times during the ceremony to this playful knife, somewhat in the nature of the hand on the bannister in The Old Dark House, and as the lovely bride is receiving the sacrament, the knife raises and completes its bloody work.

Our meal of horror is not yet complete. The liqueur is still to be served. Our eyes must surely pop completely out as we watch the knife jerk out of the now unlovely corpse, raise itself into mid-air, and plunge itself quivering into the heart of the remorseful invisible man. Who, as his life's blood ebbs swiftly away, becomes gradually visible, revealing for an instant, a face so fantastically horrible that even we who are used to such dishes, close our eyes, as the sound of a dull flopping thud forces the sickening news through our other senses, that the lovers are united a last!

Finis

Whale clearly enjoyed writing his rather deliriously over-the-top treatment, which seems inspired by both *The Phantom of the Opera* and *Dr. Jekyll and Mr. Hyde.* He's spiced it with the strange religious touches with which he'd daubed *Frankenstein* and *The Old Dark House* — and which would explode in *Bride of Frankenstein.* Junior Laemmle, ever in Whale's corner, green lights the treatment and Whale turns over his work to writer Gouverneur Morris to flesh out into a screenplay. The Production Code approves it too, despite the bloodthirsty cathedral finale that would have never passed the empowered Code that came into effect in June of 1934. Yet it's all for nothing - H.G. Wells rejects it.

Angry and spiteful, James Whale abandons *The Invisible Man... again.*

Part IV.
The Mummy Vs. The Panther Woman – at Yuletide

It Comes to Life!
—Promotional Copy for *The Mummy*

...The Panther Woman...Throbbing to the Hot Flush of Love.
—Promotional Copy for *Island of Lost Souls*

Friday, December 23: Universal's *The Mummy* opens at the State Lake Theatre in Chicago, the posters proclaiming the star as "Karloff the Uncanny." He wears two Jack P. Pierce makeups — the bandaged Mummy "Imhotep" of the opening (which takes eight hours to apply), and Imhotep's alter-ego, the skeletal, shriveled Ardath Bey (a 90-minute makeup, but it must be melted off every night). Zita Johann plays his soulful reincarnated love, the ravishing Anckesenamon.

Also on December 23: Paramount's *Island of Lost Souls*, based on H.G. Wells' *The Island of Dr. Moreau*, opens at the Roosevelt in Chicago, directly competing with *The Mummy*. The film stars Charles Laughton as mad, whip-cracking Moreau, Bela Lugosi as the hairy Sayer of the Law, and — in a role purring with Hollywood sensationalism and not at all in Wells' novel — Kathleen Burke as the Panther Woman, whose "stubborn beast flesh" comes "creeping back." The script, in which Moreau hopes to mate his Panther Woman with a human male, somehow gets by the Production Code, but without Wells' approval.

To make matters more potentially explosive, one of the writers is Philip Wylie — author of *The Murderer Invisible*.

There's more drama bubbling below the surface. "The Panther Woman" seems a personal jibe at Wells and author/feminist Rebecca West, who had become lovers in 1913. During intimacy, they had "pet" soubriquets; she called him "Jaguar" and he called her "Panther." In fact, West named their love child, born in 1914, Anthony Panther West (who would write the biography *H.G. Wells: Aspects of a Life*). Perhaps Wylie knows of these pet names; maybe it's just a bizarre coincidence; nevertheless, the feline presence of "The Panther Woman" naturally does nothing to endear Island *of Lost Souls* — or Hollywood – to Wells. Great Britain bans *Island of Lost Souls*, much to Wells' delight.

Universal's winning the great man's blessing for *The Invisible Man*, after the notoriety of *Island of Lost Souls*, seems more a challenge than ever.

Incidentally, neither *The Mummy* nor *Island of Lost Souls* breaks any box office records in Chicago. In its first week, *The Mummy* takes in $11,500 at the State Lake (where the high had been *Frankenstein*, at $44,000); *Island of Lost Souls* brings in $11,000 at the Roosevelt (where the high had been Marlene Dietrich's *Dishonored*, at $30,350).

Part V.
A Bull's Eye Script

"Power...Power to walk into the gold vaults of nations, amidst the secrets of kings, into the Holy of Holies! Power to make multitudes run squealing in terror, at the touch of my little invisible finger!"
–Claude Rains as The Invisible Man

Tuesday, January 17, 1933: Uncle Carl Laemmle celebrates his 66th birthday. As he cuts the giant 66-pound cake at the studio, James Whale and Boris Karloff are among the celebrants. Most of the crowd smiles respectfully, despite this morning's headline in *The Hollywood Reporter*: *Universal Closing for Short Period*. The studio's 1932 loss is $1,250,283, and the lot plans to shut down for six to eight weeks after the current productions finish shooting.

Whale is now directing *The Kiss Before the Mirror*, the saga of a lawyer (Frank Morgan, future title character in 1939's *The Wizard of Oz*) who defends a killer (Paul Lukas, future Oscar winner for 1943's *Watch on the Rhine*)

for murdering his unfaithful wife (Gloria Stuart, future leading lady of *The Invisible Man*); the lawyer meanwhile suspects his own wife (Nancy Carroll) of adultery. With Whale otherwise occupied, Junior Laemmle announces a new director for *The Invisible Man*: E.A. Dupont, who, as Louella Parsons had reported two months previously, was originally set to direct *The Wizard* (which never gets produced at all). In their book *Universal Horrors*, Tom Weaver, John Brunas, and Michael Brunas write:

German émigré E.A. Dupont came on the scene for what couldn't have amounted to more than a few weeks. (Dupont) had been brought to Hollywood by Carl Laemmle years before but returned to his native country following a disagreement

21

over his first American picture. Like Florey, Dupont also lost out on his share of landmark fright films. Besides The Invisible Man, he was announced as director of The Black Cat the following year, only to be replaced by Edgar Ulmer. When Dupont finally made his directorial bow in horror films, it was the schlocky 1953 United Artists release The Neanderthal Man, a sad commentary on the career of this once-esteemed filmmaker.

Meanwhile, John Weld is working on a script for The Invisible Man. After reviewing the "rejected scripts dumped on my desk" — including a recent draft by Laird Doyle — Weld asks for a copy of Wells' novel and learns Universal doesn't have one. Weld gets a copy from the library and follows it quite faithfully in preparing his script. Philip Wylie's The Murderer Invisible is no longer source material.

Friday, February 3: "R.C. Sherriff to Write 'Invisible Man' for 'U'", headlines The Hollywood Reporter, which writes:

Universal, after turning down several treatments prepared for The Invisible Man, has signed R.C. Sherriff to do the screen play of the story.

The writer is now in London, and starts work immediately...Picture is slated for production in April when Universal resumes after the layoff, and will be directed by James Whale.

Yes, James Whale is back again — his third announcement as director of The Invisible Man — and Sherriff has likely come at Whale's insistence. He's the author of Journey's End, which Whale had so triumphantly directed as a play and film.

Monday, February 13: "Universal Studios Closed for Six Weeks," headlines page one of The Hollywood Reporter:

Universal Studios officially closed Saturday for six weeks, with completion of work on the Slim Summerville – ZaSu Pitts film Niagara Falls. Only execs and a skeleton crew will be retained on the payroll, in addition to about 15 writers, who are preparing material for pictures to go into work when the plant reopens.

The same edition of the Reporter notes that James Whale is now taking a 12 week layoff (his contract runs 40 weeks out of 52), and when he returns, will direct The Invisible Man.

Wednesday, February 15: The Hollywood Reporter writes that Universal is preparing a script titled Bluebeard, to star Karloff with Karl Freund (who'd directed The Mummy) as director. Production is supposed to begin when Universal reopens. (How, one wonders, can Karloff do The Invisible Man and Bluebeard simultaneously?)

Tuesday, February 21: Claude Rains opens in New York in the Theatre Guild's American Dream, which traces an America family in the years 1650, 1849, and 1933.

Realizing he's not making enough money to support himself despite being an "artistic success," Rains plans to devote his time to his farm in Lambertville, New Jersey.

"I kept busy putting the place in shape," Rains will remember, "and I thought if worse came to worse, I could go into the little drugstore in town and shake up sodas."

Thursday, March 2: With Universal shut down, Junior Laemmle agrees to loan Karloff to Gaumont-British Studios to star in The Ghoul. On this date, Boris Karloff and his wife Dorothy take a plane to New York, where they will sail to England.

Friday, March 3: The Hollywood Citizen News reports on Karloff's trip:

While in London he will confer with R.C. Sherriff, who is adapting the H.G. Wells' novel, The Invisible Man, to the screen for Universal. That will be Karloff's first picture for Universal after the shutdown. James Whale, the English director, will be in charge.

There's no evidence that Karloff does any "conferring" with Sherriff, but no matter — Sherriff has a definite grasp of the story and it appears The Invisible Man might actually soon have a script that will work.

Monday, March 6: With the Depression raging, the banks have failed, and all Hollywood studios resort to cutting salaries by 50% for an estimated eight weeks.

Friday, March 24: RKO's King Kong has its official world premiere tonight at Grauman's Chinese Theatre in Hollywood, with a giant bust of Kong in the forecourt, Fay Wray in attendance, and a live stage show, including The Dance of the Sacred Ape. The film is a phenomenon and audiences are primed for more "trick" pictures — good news for The Invisible Man.

Friday, April 7: The Hollywood Citizen News announces that Gaumont-British Studios wants Karloff for two more pictures. The actor is having a grand time in England, his first return home since he left in 1909. However, as the newspaper reports, Universal has demanded that he return in May to start work on The Invisible Man.

Tuesday, April 25: The Hollywood Reporter writes that all major studios have now resumed paying full salaries, Universal having done so the previous day.

Thursday, May 4: Universal, basically shut down since early February and hoping to reopen officially next week, releases James Whale's new film, The Kiss Before the Mirror. Critically acclaimed, the film nevertheless draws the lowest gross in the history of both New York's RKO-Roxy Theatre and Los Angeles' RKO-Hillstreet Theatre.

Universal's in trouble. So is Whale, who desperately needs a hit picture.

Monday, May 8: The Hollywood Reporter notes that Universal has "cancelled the extension of a loan-out for Boris Karloff to British-Gaumont," and that the star left

London Saturday to return to Hollywood. "He goes into *Invisible Man* at Universal," writes the *Reporter*, "the production awaiting his arrival."

Saturday, May 13: It's a bombshell. "If Powell Okays, 'Invisible Man' His", headlines page one of *The Hollywood Reporter*:

Universal wants William Powell and Powell is at liberty to take on the 'U' job before he starts the four pictures with Warners. It's merely a matter of his okaying the script of Invisible Man. This being done, Universal is willing to give him $40,000 for the picture.

The "U" job, if taken, will not interfere with the RKO-Radio picture Powell will do.

Yes, *The Hollywood Reporter* is referring to urbane, dapper, impeccably mustached William Powell, who in 1934, will star in MGM's *The Thin Man*.

Tuesday, May 16: "Boris Karloff Back," headlines *The Hollywood Reporter*. He has returned, forced by Universal to leave London and abandon British film offers to come back for *The Invisible Man*, only to learn that Universal has offered it to William Powell (and with a $40,000 payday!). Powell obviously had quickly nixed the offer, as the same edition of the *Reporter* writes that Whale will direct *The Invisible Man* and that "the studio is still searching for a lead for the picture, with Boris Karloff definitely out."

There's no explanation as to why Boris is "definitely out."

Thursday, June 1: R.C. Sherriff's script for *The Invisible Man* is almost complete. He's developed a crucial element: the concept of monocaine, the drug that makes Griffin invisible, but also causes his eventual insanity. Sherriff's version delights Whale and even Wells, who gives his approval and blessing.

That same date, Karloff's option comes up at Universal. In early 1933, when the star's contract had called for a raise from $750 to $1,000 per week, Karloff had agreed to stay at $750, provided he receives his full jump to $1,250 come the next option. Now Universal refuses to keep its promise.

The betrayal with *The Invisible Man*...The crawfishing regarding his salary. It's all too much for Karloff, who's a fervent champion for actors' rights. In fact, he'll be a founder of the Screen Actors Guild, which is now evolving in the spring and summer of 1933. When the SAG officially forms in October, Karloff will hold card number nine.

What Universal has done to him is, in his opinion, unconscionable. And as *Variety* will express it, "Karloff walked."

James Whale with screen writer Robert Cedric Sherriff

Part VI.
The Monster Walks
"I think I'll throttle you!"— Claude Rains as *The Invisible Man*

June 3: The Hollywood Reporter runs the page one headline, "*Karloff Free for Two Months Stretch.*" Apparently Universal is very quick to try to make amends and actor and studio have agreed on a two month leave, during which time the star, in the *Reporter's* words, "is privileged to work for any other studio." Meanwhile, Universal

London press cartoon for THE INSECT PLAY, 1923. Note the sketch of Claude Rains, upper left center.

played by no less than Whale's future Bride of Frankenstein, 20-year old Elsa Lanchester — and hiccups in enjoyment. In Act III, Rains was the Chief Engineer Ant, supervising an assembly-line ant army. For the quirky Whale, Rains' elegantly offbeat acting had made a lasting impression.

will try to settle the contract dispute.

The same day: Columnist Harrison Carroll in the *Los Angeles Evening Herald and Express* notes that Boris Karloff is the third star to depart Universal recently due to salary battles — the other two being Lew Ayres and Garbo look-alike Tala Birell. "First result of Karloff's loss," writes Carroll, "will be a search for an actor to take the title role of H.G. Wells' *The Invisible Man.*"

Of course, Karloff was supposedly "definitely out" already for *The Invisible Man*, but by now, it's tough for the press to keep score.

Whale considers Colin Clive, his Stanhope of *Journey's End* and, of course, his Henry Frankenstein, to star in *The Invisible Man.* Clive had returned from England to star with Katharine Hepburn in RKO's *Christopher Strong*, staying on to join Lionel Barrymore in MGM's *Looking Forward*; he likes *The Invisible Man* role, considering it "down his street." However, he prefers to summer in England. Universal's front office is likely relieved; Clive's alcoholism makes him a risk on the picture.

Meanwhile, Whale has remembered an actor he'd known in Sir Nigel Playfair's London company in *The Insect Play* in the spring of 1923. His name is Claude Rains, and he'd played three different roles in the three act-play. In Act One he played The Lepidopterist, observing butterflies, played with wings and falsetto voices by actors — one of whom was 19-year old John Gielgud. In Act II, Rains was the Parasite, who devours a larva —

Whale located a screen test that Rains had done in the east for RKO, in which he'd portrayed three roles: the mad father in *A Bill of Divorcement* (which he'd played in London and in summer stock in Hartford, CT); Paul Verin in *The Man Who Reclaimed his Head* (which, as noted, he'd acted on Broadway); and Napoleon in Shaw's *Man of Destiny* (which he'd played in London in 1924). Rains had selected the three roles in hopes of showing his range and versatility.

"And they were terrible!" lamented Rains. "I was all over the place! I knew nothing about screen technique, of course, and just carried on as if I was in an enormous theatre. When I saw the test, I was shocked and frightened." In his excellent book *An Actor's Voice: Claude Rains*, written with the authorization of Rains' daughter Jessica, David J. Skal writes, "...legend has it, the awful screen test was circulated in Hollywood as a kind of joke reel."

Whale tracks down the notorious test, watches, and later admits he "howled with laughter." Yet Rains' throaty, dynamic voice captivates him. Just as Whale had demanded a largely unknown Boris Karloff play the Monster in *Frankenstein*, as opposed to the studio's first choice of Bela Lugosi, Whale now insists on a star for *The Invisible Man* who's never been in an American movie at all.

"I don't give a hang what he *looks* like!" Jimmy Whale vows. "That's how I want him to *sound* - and I want *him!*"

Part VII.
The Woes and Wives of "Willie Wains"
"It's cold outside when you have to go about naked!"
—Claude Rains, *The Invisible Man.*

Claude Rains was a Great Actor who — while standing on boxes to look Great Actresses in the eye — became (in Bette Davis's words), "a contributor to the dignity of Hollywood."

William Claude Rains was born Sunday, November 10, 1889 — "on the wrong side of the Thames," as he put it. His parents were poor; most of their children died very young. The boy had a serious lisp — "Willie

Wains" was how he pronounced his name. Children teased him. He loathed school. He joined a choir as a soprano and on a very memorable date in his life — August 31, 1900, — the ten-year old Willie sang with the choir in a crowd scene in *Sweet Nell of Old Drury* at London's Haymarket Theatre. The boy was enchanted. Acting, he decided, would be his life.

The speech impediment blocked the way, and Rains

became a call-boy at His Majesty's Theatre. 50 years later, when Rains received the Medal for Good Speech on the Stage in New York, he remembered:

...I had to summon actors from their dressing rooms to the stage. It was difficult to be taken seriously, because I had an impediment in my speech. I had no "R's"...I discovered that I had a lazy tongue, the muscle of which had never been properly used because my mother thought that I talked "pwettily"!

He took all variety of backstage jobs while studying Elocution. He also sometimes landed "supernumerary" (i.e. "extra work") in scenes where speech wasn't necessary. One of his first such stints was in a production of *The Mystery of Edwin Drood*:

I was fourteen or fifteen then. I played a silent Lascar in a dope scene. Herbert Tree, who was running His Majesty's in those days, told me after my first performance that I was one of the finest over-actors he'd ever laid eyes on!

Ironically, 20 years later, Rains will star in Universal's *Mystery of Edwin Drood* (1935) as the opium-addicted choirmaster and murderer, John Jasper — a performance, the *New York Times* will report, that "makes your flesh crawl."

On June 28, 1911, Claude Rains — 5'6"-tall, 21-years old and victorious over his speech impediment — made his official acting debut as Slag, a beggar in Dunsany's *The God of the Mountain* at London's Haymarket Theatre. He later toured Australia, gained credits on the London stage and in 1914, came to the U.S. as general manager and actor for impresario Granville Barker.

World War I. Rains returned to England. He enlisted in the "London Scots" because, as he will recall, his dramatic nature made him yearn to wear a kilt. At Vimy Ridge, he was the victim of poison gas, which nearly blinded him in his right eye and left him the sensually husky voice that will become world-famous. By the time he left the Army in 1919, he was Captain Claude Rains.

Back on the London stage, he acted constantly: a bloodthirsty Casca in Shakespeare's *Julius Caesar* (St. James Theatre, January 9, 1920); insane Hilary Fairfield in *A Bill of Divorcement* (St. Martin's Theatre, March 14, 1921); Billy in *The Bat* (St. James Theatre, January 23, 1922); gigolo Max in *The Love Habit* (Royalty Theatre, February 7, 1923). Another irony: When *The Love Habit* opened a month later in New York, the actor playing Rains' role of Max was Dwight Frye — fated to make his own indelible mark in Universal Horror as the fly-eating Renfield in *Dracula* and the hunchbacked Fritz in *Frankenstein*.

Meanwhile, Rains taught at London's Academy of Dramatic Art, where his students included Laurence Olivier and John Gielgud. In his 1973 book *Distinguished Company*, Gielgud will write:

By the time I met him in the Twenties he was already much in demand as a successful character actor. He lacked inches and wore lifts in his shoes. Stocky but handsome, with broad shoulders and a mop of thick brown hair that he brushed over one eye... He had piercing dark eyes and a beautiful throaty voice, though he had, like Marlene Dietrich, some trouble with the letter "R." Extremely attractive to women.... all the girls in my class at the Royal Academy of Dramatic Art, where he was one of the best and most popular teachers, were hopelessly in love with him.

Rains himself was hopelessly in love — many times. David J. Skal's *An Actor's Voice: Claude Rains*, provides the intimate details. There will eventually be six wives in all; as for the first three:

Wife Number One: Actress Isabel Jeans, who played such roles as Titania, Queen of the Fairies in *A Midsummer Night's Dream*, wore "wonderful wigs" in real life (Rains discovered her own hair was very thin), and cheated on Rains while he was away at war. They divorced. (Ms. Jeans later appeared in such films as Alfred Hitchcock's 1941 *Suspicion* and Vincente Minnelli's 1958 *Gigi*.)

Wife Number Two: Actress Marie Hemingway, an alcoholic who, on their wedding night, got drunk, became (as Rains remembered it) "lusty," and, when her disgusted bridegroom refused to make love to her, threatened to throw herself out a window. They wed in 1920 and divorced the same year.

Wife Number Three: Actress Beatrix Thomson, "a fragile, dark-haired girl," who'd won the Royal Academy's Silver Medal as "Most Talented Actress" of 1922. They wed in 1924, and when Beatrix won the plum role in *The Constant Nymph* in New York in 1926, Rains resigned from the Royal Academy and took the supporting role of Roberto the butler in the play to accompany his wife to America.

Strange are the ways of the Theatre: When Rains played Faulkland in *The Rivals* in March of 1925, his female co-players included not only wife Beatrix, but also ex-wives Isabel and Marie!

In New York, Rains eventually emerged from his wife's shadow, taking over the male lead in *The Constant Nymph*. He signed with the illustrious Theatre Guild, which engaged Rains to tour as *Volpone* and as Chu-Yin in *Marco's Millions*, replacing Dudley Digges, who'd scored in both roles that season.

Again, strange are the ways of the Theatre, and Movies: Digges, whom Rains replaced, will play the Chief Inspector who fatally shoots *The Invisible Man*.

Rains became the Theatre Guild's top character star. He starred in such plays as *The Camel Through the Needle's Eye* (with Miriam Hopkins, Martin Beck Theatre, April 15, 1929) and *Karl and Anna* (with Otto Kruger and

Alice Brady, Guild Theatre, October 7, 1929). He enjoyed a special success as Proteus in Shaw's *The Apple Cart* (Martin Beck Theatre, February 24, 1930).

Meanwhile, Beatrix Thomson, her ego bruised, left Rains and went home to England. He eventually divorced her on the charge of desertion.

The Depression left its scar on the Theatre. The Theatre Guild collapsed along with Rains' marriage. Rains had achieved no financial security. He was at a mid-life crisis when Hollywood called.

Rains filmed a new test in the east — "The scene," according to the *New York Times*, "where Jack Griffin explains to Dr. Kemp his maniacal scheme for bringing the whole world under his sway." Universal officially approved and offered Rains a two-picture contract, with promise of top-billing in *The Invisible Man*.

Saturday, June 17: Louella Parsons runs a portrait of Rains in her column, writing in the *Los Angeles Examiner*:

You probably will say when I mention Invisible Man, *goodness, hasn't that been filmed yet? The delay in filming has been the search to get just the right leading man. Carl Laemmle, Jr. considers he has just that person in Claude Rains, New York stage actor and an Englishman who was particularly successful on the stage in* The Man Who Reclaimed his Head, The Apple Cart, *and other plays. He gets here tomorrow... Wonder what happened to Boris Karloff, wasn't he supposed to play the part?*

Part VIII.
A Good Cast Is Worth Repeating
"Here we go gathering nuts in May,
On a cold and frosty morning – Woops!"
–Claude Rains, singing in *The Invisible Man*.

James Whale selects actors for the various major roles in *The Invisible Man*:

Gloria Stuart

Flora: As the melodrama's heroine, Whale cast Gloria Stuart, Universal's beautiful blonde who, over 60 years later, won glory via her Oscar-nominated performance as "Old Rose" in the blockbuster *Titanic*. Born in Santa Monica on the 4th of July, 1911, Gloria attracted talent scouts from Paramount and Universal with her performance in Pasadena Playhouse's *The Sea Gull*. Both studios wanted her and agreed to a coin toss. As Gloria told me in a 1986 interview, more with humor than bitterness:

Unfortunately, Universal won! Paramount was really a major studio, while Universal was dedicated to westerns and horror movies...Paramount had marvelous stars and directors; Universal had nobody, except Boris Karloff and James Whale.

Gloria had worked with Karloff and Whale in Universal's *The Old Dark House* (1932); Whale even designed the pale pink, Jean Harlow-style satin velvet evening dress that Gloria wore in the film.

"Boris is going to chase you, up and down the corridors," Whale told her, "and I want you to appear like a white flame!"

"Okay," said Gloria. "I'm a white flame!"

Gloria admires Whale tremendously, and her relationship with the gay director takes a curious turn:

I was separated from my first husband at the time, and James took me to the theatre many times – Jane Cowl, Katharine Cornell, all the greats who came to Los Angeles – and he was a wonderful companion. Off the set he had a very sharp sense of humor, and he could be very cutting too – he could really cut you off at the pass. Away from the set he was charming, but back on the set the next morning...it was 'Ach-Tung' time!

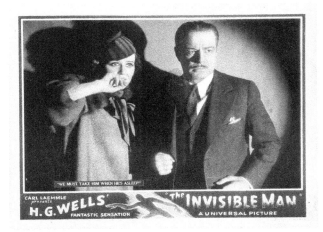

Henry Travers as Flora's father

Dr. Kemp: The cowardly villain of *The Invisible Man* was in fact, like Claude Rains, a World War I hero. It was Captain William Harrigan who had led a relief column to aid the famed "Lost Battalion" and his resultant wounds had caused him to spend four months in French hospitals. Born in New York City in 1886, Harrigan, who'd won Broadway stardom in Eugene O'Neill's *The Great God Brown* (1926), hailed from a theatrical family who dated back its stage roots (without a break!) to 1660. His father was "Ned" Harrigan of the "Harrigan and Hart" act, his mother was actress Annie Braham Harrigan, and his sister was Nedda Harrigan — who played "Miss Wells," the maid in Broadway's 1927 *Dracula* with Bela Lugosi. (She'd later be leading lady of Warner Bros'. 1938 *Devil's Island* with Boris Karloff and, in 1945, married Broadway writer and director Joshua Logan.)

The role of Jack Griffin's romantic rival for Flora's hand and treacherous "friend" had been set for Chester Morris. However, Morris, who'd recently co-starred with Jean Harlow in MGM's notorious *Red-Headed Woman* (1932), was dismayed to learn how unflattering the role of Kemp was and that Rains would have top-billing, so he bailed. Harrigan is a fine choice as a replacement. He's so appropriately bland and snively as Kemp that it's hard to imagine that, in 1927, he'd played New York's Palace in *Memories of Harrigan and Hart*, performing many of his father's old musical numbers.

Notable too: William Harrigan had appeared on Broadway in the play *The Moon in the Yellow River* (February 29, 1932), co-starring with Claude Rains.

Dr. Cranley, Flora's Father: Henry Travers' most famous role will be Clarence, the angel trying to win his wings, in Frank Capra's *It's a Wonderful Life* (1946). Born Travers John Hegerty in Northumberland, England in 1874, he'd been a star athlete in school, notably as a long distance runner. (He decided to forsake running after collapsing under a bridge during a meet; his classmates fortunately saved him before the water rose!) Travers began his acting career in stock in England; in New York, he too was a member of the Theatre Guild, acting in such plays as *Caesar and Cleopatra* (with Lionel Atwill and Helen Hayes, 1925) and *The Camel Through the Needle's Eye* (with Claude Rains and Miriam Hopkins, 1929). Travers came to Hollywood to reprise his stage role of Herr Krug in *Reunion in Vienna* (1933), and Universal borrowed him for *The Invisible Man.*

Jenny Hall, Proprietress of The Lion's Head Inn: Perhaps what we remember best about her is her scream — a wild, piercing, caterwauling shriek, the scream of a witch whose wig blew off as she flew her broom past the moon on Halloween night. It's a specialty of Una O'Connor, born Agnes McGlade in Belfast, Ireland in 1880. She had loved playing "Dress-up" as a little girl, and became a member of the famed Abbey Players, where her favorite role was the Third Witch in *Macbeth*:

Jenny Hall, Proprietress of The Lion's Head Inn, portrayed my Una O'Connor

Double, double toil and trouble,
Fire burn and cauldron bubble!

She worked on the London and New York stage, achieving one of her greatest successes as Ellen Bridges, the charwoman in the original London production of Noel Coward's *Cavalcade*. Fox Studios in Hollywood sent for Una when they produced *Cavalcade*, but the actress almost never arrived. Sailing to the U.S. on the liner *Paris*, the 50-year old Una was found at Ellis Island to have (as the press reported) "a leaky heart she never knew she had." Fearing the actress might become "a public charge," Ellis Island authorities detained her. Eventually she won clearance, got to Hollywood, and played in *Cavalcade*, which premiered at Grauman's Chinese Theatre on the night of January 12, 1933 and went on to win 1933's Best Picture Academy Award.

A strongly religious "maiden lady" who professed to have been in love "a dozen times" ("I always found out he was not the right man, or I was not the right woman"), Una enjoyed reading, swimming in the Pacific, and sculpting – she'd create busts of such stars as Joan Crawford and Norma Shearer. She rarely stopped working, and James Whale awarded her the plum role of Jenny in *The Invisible Man*.

One of Una's best lines (after the Invisible Man has tossed her husband down the stairs): "He's *homey-cidal!*"

Mr. Herbert Hall, Proprietor of The Lion's Head Inn: The role of Jenny Hall's hapless husband – he who's tossed down the stairs — goes to Forrester Harvey, born in County Cork, Ireland in 1890. He had worked in regional theatre in Ireland and England, acted in London's West End and on Broadway, and had appeared in two of Alfred Hitchcock's British films — *The Ring*

Mr. Herbert Hall, Proprietor of The Lion's Head Inn

"There's breathing in my barn!"

(1927) and *The Farmer's Wife* (1928). In Hollywood, Harvey appeared in such 1932 MGM films as *Tarzan the Ape Man*, the Clark Gable/Jean Harlow sex saga *Red Dust* (1932), and the horror film *Kongo* (a remake of *West of Zanzibar*, with Walter Huston in the late Lon Chaney's role of "Dead Legs").

P.C. Jaffers: Perfectly cast as walrus-mustached, bloodhound-faced Constable Jaffers — who marvels "Look! E's al eaten away!" as the Invisible One merrily unwraps his bandages – is E.E. Clive, born Edward E. Clive (and no relation to Colin Clive) in Monmouthshire, Wales in 1879. Clive has learned his acting rubrics with "the Penny Gaff," a caravan of wagons bearing actors, props, scenery and benches for spectators, that toured the British Isles in the early 1900s. Arriving in New York in 1912, Clive played Marley's Ghost in *A Christmas Carol* and made Boston theatre history as manager of The Copley Players. Clive was especially proud of the free performances he and the Copley players presented at Massachusetts State Prison

and the appreciative letters he received from inmates for many years afterward.

Clive will relish some of the best lines in *The Invisible Man* — such as, "'E's *invisible*, that's what's the matter with him. If he gets the rest of them clothes off, we'll never catch him in a thousand years!"

Chief of Detectives: Dudley Digges, Irish actor and Theatre Guild confrere of Rains, played Casper Gutman ("The Fat Man") in the original 1931 film version of *The Maltese Falcon*. Here, as the Chief Inspector, he has a dynamic role and a break from his usual screen villainy. Indeed, as the unspeakable reform school head in Warner Bros.' *The Mayor of Hell*, Digges had experienced the most spectacular demise of any 1933 Hollywood heavy short of King Kong: chased in the night by the bloodthirsty reform school kids with torches (a la *Frankenstein*), taking refuge atop a barn, falling, landing on a barbed wire fence, and tumbling into a pen of hogs.

The remainder of the cast is excellent. Holmes Herbert, who played Dr. Lanyon in Paramount's *Dr. Jekyll*

E.E. Clive (center) as P.C. Jaffers

and *Mr. Hyde* (1931), signs to portray the Chief of Police. Harry Stubbs accepts the role of Inspector Bird, the Invisible Man's first murder victim, and will portray a showy piece of mime – pretending the Invisible One is strangling him to death. Merle Tottenham, who'd acted with Una O'Connor in *Cavalcade*, will play Millie, slovenly maid of The Lion's Head Inn.

Also landing jobs in *The Invisible Man* are two character players on the eve of Hollywood success. Walter Brennan plays a yokel whose bicycle the Invisible Man steals and rides; Brennan will soon win the first of his three Academy Awards for *Come and Get It* (1936). And

playing an Informer, in derby hat and droopy mustache, is John Carradine, three years away from his triumph as the sadistic jailer of John Ford's *The Prisoner of Shark Island*.

Finally, for fans of Classic Universal Horror, there will be a shocker in *The Invisible Man*. Popping up as an anonymous, bespectacled reporter will be Dwight Frye, who chewed up the scenery (and the flies) as Renfield in *Dracula* and tortured Karloff's Monster as Fritz in *Frankenstein*. After enjoying these richly macabre roles, Frye, hopelessly typecast, accepts this virtual bit with only four lines of dialogue. Whale, an admirer of Frye's

talent, cast him wherever he could (and will do much better by him in *Bride of Frankenstein*, with Frye superb as the grave-robbing ghoul, Karl).

Meanwhile, a true superstar of *The Invisible Man* will be forever off-screen. He's John Fulton, Universal's 31-year old, Nebraska-born Special Effects wizard, known at the studio as "The Doctor" as he worked his magic on such films as *Frankenstein*, John Ford's *Air Mail* (Fulton was an aviator), and *The Mummy*. Fulton takes on the monumental challenge of *The Invisible Man* — if the Special Effects are unconvincing, audiences will laugh the film off the screen and the failure could be the downfall of Universal City.

Perhaps as critical as the Special Effects, however, is the very moving sensitivity that R.C. Sherriff has invested in his script. He's given strange nobility to the title horror character – a man with a dream that inspires him to conquer an early life of want and poverty. When Flora asks Jack Griffin why he pursues his mad science, he responds:

For you, Flora...Yes, for you, my darling. I wanted to do something tremendous. To achieve what men of science have dreamt of since the world began. To gain fame and wealth and honor. To write my name among the greatest scientists of all time. I was so pitifully poor. I had nothing to offer you, Flora. I was just a poor, struggling chemist. I shall come back to you Flora. Very soon now...

This surely appeals to Jimmy Whale. While he's led most of Hollywood to believe he's an English aristocrat, educated by private tutors, he's truly a poor boy from Dudley, England, who'd had his first taste of Drama staging shows at a POW camp in Germany — and had conquered his many challenges to become an acclaimed film director. And the approach surely appeals to Claude Rains, who's overcome poverty, a speech impediment, semi-blindness, diminutive height, and a traumatic love life to be starring in a major motion picture.

Both director and star can relate to this tragedy about the desire for power and glory. The project becomes oddly, deeply personal. In late June of 1933, *The Invisible Man* begins shooting.

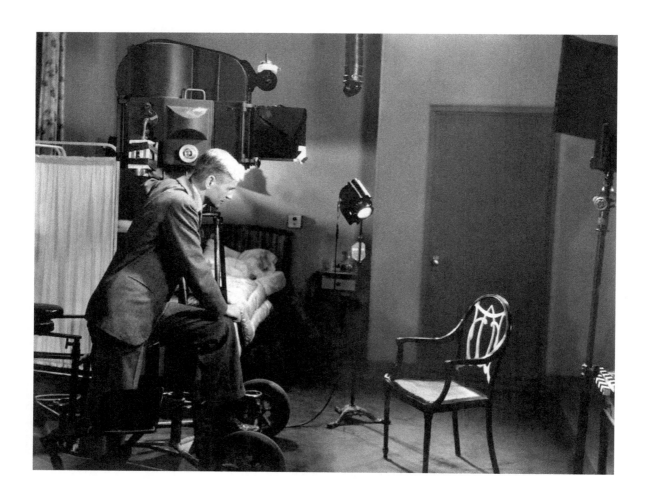

James Whale directing "The Invisible Man"

James Whale directing "The Invisible Man"

35

Part IX.
The "Cock-a-Hoop"
"An Invisible Man can rule the world! Nobody will see him come, nobody will see him go! He can hear every secret! He can rob and wreck and kill!"

—Claude Rains as *The Invisible Man*.

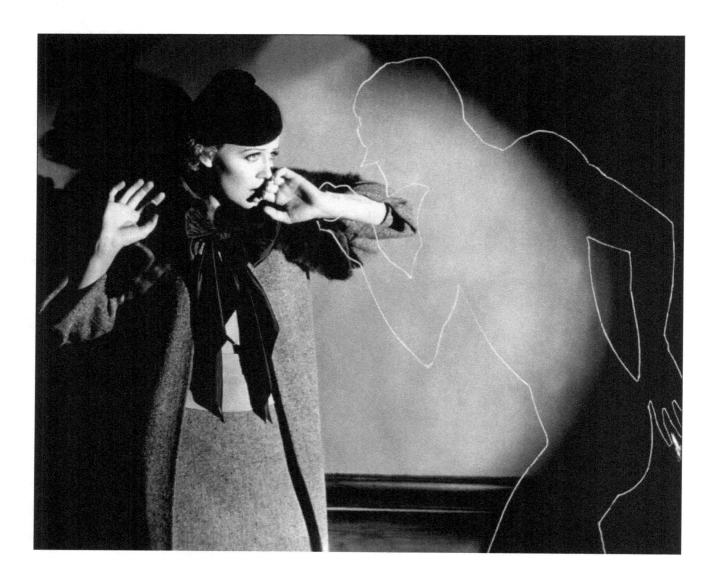

Claude Rains takes quarters at the Hollywood Knickerbocker Hotel as production of *The Invisible Man* begins with the "straight" scenes. Rains will tell reporter Eileen Creelman:

For five years, five years, mind you, I was prating to the Theatre Guild about my "artistic integrity." I was so cock-a-hoop about it. My "artistic integrity." Then the first day at the studio James brought over some bandages. I asked him about them, and he said, Oh yes, I was to be bandaged during most of the picture. And there I had been fighting with the Theatre Guild about my "artistic integrity." Oh, it served me right!

Rains laughs about it in later years, but in the summer of 1933, *The Invisible Man* is no laughing matter for the actor, who has learned only after his arrival in Hollywood that his face will not be seen.

"Not my eyes?" laments Rains, proud of his piercing features. "Not even *just my eyes?*"

There's immediate trouble. Whale sends Rains to the Universal laboratory "to have a cast made," as Rains later tells Andre D. Sennwald in a *New York Times* interview (December 3, 1933):

That should have been a warning. The laboratory had an odd look. There were all sorts of casts about, in papier-mâché, clay and plaster. Men in white coats walked about without noise. "Have you ever done this before?" one of them asked me. "No," I answered, getting apprehensive. "Well, we'll get you a shirt. It's a dirty business," he said. He asked if I had shaved. I said rather indignantly, you know, that I had. "Well, we'll get you some Vaseline for your face, then," he said.

They made a cast and nailed me in. Just my head stuck out. They smeared me with Vaseline and then stood off and threw plaster at my head. I thought I was going to die. It was a most alarming operation. Really, I'm afraid I behaved rather badly!

Rains, nailed into his cast, genuinely battles hysteria as the "men in white coats," having thrown the plaster at him so it stuck to his face, put straws up his nose so he can breathe. He battles not only claustrophobia and his own bantam temperament, but also memories of his hospitalization during the war. At last the ordeal ends.

"I went back the next day," Rains will recall, "and saw masks and half-masks of my head all over the place."

As the Universal lab works on the helmet necessary for the Special Effects scenes, Rains, former Theater Guild "cock-a-hoop," reports to a sound stage — dingy bandages around his head, goggles over his beautiful eyes, sporting a fake beak of a nose, a ratty toupee peeking here and there through the bandages like a misplaced bird's nest. The ego bridles, and Rains, in a desperate stab at matinee idol style, cocks his homburg hat over his bandaged head whenever he's outside the soundstage.

Unfortunately, the sight of the dapper, goggled mummy in the homburg hat causes Universal-at-large to burst into laughter. Rains fumes.

The press, aware of the bizarre nature of Rains' role and perhaps his hair-trigger temperament, enjoys its pot shots too. On July 20, Harrison Carroll writes in *The Evening Herald* and *Express*:

It's the gate-man gag, but it actually happened and they're getting a great laugh out of it at Universal.

The other day, Claude Rains, newcomer from the stage, was stopped as he tried to drive his car on the lot.

"Who are you?" asked the gateman.

"I'm Claude Rains," the actor explained. "I'm playing out here in The Invisible Man.*"*

The movie St. Peter looked bored. "Oh yeah," he said. "Well, you'll have to make your car invisible too. I can't let you in."

Now and then the press runs a notice on another player from *The Invisible Man*. Rosalind Shaffer, Hollywood correspondent of the *Chicago Daily Tribune*, files this report (July 6, 1933):

When Una O'Connor, Irish actress now appearing in Universal's The Invisible Man, *first met Joseph McDonough, assistant director at Universal, she gave McDonough something to ponder about. "The assistant director of the first play I appeared in, in Ireland, was named McDonough," she reminisced. "He was an ardent Sinn Feiner, and not long after our play he was active in the Easter rebellion and was hanged. I'm glad to know you too, Mr. McDonough."*

McDonough just wonders.

However, it's Claude Rains who fascinates Hollywood, which basically considers him a freak attraction as he stars as the Invisible One. His anger and insecurity swell. Little wonder that such flamboyant, r-trilling passion rings in Rains' voice as Jack Griffin raves at The Lion's Head yokels:

Alright, you fools! You brought it on yourselves! Everything would have come out right if you had left me alone! You've driven me near madness with your peering through the keyholes and peeping through the curtains. And now, you'll suffer for it! You're CRRRAZY to know who I am, aren't you? Alright — I'll show you!

Off comes the nose, the toupee, the bandages — and Rains unleashes one of the wildest, most unforgettably insane laughs in the Movies.

No other candidates for the Invisible Man role could have possibly matched Rains' bravura in this classic scene. William Powell would have delivered this speech merely with an insouciant tongue-in-cheek. Karloff's lisp would have ill-served such lines as "peering through the keyholes and peeping through the curtains." And Colin Clive's fraught, "It's Alive!"- style hysteria as he laughed insanely would have over-chilled audiences — fearful that his mad cackling might never stop.

In a happy dash of Hollywood destiny, Claude Rains *is* — madly, movingly, and apocalyptically — The Invisible Man.

Of course, as star of the show, Rains quickly discovers he has much to dominate: Una O'Connor's scream, E.E. Clive's deadpan, and the stunningly blonde beauty of Gloria Stuart. Rains suffers more shame as Whale notes that Gloria — in her high heels — is taller than Claude. In their big scene together, Rains, still bandaged and goggled (but costumed in a beautiful dressing gown and ascot) finds himself standing on a box beside his gorgeous co-star. He retaliates by trying to scene-steal from his leading lady - mercilessly. Almost 60 years later, Gloria talked with me about the upstaging antics of her Invisible Man:

In the profession, we have a saying — "He's an actor's actor." It's a little deprecating – it means enormous ego, enormous self-involvement, and so forth. Well...Claude was "an actor's actor's actor"! A very nice person and a brilliant actor. But the first day on the set was a little difficult...he started to back me into the scenery!

I turned and said, "James – Look what he's doing!"

And James said, "Now Claude, be nice to Gloria, because this is not the stage. If you back her into the scenery on the stage, that's it. But we can take it over again and over again and over again, so she gets her share of the camera. And this is how it's done!"

Claude was completely cold, only thinking of his performance...There was no camaraderie, no feeling about any concern for the other actor. He was not one of my favorite people, I'm afraid; he never extended himself in any direction as far as being gracious, or saying "Hello"...No, it was very difficult with him. I didn't suffer with Claude, because I had a very strong director, but I didn't enjoy it at all. Of course, it didn't help that Claude was shorter than I was, so he was always standing on a box while I was always in my stocking feet – and in a trench!

As revealed in the film, Whale eventually handles the height problem quite easily: He has Rains and Gloria act most of their key scene together seated.

Whale, meanwhile, has a grand time directing *The Invisible Man*. Indeed, having been an actor in London, appearing in such plays as 1928's *A Man with Red Hair* (with Charles Laughton as the title role sadist, and Whale as his lunatic son), he likely wishes he could play the Invisible One himself. The director delights in the snowy night opening at The Lion's Head Inn, with its host of eccentrics the director bases on his own "Black Country" youth in Dudley, England: A derby-sporting hambone playing a player piano; a gaggle of old women drinking by the staircase; the dart-throwing villagers. He works as smoothly as ever with his cinematographer Arthur Edeson, cameraman of *All Quiet on the Western Front* and Whale's *Waterloo Bridge*, *Frankenstein*, *The Impatient Maiden* and *The Old Dark House*. Director and cinematographer treat Rains to a deluxe entrance, with three quick, increasing close-ups — just as Karloff had received in *Frankenstein*. Whale enjoys the atmosphere of the village of "Iping," built on Universal's back lot, and copes with a misadventure: The barn, scheduled to be set afire by the police as they stalk the Invisible Man and shoot him in the snow, actually does catch fire and burn to the ground when a smudge pot overturns, setting the hay afire. The crew hastily rebuilds the barn and the following night, it goes up in flames on cue.

Ever the perfectionist, Whale fires off this August 1, 1933 memo about "Red Light Signals" - i.e., a flashing light that warns anyone outside a soundstage that a scene is being shot:

Time after time the perfect take has been ruined by motor cars and trucks driving past the red light signal outside the Invisible Man *stage. If a general warning does no good, I think a watchman would save the company at least twelve times his salary.*

James Whale

Always, Whale enjoys puncturing the ego of his star. Rains constantly begs Whale to let him act even more emotionally.

"I thought at least I could try to express something with my eyes," Rains will remember. "Then Whale would say, 'But Claude, old fellow, what are you going to do it with? You haven't any face!'"

Part X.
The Doctor's Black Magic

There are one or two things you must understand, Kemp. I must always remain in hiding for an hour after meals. The food is visible inside me until it is digested. I can only work on fine, clear days. If I work in the rain, the water can be seen on my head and shoulders. In a fog, you can see me, like a bubble. In smoky cities the soot settles on me until you can see a dark outline. You must always be near at hand to wipe off my feet. Even dirt between my fingernails would give me away. It is difficult at first to walk down stairs, we are so accustomed to watching our feet...
—Claude Rains, *The Invisible Man*

Whale completes the "straight" scenes in mid-August. Incidentally, Boris Karloff, his new pact with Universal announced by Harrison Carroll in the *Evening Herald Express* on July 10, comes back to the fold, the publicity promising that he'll reprise the Monster in *The Return of Frankenstein* (which morphs into 1935's *Bride of Frankenstein*). A good sport and a gentleman, Karloff pays a friendly visit to *The Invisible Man* set. (He sticks to his two-month leave, however — departing in August for the Arizona desert to play the religious lunatic in John Ford's *The Lost Patrol* for RKO.)

It's now time for "the Doctor," John P. Fulton, to work his Special Effects magic. There are several key techniques:

A. The easiest gimmickry comes in scenes where props move "by themselves." The crew attaches thin wires to the props (books, a drawer of money, etc.) and moves them from overhead. For example, in the scene where the Invisible Man rides a bicycle through the village, wires from a "boom" or "dolly" actually perform the action.

B. For the unforgettable shot where Rains, in ghoulishly good humor, unwraps his bandaged head to reveal to the villagers – nothing! – Rains' own head is hidden below his collar, the bandages actually wrapping a thin wire fame invisible on the screen.

C. The vast majority of Trick Shots in *The Invisible Man*, however, require a far more complex procedure: a "multiple printing" technique, blending four different pieces of film together.

In September of 1934, a year after Universal completes *The Invisible Man*, Fulton explains his trickery in *American Cinematographer* magazine:

The wire technique could not be used, for the clothes would look empty, and would hardly move naturally. So we had recourse to multiple printing – with variations. Most of these scenes involved other, normal characters, so we photographed these scenes in the normal manner, but without any trace of the Invisible Man. All of the action, of course, had to be very carefully timed, as in any sort of double exposure work. The negative was then developed in the normal manner.

Then the special process work began. We used a completely black set – walled and floored with black velvet, so to be as nearly non-reflective as possible. Our actor was garbed from head to foot in black velvet tights, with black gloves, and a black headpiece rather like a diver's

"Invisible Man" Cameraman, Make-up Artist and Art Director Divide Honors

Another of those weird pictures that have made Universal famous was brought to the screen in H. G. Wells' fantastic story, "Invisible Man." This time the horrors have even honors with many peculiar situations that brought hearty laughter to the preview audience, but were entirely plausible. No doubt many of you know H. G. Wells' story of the scientist who discovered a chemical that will make him invisible to the human eye with its attendant results.

The honors of this production go equally to Arthur Edeson, whose camera effects made this picture possible; to Charles D. Hall for his art direction, and Jack Pierce, make-up artist, for the weird result attained by the "Invisible Man." James Whale directed skillfully the splendid cast that held the audience spellbound at times with the many surprising situations. Claude Rains, who was brought from New York to play the role of the invisible man, did a splendid piece of work with his vivid characterization. In fact, we don't know of any other player who could have given the character so much dignity and realism. Gloria Stuart was particularly satisfying and lovely as Flora Cranley, the girl who was in love with the invisible man, while Dudley Digges gave his usual fine performance as the chief detective.

Special mention must be made of Una O'Connor and Forrester Harvey, owners of the English Pub where most of the action takes place. Henry Travers, Donald Stuart, Merle Tottenham, Harry Stubbs and E. E. Clive were adequate in the other characters.

For those who enjoyed the former horror pictures produced by Carl Laemmle. Jr., will find this one the best produced so far: it should reap a heavy harvest at the box-office.

From Jack Pierce's scrapbook - formerly owned by Doug Norwine

helmet. Over this, he wore whatever clothes might be required. This gave us a picture of the unsupported clothes moving around on a dead black field. From this negative, we made a print, and a duplicate negative which we intensified to serve as mattes for printing. Then, with an ordinary printer, we proceeded to make our composite: first we printed from the positive of the background and the normal action, using the intensified, negative matte to mask off the area where our Invisible Man's clothing was to move. Then we printed again, using the positive matte to shield the already printed area, and printing in the moving clothes from our "trick" negative. The printing operation made our duplicate, composite negative to be used in printing the final masterprints of the picture.

The two principal difficulties, photographically speaking, were matching up the lighting on the visible parts of my shot with the general lighting used by Arthur Edeson, A.S.C., for the normal parts of the picture; and eliminating the various little imperfections – such as eye-holes, etc. – which were naturally picked up by the camera. This latter was done by retouching the film –

frame by frame – with a brush and opaque dye. We photographed thousands of feet of film in the many 'takes' of the different scenes, and approximately 4,000 feet of film received individual hand-work treatment in some degree.

John J. Mescall, who will be cinematographer of Edgar G. Ulmer's *The Black Cat* (1934) and Whale's *Bride of Frankenstein* (1935), works with Fulton on these critical sequences, as well as on the shooting of the miniatures. Although Fulton was willing to reveal his methods after the film's release and original reception, all of the magic of *The Invisible Man*, as Gloria Stuart will recall, develops in utmost secrecy as the production progresses. Rains watches the wire trickery – e.g., the Invisible Man riding a bike – and says, "I sat about for hours watching them do it, and I never had such a lark in my life!"

Yet the Special Effects magic takes a terrible toll on the star. In his black velvet tights, gloves, and black helmet with air hoses attached, Rains evokes some horrid deep sea diver mutant; he's able only to hear clearly the

41

To Stanley Best wishes Gloria Stuart

rush of his own air supply as Fulton tries desperately to shout to him through a megaphone; he must be perfectly precise in his movements, under merciless lights on a hot soundstage in summer heat. A tendency to place accidentally his black-gloved hand over a part of his visible costume results in as many as 20 agonizing "takes."

At least once — due to the heat, a faulty air hose, exhaustion, or all of these — Rains faints on the set.

Still, the actor endures, sometimes relieved by a double. And, perhaps as a wry comment on the outrageousness of this whole mad business, Rains still wears his homburg hat between scenes — now cocked atop his diving helmet.

It's all over, for the most part, by late September. Charlie Baker performs wonders in the film — including the Invisible One's terrorizing execution of a spectacular train wreck - in the studio's miniature department. John Fulton is still retouching individual frames of film and Universal despairs about meeting *The Invisible Man's* arranged shipping dates.

In fact, the trickery of *The Invisible Man* is so superb that one mystery has remained unsolved to this day: the fade-out appearance of Jack Griffin on his deathbed. Is it Rains or a dummy? Fulton claimed it was Rains: that the Special Effect began with the head's indent on a plaster pillow and a blanket made of papier-mâché; then came a lap dissolve of a real skeleton; then several lap dissolves of a dummy of Rains; and finally Rains himself.

"But my eyes are closed!" Rains supposedly protests.

Others argue that what audiences will see is a life mask with a wig. The mystery perpetuates. (Note: Jessica Rains, the actor's daughter, firmly believes it's her father in the flesh in the fade-out.)

All in all, Rains comes to savor the experience of *The Invisible Man*, and Hollywood. He gallantly speaks to a British reporter, offering only upbeat remarks:

This new film work of mine is an adventure. It is a strange, exotic, thrilling experience…a most enjoyable experience, particularly since I had such a sympathetic, patient and charming director as Jimmy Whale.

And Gloria Stuart is a grand girl; Una O'Connor, too. Last night I had a most enjoyable time. I motored to the summit of Mount Wilson and from the observatory indulged in my hobby of astronomy. And today I am going to the Huntingdon Library to enjoy that great collection of Gainsborough's. Cheerio!

After all his pains on *The Invisible Man*, the studio has no new assignment for him. Rains cocks his homburg hat and heads home to his New Jersey farm.

"I was very depressed," Rains will remember. "I was not married then — I was alone, so I wept and wailed and carried on all by myself."

It might be a hard winter on the farm.

Part XI.
A NASTY PUMPKINHEAD

...unlimited exploitation angles...The pressbook will be full of them, undoubtedly; there are a million more you can concoct, not the least of which are those that can be applied to women to stir their curiosity. How would you like to be embraced, kissed, by an invisible lover, an invisible man prying into their inmost secrets, an invisible man prowling the streets, a man they never see until he's dead....

- *Film Daily,* writing about the "sex sell" of *The Invisible Man,* November 4, 1933.

Heinz Roemheld - Photo by Jack Freulich
(Courtesy of Randall D. Larson)

The Universal scoring stage in the 1930s

Heinz Roemheld, who later scores Universal's *The Black Cat* (1934) and *Dracula's Daughter* (1936), and who will win an Academy Award for Warner Bros.' *Yankee Doodle Dandy* (1942) composes a score for *The Invisible Man* that is full of both whimsy and melodrama. It's also peculiar in its use: heard only in the opening and closing credits, and the last seven minutes of the film.

John P. Fulton works to the absolute last minute on the Special Effects. The final cost of *The Invisible Man:* $328,033. The promotional catch phrase: "Catch Me if You Can!"

Thursday, October 26, 1933: The Invisible Man plays a press preview at the Fairfax Theatre on Beverly Boulevard. UNIVERSAL'S INVISIBLE MAN IS BIG BET FOR SHOWMEN, headlines *The Hollywood Reporter* the next morning:

As we came out of the theatre someone near us said, "Here's the answer to a showman's prayer." And about all we can add to that is to remark that if the showman doesn't know how to use it he had better quit saying his prayers. There's no hope, here or hereafter.

Invisible Man is a legitimate offspring of the family that produced Frankenstein *and* Dracula, *but a lusty, healthy, willing-to-laugh youngster, who can stand on his own feet. And while we are indirectly comparing, we may as well add that it is a picture that will fare better in the neighborhoods than either of its predecessors, for while it is "horror" it is in reality "horror comedy" – they get their laughs with the shrieks, and the kiddies won't go home to sport in nightmares through the slumbering hours...*

We could dispose of all the credits by saying that all concerned did a great job. But if names must be mentioned, let's start with James Whale for a concept and execution, timing, tempo and change of pace, that are masterly. Some of that credit should naturally be split with the author of the screenplay, R. C. Sherriff.

It's tough on Claude Rains to make his debut in a part in which he isn't seen until the last few feet, and then as a corpse, but perhaps that's all the more reason to compliment him on the sport of acting that DOES put the character over...

Friday, November 10: It's Claude Rains' 44th birthday, and *The Invisible Man* opens at the Palace Theatre in Chicago. "This Thriller Is No Movie for Nervous," headlines critic Mae Tinee (who clearly bases her *nom de plume* on "matinee") in *The Chicago Tribune*:

This is a thriller, all right...Through much of the action, Claude Rains, that fine young Theatre Guild player, is only a voice...He has excellent support, and smart direction and marvelous trick photography combine to raise The Invisible Man *well above the standard of the average horror cinema...*

The Invisible Man plays a week at Chicago's Palace, with a take of $24,500. (The high at the Palace had been *Morning Glory*, at $37,000; the low, *Below the Sea*, at $14,000.)

Monday, November 13: In the New York City-based trade paper *The Film Daily*, Phil M. Daly (who obviously bases his *nom de plume* on *Film Daily*) praises *The Invisible Man* in his "Along the Rialto" Column, predicting great things as the movie approaches its New York and Los Angeles premieres:

A showman who has never yet gone overboard in any advance statements about a picture cuts loose for the first time in talking about Universal's Invisible Man, *scheduled to play the Roxy...Publicity director Morris Kinzler told us, "If this picture hasn't got it, I'm ready to go out of show-biz"...The reasons for his enthusiasm are easily understood. Director James Whale has done the seeming impossible in* The Invisible Man...*the sum total is a Novelty Thriller that ranks Mister Whale among the greatest directors of all time.*

Friday, November 17: *The Invisible Man* opens at the RKO-Hillstreet Theatre in Los Angeles and at the Roxy Theatre in New York City. Again, the reviews are raves. *The Los Angeles Times* headlines "INVISIBLE MAN APPEARS!" and writes:

...The Invisible Man is like no other film drama you have ever experienced....Not, strictly speaking, a horror story at all, the Wells fantasy is really a humorous grotesquerie of unique pretensions. And so peculiarly suited to the cinema is it that it may well rate as the most ingenious effort of its kind in years...Spiritedly directed, as it were, by James Whale....Rains is admirable as the hunted one; at least he sounds admirable... The Invisible Man *is movie legerdemain at its best.*

The New York Times writes:

No actor has ever made his first appearance on the screen under quite as peculiar circumstances as Claude Rains does in the picturization of H.G. Wells' novel The Invisible Man... *The eerie tale evidently afforded a Roman holiday for the camera aces. Photographic magic abounds...The story makes such superb cinematic material that one wonders that Hollywood did not film it sooner. Now that it has been done, it is a remarkable achievement.*

Despite the reviews, Universal despairs: *The Invisible Man* is playing to a near-empty house at L.A.'s RKO-Hillstreet. However, lightning has struck at New York's Roxy: In its first three days there, *The Invisible Man* takes in a walloping $26,000.

Monday, November 20: *Time* magazine reports:

While other Hollywood producers confine themselves to the humdrum mishaps of prostitutes, millionaires, and college footballers, Carl Laemmle Jr.'s Universal Studio specializes darkly in supernatural pasquinades. The hero of The Invisible Man *is as nasty a pumpkinhead as Frankenstein's Monster or* The Mummy...*Claude Rains gives an alarming performance, almost as frightening when he is present as when he is not.*

"The strangest character yet created by the screen roams through *The Invisible Man*," reports *Variety*, the "show business Bible," and Universal enjoys its greatest horror hit since *Frankenstein*. At the Roxy in New York, the film tallies a week's take of $42,000, breaking the house record for the previous three-and-half years. It does $23,000 in its second week, then moves to two theatres — the Radio City Roxy and the RKO Palace — to continue big business. Oddly, in L.A., *The Invisible Man* never picks up, laying an egg at the RKO-Hillstreet, its excruciatingly bad $4,300 week's take blamed on lack of promotion and exploitation.

In London, *The Invisible Man* opens January 28, 1934 at the Tivoli Theatre, and is a smash. The management erects a huge sign of the Invisible Man outlined in neon tube lighting, now and then obliterated by jets of steam. *Motion Picture Herald* (March 17, 1934) reports on pre-opening publicity in the streets of London:

Four days in advance, a bannered roadster was put on the streets and by an ingenious control device it was made to appear as though an invisible man was driving...white gloved hands appearing to drive the car with no driver in view...

The car bore the words, "This Car Driven by the INVISIBLE MAN Now on his Way to the TIVOLI." As *Motion Picture Herald* wrote,

The gag went over enormously, so much so that the publicists were arrested and fined for breaking the city ordinance against ballyhoos of theatre. However...the Universal-ites were not at all cast down as a result of the forthcoming publicity.

The laurels keep coming. The *New York Times* awards *The Invisible Man* the #9 spot on its 1933 "Ten Best" List. The Venice Film Festival awards James Whale a "Special Recommendation" prize. Even H. G. Wells praises the film, especially the trick photography and the performances of Una O'Connor and Forrester Harvey. Most exhibitors love *The Invisible Man* — e.g., William A. Crute of the Victoria Theatre in Vancouver, British Columbia, who writes to *Motion Picture Herald*:

Society beware! The Invisible Man is on the loose!

(April 28, 1934):

This is a box office natural. We broke records with this picture. The first night we had the house sold out before we started and held them out until the second show and filled it again. The second night came up to expectation, too...

James Whale has reversed his recent flops, directed a new super-hit, and sails home in glory for a 12-week vacation in his native England, where he, R.C. Sherriff and H.G. Wells all appear at a trade reception for *The Invisible Man*. Claude Rains wins international fame . Andre D. Sennwald of the *New York Times* arranges an interview, writing he awaits Rains "with fingers crossed and an ancient Spanish formula for expelling devils." Instead, he meets a high-spirited actor, rejoicing in his triumph.

"Mr. Rains came in at the door with a loud and tangible guffaw," reports Sennwald, "and announced that if the cinema kept throwing money at him he planned to buy a flock of sheep for his farm in New Jersey."

Before going back to Hollywood, however, Rains signs for a Broadway play, *They Shall Not Die*, in which he plays Nathan G. Rubin, defense attorney of unjustly accused blacks in the controversial Scottsboro case. The plays opens at the Royale Theatre on February 21, 1934, and Rains wins cheers nightly with his climactic courtroom speech. While he's in the play, writers Ben Hecht and Charles MacArthur sign Rains to star in his second film, *Crime Without Passion*, which they themselves direct in New York. Rains' role: a flashy criminal lawyer who murders a woman and goes insane.

Eventually, Universal recalls Rains for two films: *The Man Who Reclaimed his Head* (1934), in which he reprises his stage role of mad Paul Verin, and *Mystery of Edwin Drood* (1935), based on Dickens' unfinished novel, with Rains as dope-addicted John Jasper. He performs Poe's "The Tell-Tale Heart" on Rudy Vallee's radio show (April 4, 1935). His life continues with drama — his New Jersey farm burns down, due either to lightning or arson — and his marital adventures continue. In April of 1935, only hours after his divorce from Beatrix Thomson becomes final, he marries his fourth wife, Frances Propper, whom he'd met in the Theatre Guild. A famous headline reads:

INVISIBLE MAN DIVORCES WIFE

Part XII.
The Impact

I meddled in things that man must leave alone.

Claude Rains in The Invisible Man.

Today, almost 80 years after its premiere, *The Invisible Man* is still a macabre masterpiece. It is, certainly, a James Whale picture; indeed, how splendidly does the director mix Claude Rains' suave, rising hysteria and John P. Fulton's dazzling Special Effects magic with his own bravura, theatrical style. And how strikingly does he spike the film with his odd, misanthropic comedy!

In the movie's windy, snowy opening, on that fateful night at The Lion's Head Inn, we hear a Cockney morbidly explaining how a neighbor's "little Willy" was extracted from a ten-foot snow drift – "Brought the fire engine around, put the hose part in, pumped it backwards, and *sucked* him out!" – followed by a shriek of sadistic, communal laughter. It's Whale's attack on the narrow fearful minds and petty savagery of basic society – an attack he'll have in common with his title character. Indeed, from the moment that The Invisible One throws open the inn door in a blast of howling wind and snow, and poses for those three classic Whale close-ups....

Society beware!

With a glorious, charismatic insanity, for which the village yokels are no match, Rains' Jack Griffin carries out Whale's charge - hurling a bottle at Una O'Connor's picture, throttling dense policeman Clive, dumping a baby out of a carriage, stealing a bicycle, throwing an old man's hat into a pond. He causes a jolly riot in the village streets by removing a drawer of cash from a bank, throwing it about outside, singing "That's the Way the Money Goes" to the tune of "Pop Goes the Weasel" as the oafish villagers battle to grasp the fluttering bills. Of course, the "mischief" eventually escalates to true horror, as Griffin destroys the train. And his execution of Kemp becomes a horrible carnival ride, Rains a grotesque barker:

I hope your car's insured, Kemp. I'm afraid there's going to be a nasty accident in a minute – a very nasty accident... Just sit where you are. I'll get out and take the handbrake off and give you a little shove to help you on. You'll run gently down and through the railings. Then you'll have a big thrill for a hundred yards or so until you hit a boulder. Then you'll do a somersault, and probably break your arms. Then a grand finish-up with a broken neck. Goodbye, Kemp! I always said you were a dirty little coward. You're a dirty, sneaking little rat as well. Goodbye!

And he laughs in celebratory, hysteric joy as the car plunges over the cliff and explodes into flames.

It's a brilliant, funny, frightening and strangely personal film. And when *The Invisible Man* presents a pair of pants, merrily skipping down a country lane at night, singing "Here We Go Gathering Nuts in May" and chasing a fat, screaming woman, it's as if a 2013 audience is seeing (or *not* seeing!) the sardonic ghost of Jimmy Whale, enjoying his own mad, wonderful romp of a movie.

*

46

Boris Karloff visits James Whale on the set of The Invisible Man after resolving his contract dispute with Universal.
(Courtesy of the late Richard Bojarski)

Come the early 1940s, Universal produced an Invisible Man series. *The Invisible Man Returns* (1940) starred Vincent Price as Frank Griffin, brother of Jack, who's improved monocaine so it's now duocaine; the villain was Sir Cedric Hardwicke, Joe May directed, and the film afforded the Invisible Man a happy ending. *The Invisible Woman* (1941), basically a slapstick comedy, starred a wheezing John Barrymore as a mad scientist who makes Virginia Bruce invisible (she promptly gets drunk and goes prancing about in just her stockings); A. Edward Sutherland directed. *Invisible Agent* (1942) presented an invisible Jon Hall battling Nazi Sir Cedric Hardwicke and Japanese Peter Lorre, aided and abetted by femme fatale spy Ilona Massey; Edwin Marin directed. Jon Hall returned for the title role in *The Invisible Man's Revenge* (1944); the mad scientist was John Carradine (who walks an invisible Great Dane on a leash), the leading lady was Evelyn Ankers, and the director was Ford Beebe. John P. Fulton worked on the entire series, winning Special Effects Oscar nominations for *The Invisible Man Returns*, *The Invisible Woman* and *Invisible Agent*.

While the grosses on the original *The Invisible Man* aren't available, the following figures show the popularity of Universal's series:

The Invisible Man Returns: Cost, $281,743. Total gross, $815,100.

The Invisible Woman: Cost, $269, 062. Total gross, $659,600.

Invisible Agent: Cost, $322, 291. Total gross, $1,041,500.

The Invisible Man's Revenge: Cost, $314, 790. Total gross, $765, 700.

The Invisible Man (with voice courtesy of Vincent Price) turned up in a "cameo" for the fadeout laugh of Universal-International's super hit *Abbott and Costello Meet Frankenstein* (1948). In 1951, *Abbott and Costello Meet the Invisible Man* had Arthur Franz sharing the title spot with the comics.

One of the most enjoyable offspring of the original *The Invisible Man* came in *Son of the Invisible Man*, one of the episodes in the satire feature *Amazon Women of the Moon* (1987). Carl Gottlieb directed this skit in which Ed Begley, Jr. (in an inn remarkably like the one in the 1933 film) *thinks* he's invisible — with hilarious results.

Part XIII.
The Posterity

Good men, while slated to inherit the earth and the kingdom of Heaven too, are rarely as captivating to the eye as a polished blackguard. Or to the mind, for that matter. People can't help saying, "My, my. If only the rascal had turned his talents in the proper channels – what a power for good he would have become!" It's the reforming instinct in mankind, I guess.
–Claude Rains, 1941

As for the major talents of *The Invisible Man*:

Gloria Stuart, "Flora," wed writer Arthur Sheekman, co-scripter of such Marx Brothers classics as *Monkey Business* and *Duck Soup*. They had a daughter, Sylvia. Gloria later joined 20th Century-Fox, where she starred in such films as John Ford's *The Prisoner of Shark Island* (1936) and with Shirley Temple in *Poor Little Rich Girl* (1936) and *Rebecca of Sunnybrook Farm* (1938). She later worked on the stage and then devoted herself to being a mother, artist and hostess. After Sheekman's death in 1978 Gloria gradually reactivated her career, appearing in such films as *My Favorite Year* (1982) and, ultimately, the $250,000,000 spectacular, *Titanic* (1997), for which she received a Best Supporting Actress Oscar nomination. (She lost to Kim Basinger for *L.A Confidential.*) She published her memoir, *I Just Kept Hoping*, written with her daughter, Sylvia Thompson, in 1999, and on August 24, 2001, appeared as the grandmother to Darien Fawkes (Vincent Ventresca), the title character in the Sci-Fi Channel's *The Invisible Man*. Gloria Stuart died September 26, 2010, at the age of 100.

William Harrigan, "Kemp," after completing *The Invisible Man*, promptly went back to Broadway and played Charlie Chan in *Keeper of the Keys* (October 18, 1933), in which his *The Invisible Man* colleague Dwight Frye co-starred as an aged Chinaman. A highlight of Harrigan's career was enacting the tyrannical Captain in Broadway's *Mr. Roberts* (February 18, 1948), which he played for almost three years and 1,158 performances. He acted in many films including *G-Men* (1935), *Flying Leathernecks* (1951), and his last, *Street of Sinners* (1957). William Harrigan died February 1, 1966 in New York City at the age of 79. He was buried with full military honors at Arlington National Cemetery.

Henry Travers, "Dr. Cranley," returned to Broadway in the Moss Hart/George S. Kaufman Pulitzer Prize winner, *You Can't Take It With You*, which opened December 14, 1936. (He suffered a great disappointment when he came back to Hollywood to star in Frank Capra's 1938 film version, only to be replaced at the last minute by Lionel Barrymore.) He'd act in over 50 films, notably as the old rose gardener in *Mrs. Miniver* (1942, winning a Best Supporting Actor Oscar nomination) and of course, Clarence the angel in Capra's *It's a Wonderful Life* (1946). Travers retired from films in 1949 and died at Villa Gardens Convalescent Hospital in Los Angeles on October 18, 1965, at age 91.

Una O'Connor, "Jenny Hall," tallied a grand repertoire of roles in classic 1930s films — Victor McLaglen's saintly mother in *The Informer* (1935), Bess, maid to Olivia de Havilland's Maid Marian in *The Adventures of Robin Hood*, and, of course, Minnie, the screaming maid of James Whale's *Bride of Frankenstein*. She carried on in such movies as *The Sea Hawk* (1940) and *The Bells of St. Mary's* (1945), off-screen being very hospitable and generous to servicemen stationed in Los Angeles. Come the late 1940s, Una acted in such films as *The Adventures of Don Juan* (1948) and was in two Broadway flops with Boris Karloff: *The Linden Tree* (1948) and *The Shop at Sly Corner* (1949). She had her last success as the deaf Scottish maid Janet Mackenzie in Broadway's *Witness for the Prosecution* (December 16, 1954). Una was 74 years old, and her weakened heart forced her to rest all day in bed for her performance — which always brought down the house. She reprised her role in Billy Wilder's film version of *Witness for the Prosecution* (1957), starring Charles Laughton, Marlene Dietrich and Tyrone Power — her final film. Una O'Connor died at the Mary Manning Walsh Home, an institution of Carmelite nuns in New York City, on February 4, 1959. She was 78. James Whale, a fan of Una personally and professionally, had left her $10,000 in his will.

Forrester Harvey, "Mr. Hall," remained one of Hollywood's familiar faces, and also acted in several Universal horrors. In *Mystery of Edwin Drood* (1935), he played Durdles, the cemetery caretaker whom Claude Rains' John Jasper bribes with booze to take him on a moonlight tour of the graveyard. He also played in *The Invisible Man Returns* (1940) as bumbling Ben Jenkins, and in *The Wolf Man* (1941) as Mr. Twiddle, nervous assistant to constable Ralph Bellamy. Forrester Harvey died of a stroke in Laguna Beach, California on December 14, 1945, at age 55.

E.E. Clive, "P.C. Jaffers," became a James Whale favorite: he acted again for the director in *One More River* (1934), *Remember Last Night* (1935), *Show Boat* (1936), *The Road Back* (1937), *The Great Garrick* (1937), and most memorably, as the blustery Burgomaster ("Monster indeed!") in *Bride of* Frankenstein (1935). As one of Hollywood's busiest character actors, he also appeared in such films as *Dracula's Daughter* (1936) and Alfred Hitchcock's *Foreign Correspondent* (1940). On June 6, 1940, E.E. Clive suffered a fatal heart attack in North Hollywood while holding a cup of tea. He was 60. His widow sent his ashes to Boston, where (rumor claims) the ashes were scattered around the site of the long-demolished Copley Theatre.

Dudley Digges, "Chief of Detectives," later acted in such films as *Mutiny on the Bounty* (1935) and created the role of "Gramps," who chases "Death" up a tree in the play *On Borrowed Time* (1938). (Lionel Barrymore acted Gramps in MGM's 1939 film version.) Digges became one of the most beloved actors on the American stage and died in New York City October 24, 1947, at age 68.

Cinematographer Arthur Edeson later was cameraman on such classics as *Mutiny on the Bounty* (1935), *The Maltese Falcon* (1941), and *Casablanca* (1942). He died February 14, 1970, age 78.

John P Fulton

Arthur Edeson

John P. Fulton left Universal in 1945 and joined Samuel Goldwyn Studios, winning his first Special Effects Oscar for *Wonder Man* (1945). He later headed Paramount Studios' Special Effects lab and won two more Oscars - for *The Bridges at Toko-Ri* (1954) and Cecil B. DeMille's *The Ten Commandments* (1956), in which he masterminded the parting of the Red Sea. After Paramount cut its Special Effects department, Fulton stayed busy, and even co-wrote *The Bamboo Saucer* (1968), for which he provided the effects. While in Spain working on *The Battle of Britain*, Fulton contracted a rare infection and died in a hospital in Buckinghamshire, England, on July 5, 1966. He was 63.

Herbert George Wells died in London on August 13, 1946, at age 79. Many believe *The Invisible Man* to be the best cinematic treatment of any of his works.

Philip Wylie saw his novel *When Worlds Collide* become a classic science fiction film, produced by George Pal for Paramount Pictures and released in 1951. Wylie died in Miami, Florida on October 25, 1971, at age 69.

As for the legendary James Whale....he followed at Universal with what many consider his masterpiece, 1935's *Bride of Frankenstein*. He enjoyed another triumph with the 1936 version of the musical *Show Boat*, but his career nosedived after Uncle Carl Laemmle and Junior sold Universal in 1936. By 1941, his film career was virtually finished. He directed on the stage, traveled, and painted, basically content in his wealthy retirement. Tormented by a stroke, Whale wrote a sad note on May 29, 1957, addressed "To ALL I LOVE," threw himself into the swimming pool behind his house in Pacific

James Whale - circa 1950s, in his artist studio at his Pacific Palisades Home.

Palisades, and drowned. His ashes are in the "Columbarium of Memory" in the Great Mausoleum in Forest Lawn, Glendale, California. *Gods and Monsters* (1998), based on Christopher Bram's novel and featuring Ian McKellen's Oscar nominated portrayal of Whale, has sparked interest in the man and his career.

And finally, as for Claude Rains. He became one of the cinema's greatest character actors — a powerhouse at Warner Bros'. in such films as *Anthony Adverse* (1936), *They Won't Forget* (1937), and *The Adventures of Robin Hood* (as King John, 1938). He garnered four Best Supporting Actor Oscar nominations: for *Mr. Smith Goes to Washington* (Columbia, 1939), as tarnished Senator Joe Paine; *Casablanca* (Warners, 1943), as womanizing Captain Louis Renault; *Mr. Skeffington* (Warners, 1944), in the sympathetic title role; and *Notorious* (RKO, 1946), as Nazi mamma's boy Alexander Sebastian. He also added to his laurels in two more Universal horror classics: *The Wolf Man* (1941), as Sir John Talbot, fatally proud father of Lon Chaney Jr.'s tragic lycanthrope; and *Phantom of the Opera* (1943), bringing power and pathos to the title role — in Technicolor. (A Universal horror role Rains declined: Dr. Wolf von Frankenstein in 1939's *Son of Frankenstein*, ultimately played by Basil Rathbone.)

In 1938, Rains became an immensely proud father with the birth of his only child, Jennifer (known today as Jessica Rains, formerly an actress, now a producer). From the early 1940s until the late 1950s, Rains lived on "Stock Grange," a pre-Revolutionary War farm in Brandywine country in West Chester, PA. Rains would travel to Hollywood for a film, then hurry home across the country to his wife Frances, daughter Jennifer, and his "beautiful old barn" as soon as the film was finished. He returned to England as George Bernard Shaw's personal choice to star with Vivien Leigh in Shaw's *Caesar and Cleopatra* (1946), and later acted in England in another film based on an H.G. Wells' tale, *One Woman's Story* (1949).

The awards that had eluded Rains in film came his way in theatre as he triumphed in Sidney Kingsley's play *Darkness at Noon*, which opened at Broadway's Alvin Theatre January 13, 1951. As Rubashov, an old revolutionary victimized by Communist "justice," Rains won virtually every award in the New York theatre, including the Tony Award, the Donaldson Award, the Delia-Austria Award, and the New York Drama Critics Award. He also won the American Academy of Arts and Letters' Medal for Good Speech on the American Stage — a special honor for a man who had to conquer a major speech impediment to begin his career in the theatre.

In 1956, Rains' wife of over 20 years, Frances, divorced him. He'd developed an alcohol problem by that time, and soon gave up his farm. A fifth marriage, to Hungarian pianist Agi Jambor in 1959, lasted only six months. He kept working, and among his credits: returning to Broadway for a final time in Arch Oboler's science fiction play *Night of the Auk* (December 3, 1956 lasting only eight performances); playing a singing Mayor in the NBC special *The Pied Piper of Hamelin* (November 26, 1957); and acting a red-haired and bearded Dr. Challenger in Irwin Allen's dinosaur saga, *The Lost World* (1960).

In 1960, only days (possibly hours) after his fifth divorce, Rains married for a sixth time: M. Rosemary Clark, whom he met while searching for someone to ghost-write his memoirs. He was 70; she was 42. Rains and his new wife and her children settled in Sandwich, New Hampshire as Rains continued expertly practicing his craft: a guest spot on *Alfred Hitchcock Theatre* ("The Horseplayer," March 14, 1961, directed by Hitchcock himself, who'd directed Rains in *Notorious*); a brief appearance as Mr. Dryden in *Lawrence of Arabia* (1962); a 1964 play, *So Much of Earth, So Much of Heaven*, which he had to leave due to illness and which never made it to Broadway; and two final films, *Twilight of Honor* (as a kindly old Texas lawyer, 1963) and *The Greatest Story Ever Told* (as a not-so-kindly King Herod, 1964). After Rosemary Rains died of cancer on New Year's Eve, 1964, Rains, old and ill, had little stamina left for acting. Offered the role of a blind sculptor in *Blind Man's Bluff*, shot in Madrid, Rains was too weak to accept and Boris

Karloff—whom Rains had replaced over 30 years before in *The Invisible Man*—played the part.

Tuesday, May 30, 1967: Claude Rains died of an intestinal hemorrhage at Lakes Region Hospital in Laconia, New Hampshire. He was 77 years old. He was buried beside his last wife, Rosemary, in Red Hill Graveyard near Squam Lake, New Hampshire. His tombstone reads:

CLAUDE RAINS
1889-1967
"All things once
Are things forever.
Soul once living,
Lives forever."

In 2008, the Library of Congress added *The Invisible Man* to the United States National Film Registry as a movie that is "culturally, historically, or aesthetically significant."

In 2012, Universal Studios, celebrating its 100th birthday, released a beautifully restored version of *The Invisible Man*, as it did for *Dracula*, *Frankenstein*, and *Bride of Frankenstein*. The studio engaged Technicolor Creative Service to prepare the new print, which combined Universal's preservation acetate dupe negative and a nitrate dupe found at the British Film Institute. The new print now features long-missing frames, digital repair of scratches and stains, and improved sound; happily, there was no need to touch up the original Special Effects. As Glenn Erickson writes in *DVD Savant*, "It's just a super, super restoration of a film we know and love."

So...79 years after its original release, James Whale's *The Invisible Man* has a new, happy, unholy lease on life. For acolytes of Classic Horror, and for new audiences just discovering the magic, Claude Rains' Invisible One robs and wrecks and kills again — meddling in things, wickedly, hilariously, and gloriously, that man must leave alone.

The End

The Invisible Man

Studio: Universal
Producer: Carl Laemmle, Jr.
Director: James Whale
Screenplay: R. C. Sherriff (based on H.G. Wells' novel, *The Invisible Man*)
Cinematographer: Arthur Edeson
Art Director: Charles D. Hall
Music: Heinz Roemheld
Film Editor: Ted Kent
Special Effects Photography: John P. Fulton
Miniatures: Charlie Baker
Makeup: Jack P. Pierce
Sound: William Hedgcock
Assistant Director: Joseph A. McDonough
Additional Photography (Uncredited): John J. Mescall
Running Time: 70 minutes.
Chicago Premiere: Palace Theatre Nov. 10, 1933
New York Premiere: Roxy Theatre, Nov. 17, 1933
Los Angeles Premiere: RKO-Hillstreet Theatre, Nov. 17, 1933

The Players

Jack Griffin, the Invisible One............Claude Rains
Flora Cranley.......................................Gloria Stuart
Dr.Kemp..William Harrigan
Dr.Cranley...Henry Travers
Jenny Hall...Una O'Connor
Herbert Hall..................................Forrester Harvey
Chief of Detectives......................Dudley Digges
Police Constable Jaffers............................E.E. Clive
Chief of Police...............................Holmes Herbert
Police Constable Bird.........................Harry Stubbs
Inspector Lane..................................Donald Stuart
Millie...Merle Tottenham
Reporter...Dwight Frye
Bicycle Owner................................Walter Brennan
Informer..............................John Peter Richmond
                                                    (aka John Carradine)
Newsboy..John Merivale
Farmer..Robert Brower
Woman................................Violet Kemble Cooper
Chubby Policeman........................Monty Montague
Doctors...Jameson Thomas
                                                            Crauford Kent
Officials..Bob Reeves
                                                        Jack Richardson
                                                            Robert Adair
Villagers..Ted Billings
                                                          D'Arcy Corrigan
Chased Woman................................Mary Gordon

"INVISIBLE MAN" — A UNIVERSAL PRODUCTION PRINTED IN U. S. A.

53

The end of the Invisible Man

H.G. Wells, *author of* The Invisible Man

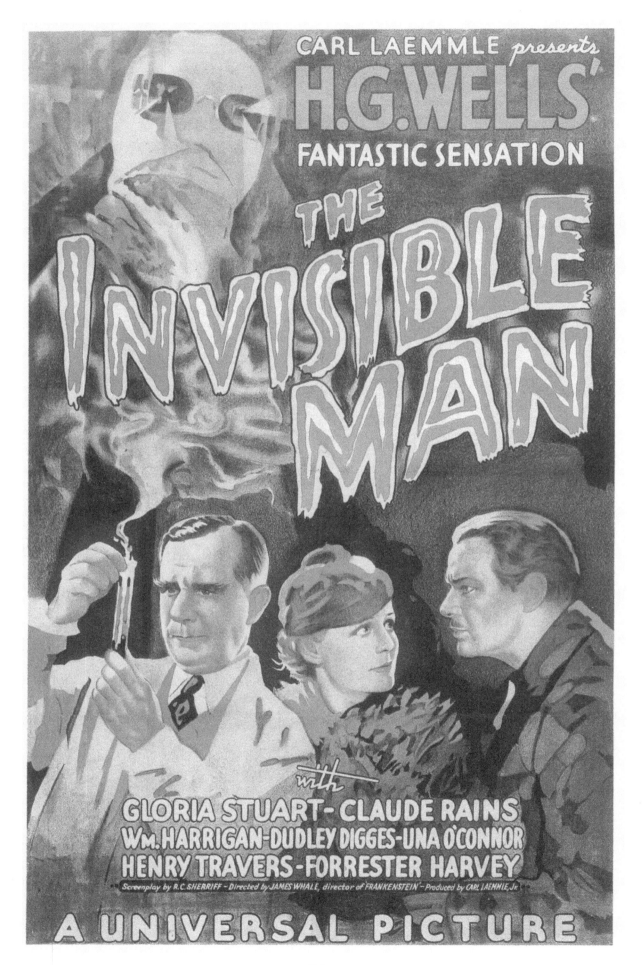

"THE INVISIBLE MAN"

IMPORTANT   NOTICE

This script is the property of Universal
Pictures Corporation and is merely loaned
to you for use in connection with the
picture for which it is issued.

You have accepted this script upon the
distinct understanding that if same is not
returned to the Stenographic Department
immediately after the completion of your
work in connection with this picture, you
will pay to Universal Pictures Corporation
the sum of Twenty-five dollars for its
retention.

                              CARL LAEMMLE JR.
                              General Manager

SCRIPT NO:____ 22

SEQUENCES	SCENES	PAGES
A	42	11 - 2 - 25 - 34 - 38 - 4?
B	72	11 - 19 - 21 - 24 - 25 - 2~ 53 - 58 - 6?
C	12	5
D	79	21 17 - 34 - 37 - 42 - 44 - 62 - 71 -
E	123	33 2 - 15 - 16 - 34 - 43 - 44 - 5??
F	83	20
G	57	12
H	11	4 - 3 - 4 - 7
TOTAL: 8	479	117

113 - 114 - 117

E 3 - 77 - 78 - 75 - 82 - 86 - 88 - 96 - 98 - 99 - 101 - 104 - 106 -
F 3 - 12 - (18) 14 - 21 - 30 - 32 - 68 - 81
G 12 - 1 - 30 - 23 - 24 - 34 - 2
38 - 45 - 48 - 49 - 50 - 55 -

"THE INVISIBLE MAN"

SEQUENCE "A"

A-1   A BARREN, WINDSWEPT ROAD..DEEP
        IN SNOW...LONG SHOT
        _____

        So deep that a forlorn wire
        fence to either side is all
        that shows its course. The
        surrounding country is destitute,
        of life and vegetation. It is
        twilight. The wind moans; snow
        shirls across a leaden, darken-
        ing sky. Out of the shadows
        from background comes a man,sil-
        houetted against the darkened
        sky. He is bending to the wind,
        stubbornly holding down a wide
        brimmed hat, a small dark bag
        clutched in his other hand. As
        he comes to foreground, we...
        CUT TO:

A-2   EXT. ROAD..MEDIUM SHOT SIDE ANGLE
        ON MAN
        _____

        As the man comes to camera and
        passes closely by; tall and gaunt;
        his clothes flap around him, and
        give an eerie, scarecrowish appear-
        ance.
        CUT TO:

A-3   EXT. ROAD..NIGHT..CLOSE SHOT
        OF MAN
        _____

        WE catch a fleeting glimpse of his
        face, thru the whirling snow, as
        he passes by - of something strange
        that is lost too quickly to under-
        stand -- of a thin long nose protrud-
        ing from a mass of bandages; of two
        round black goggles -- and then the
        head is bent to the wind again, and
        all we can see is the brim of a hat
        and coat collar high up over the chin.
        CUT TO:

A-4   EXT. ROAD NIGHT..DOLLEY SHOT WITH
        MAN
        _____

        CAMERA on DOLLEY follows the strange
        lonely figure down the road as he
        goes his way, head bent down, seek-
        ing shelter from the elements. He
        halts as he comes to a sign post
        and looks up.
        CUT TO:

A-5   EXT. ROAD..CLOSE SHOT ON SIGN
        POST
        _____

        "TO IPING ½ MILE".

        CUT BACK TO:

A-6   EXT. ROAD..MEDIUM LONG SHOT
                WITH MAN IN FOREGROUND
                _____

                The man has just turned from
                reading the sign and starts
                towards CAMERA which DRAWS
                BACK as we see below us, in a
                velly, a little group of houses-
                dark walled, white roofed - grey
                smoke zigzagging to the gust of
                wind. The man moves forward dark-
                ening the picture which...

                DISSOLVES TO:

    A-7   INT. VILLAGE INN (NIGHT.) LONG
                SHOT.
                _____

                High CAMERA shooting down on the
                people in the Inn. A striking con-
                trast to the bitter loneliness of
                the world outside. An automatic
                piano is playing joyfully in a cor-
                ner, and the saloon is crowded with
                men, possibly one giggly woman.
                Tobacco smoke, talk and laughter
                fill the air. We hold on this long
                enough to get a general impression
                of the atmosphere of the Inn.
                CUT TO:

    A-8   INT. VILLAGE INN...AT BAR
                _____

                A cheery party lounging against
                the bar; rough, sturdy country types-
                each with his glass of beer.

                                    FIRST CUSTOMER
                                Did you hear about Mrs.
                                Mason's little Willy. Sent
                                him to school and found him
                                ten foot deep in a snow
                                drift!

                                SECOND CUSTOMER
                                How'd they get 'im out?

                                FIRST CUSTOMER
                                Brought the fire engine
                                along. Put the hose pipe in-
                                pumped it backwards - and
                                sucked 'im out!

                A gust of laughter greets this
                sally as the CAMERA MOVES across
                the saloon to a beery looking
                individual who is pretending to
                play the automatic piano -- he
                runs his fingers over the keys,
                swaying his head dreamily to and
                fro. The music stops - he lowers
                his hands to his knees, swings
                around and bows and smiles.
                CUT TO:

A-9   INT. VILLAGE INN. CLOSE SHOT

    Man, with a large mustache, who
    has been standing beside the
    piano, drops in another penny.
    CUT BACK TO:

A-10   INT. VILLAGE INN...TWO SHOT

    The music starts again and the
    beery looking man hastily swings
    round to pretend once more that
    he is playing -- just too late to
    carry out the illusion to the
    audience.
    CUT TO:

A-11   INT. VILLAGE INN...DOLLEY SHOT.
    MEDIUM

    CAMERA leaves the two men at the
    piano and MOVES AROUND the saloon
    getting in the different types-
    to a party of earnest villagers
    playing at darts in a corner by
    the door.
     CUT TO:

A-12   INT. VILLAGE INN. CLOSE SHOT

    We see the set profile of a
    competitor as he raises a dart
    and throws it. CAMERA SWINGS TO
    MEDIUM SHOT taking in the darts
    board and the door beside it. We
    see a dart fly, to bury itself,
    quivering, amongst other darts on
    the board, as there comes a per-
    emptory rap on the door. A moment's
    pause, then the door abruptly opens
    to reveal the wierd stranger, stand-
    ing on the threshold.
    CUT TO:

A-13   INT. VILLAGE IN...MED. CLOSE ON
    STRANGER...LOWY CAMERA

    WE can see him clearly now for the
    first time; the light of the room
    on him; the darkness of the night
    beyond. The borad brimmed hat is
    pulled low over his eyes -- covering
    his ears and forehead. The two
    eerie goggles slowly glare around
    the room. Beneath it is the long,
    peaked nose-- and beneath that only
    the high buttoned collar of his
    coat. The bandaged cheeks are
    practically hidden.

    CUT TO:

CG   A-14   INT. VILLAGE INN..MED. LONG
              SHOT ON DOLLEY

              AS the stranger advances. There
              is a power and authority in his
              slow stride; the surprised dart
              players instinctively fall back.
              CAMERA moves into TWO SHOT --
              as stranger without pause goes
              to the bar and stands looking over
              it st Mr. Hall, the plump little
              keeper of the Inn. There is a
              moment of silence before the
              stranger speaks.
              CUT TO:

      A-15   INT. VILLAGE INN..CLOSEUP
              STRANGER

              SHOOTING over Mr. Hall's shoulder
              on the stranger as he speaks - his
              voice is strong and even.

                                THE STRANGER
                                I want a room -- and a
                                fire.
              CUT TO:

      A-16   INT. VILLAGE INN..MEDIUM SHOT

              Mr. Hall standing behind the bar.
               The stranger facing him. Mr. Hall
              with difficulty tears his gaping
              face away from the strange apparition,
              and calls into the passage beyond.

                                  MR. HALL
                                Janny!

                                MRS. HALL   (offstage)
                                'Ullo!

              A short, exceedingly fat lady
              pops a round fat face round the
              corner of the door.
              CUT TO:

      A-17   INT. VILLAGE INN. CLOSEUP OF MRS.
              HALL.

              AS Mrs. Hall looks off in the
              direction of the bar.

                                MR. HALL   (offscene)
                                Here's a gent wants a room
                                and a fire.

              CAMERA DRAWS BACK to a THREE
              SHOT as Mrs. Hall comes forward
              surprised and flushed.
                                MRS. HALL
                                What? A room!

          (CONTINUED)

CG   A-17   (CONTINUED)

                                          THE STRANGER (in a patient,
                                                    level voice)
                                          I said a room.

                                          MRS. HALL (eyeing the stranger
                                                    curiously)
                                          We ain't got note ready --
                                          not this time o' year. We
                                          don't usually get folks
                                          stopping except in the
                                          summer.
             CUT TO:

A-18   INT. VILLAGE INN..CLOSE PROFILE
        SHOT ON THE STRANGER
        _____

             AS he looks at Mrs. Hall, there
             is a quiet authority in his voice.

                                          THE STRANGER
                                             You can get one ready.
             CUT TO:

A-19   INT. VILLAGE INN.   CLOSE SHOT
        ON MRS. HALL
        _____

             SHe looks at the stranger.

                                          MRS. HALL
                                             Certainly, sir!

             As she turns and calls thru the
             door from which she has just
             emerged, we
             CUT TO:

A-20   INT. VILLAGE INN..MEDIUM SHOT
        ON THE THREE
        _____

             All standing at the bar - Mrs.
             Hall looking off to door.

                                          MRS. HALL
                                             Milly!

                                          THE STRANGER
                                             I Want a private sitting
                                             room, too.

                                          MRS. HALL (sensing good
                                                    business)
                                          Certainly, sir! -- Will you
                                          come thru, sir - this way!

             Mrs. Hall throws open the door
             in the bar and the stranger walks
             thru. The villagers, now silent,
             follow him curiously with their
             eyes.
             CUT TO:

A-21   INT. HALL...FOLLOW SHOT

> As the stranger followed by Mrs.
> Hall comes out into the hall door-
> way, she closes the door, picks up
> a lamp, and the stranger follows her
> as she preceeds the way up a short
> stairway to the door of the sitting
> room. CUT TO:

A-22   INT. HALL..INTO SITTING ROOM CAMERA
        ON DOLLEY

> Mrs. Hall opens the door and they
> go into the sitting room. CAMERA
> ENTERS WITH THEM. The usual type.
> A small fireplace with ornaments
> on the mantelplace - an old arm-
> chair, a round table in the centre
> of the room - various pieces of
> furniture round the walls. The
> stranger crosses to the window -
> standing rigidly with his back to
> the room. He still wears his hat,
> and overcoat with the snow clinging
> to them. Mrs. Hall goes to the fire-
> place, gets down on her knees, busy
> laying the fire.
> CUT TO:

A-23   INT. SITTING ROOM...TWO SHOT

                        MRS. HALL   (sociably)
                        It's the coldest winter
                        we've had down 'ere for
                        years. They've had all the
                        sheep and cows in for a
                        fortnight now, poor things
                        can't get a blad of green
                        grass.

> She glances up, but the stranger
> neither moves nor replies. Wonder-
> ingly, she returns to the fire -
> lights it, and rises.

> CAMERA MOVES IN CLOSERS ON THE TWO

                        MRS. HALL
                        Can I take your hat and
                        coat, sir -- and give 'em
                        a good dry in the kitchen?

                        THE STRANGER (without moving)
                        No.

> Mrs. Hall is so surprised that
> she is not sure if she heard
> aright.

> CUT TO:

CO   A-24   INT. SITTING ROOM..CLOSEUP
                  STRANGER'S HEAD ..LOW CAMERA

           There is a pause, then the
           stranger slightly turns his
           head.

                            THE STRANGER
                             I prefer to keep them on.

           He turns back to the window.
           CUT TO:

      A-25   INT. SITTING ROOM...MEDIUM SHOT
                  OF THE TWO

                          MRS. HALL
                           Very good, sir. The
                           room'll be warm soon.

                      THE STRANGER (his back to Mrs.
                               Hall)
                           I've got some luggage at
                           the station. How can I
                           have it sent?

                          MRS. HALL
                           I'll get it brought over
                           tomorrow, sir. Are you
                           going to stay a bit?

                       THE STRANGER
                           Yes
                             (pause)
                          Is there no way of getting
                          it tonight?

                         MRS. HALL
                           Not <u>tonight</u>, sir!

                      THE STRANGER
                           Very well.
                             (another pause)
                          You'll bring me some food?

                          MRS. HALL
                           Right away, sir!

           CAMERA PANS to the door with
           her as she furtively exits,
           then swings back holding the
           silent, unmoving stranger. He
           slowly puts out his gloved
           hand, and draws down the
           blind until it meets the
           curtains on the lower half
           of the curtain.
           CUT TO:

      A-26   INT. SALOON...MEDIUM SHOT

           CAMERA BEHIND BAR shooting into
           FULL SHOT of saloon. The Darts
           competition has begun again, but
           the men round the bar are discus-
           sing the stranger. They are round-
           eyed and confidential.   (CONTINUED)

A-26   (CONTINUED)

                                    FIRST CUSTOMER
                                        If you ask me, he's a
                                        criminal - flying from
                                        justice --

                                    SECOND CUSTOMER (disgustedly)
                                        Gar! He's snowblind --
                                        that's what he is. Has to
                                        wear goggles to save his
                                        eyes.

                                    FIRST CUSTOMER (leaning over the
                                                     bar and speak-
                                                     ing to Mr.Hall)
                                        Anyway, you be careful -
                                        and lock your money up!

A-27   INT. SALOON..MEDIUM CLOSE SHOT

         Mrs. Hall passes along behind
         the bar with a tray of supper.
         THE CAMERA FOLLOWS her to the
         door of the sitting room, which
         she nervously knocks at and opens.
         We follow her into the room.
         CUT TO:

A-28   INT. SITTING ROOM. MED. CLOSE
         AT DOOR

         She pauses by the door in surprise
         to see the stranger standing ex-
         actly as she left him; rigidly;
         his back to the room -- his eyes
         to the window.
                                    MRS. HALL
                                        Your supper, sir.

         CAMERA PANS with her to the
         table and takes in the stranger
         at the window. He makes no sign
         that he has heard.
                                    THE STRANGER
                                        Is there a key to that
                                        door?

                                    MRS. HALL (surprised)
                                        A key, sir? I haven't
                                        ever seen one. I don't
                                        think there was one when
                                        we came here.

                                    THE STRANGER
                                        I want to be left alone,
                                        and undisturbed.

                                    MRS. HALL
                                        I'll see nobody disturbs
                                        you, sir.

         CAMERA PANS with her as she
         leaves the room and closes
         the door -- then SWINGS BACK
         to the stranger.
         CUT TO:

CG   A-29   INT. SITTING ROOM..CLOSE SHOT
                ON STRANGER

            Slowly he turns into CAMERA -
            raises his gloved hand and be-
            gins to unbutton his coat, as we
            CUT TO:

A-30   INT. KITCHEN...FULL SHOT

            Milly, an untidy servant girl,
            is vigorously stirring a pot
            of mustard. Mrs. Hall comes in.
            Milly hastily turns and holds
            out the pot.
            CUT TO:

A-31   INT. KITCHEN..CLOSE SHOT MILLY

                     MILLY   (innocently)
                  Here's the mustard, mam!

            CUT TO:

A-32   INT. KITCHEN...FULL SHOT

            Mrs. Hall gives an exclamation
            of disgust and snatches the pot.

                     MRS. HALL
                  You'll be the death of me,
                  with your slowness! Here
                  you let me take the gentle-
                  man's supper in - and for-
                  get the mustard! and him
                  wanting to be left alone!

            She turns indignantly on her
            heel and bounces out of the
            room.

A-33   INT. HALL...MEDIUM SHOT

            As Mrs. Hall carrying the
            mustard enters and goes to
            the sitting room door and
            knocks,
            CUT TO:

A-34   INT. SITTING ROOM...MED.CLOSE
                AT DOOR

            Mrs. Hall on the threshold-stops
            with an exclamation of surprise
            and horror. The stranger is sit-
            ting at his supper, and the sight
            of him is enough to make anyone
            start back in fear.
            CUT TO:

A-35   INT. SITTING ROOM..MED. CLOSE ON
                STRANGER

            He is sitting quite still staring
            at Mrs. Hall (off) thru his great
            blue goggles.

            CUT TO:

Not a scrap of his face is visible
save the long thin nose. His fore-
head, cheeks and ears are swathed
in white bandages. A mop of untidy
brown hair escapes here and there
from the bandages that cross the
top of his head, and projects like
tails and horns in all directions,
giving him the wierdest and most
horrifying qppearance. As we
first see him he raises his gloved
hand with a lightning movement and
holds a handkerchief over his mouth
and chin.
CUT TO:

A-37   INT. SITTING ROOM..CLOSEUP OF MRS.
        HALL

She is transfixed with astonishment
and fear.
CUT TO:

A-38   INT. SITTING ROOM..MEDIUM CLOSE
        SHOT OF STRANGER

At last the stranger speaks - in
an ominous, muffled voice.

                        THE STRANGER
                            I told you not to disturb
                            me.

        CUT TO:

A-39   INT. SITTING ROOM...TWO SHOT

Mrs. Hall comes up to the table
with the mustard.
                        MRS. HALL
                            It's - it's only the
                            mustard, sir. I forgot it.
                            I'm sorry.

                CUT TO:

A-40   INT. SITTING ROOM..CLOSEUP ON
        STRANGER

He looks up at Mrs. Hall.

                        THE STRANGER
                            Thank you.
        CUT TO:

A-41   INT. SITTING ROOM..MEDIUM
        SHOT.

                        MRS. HALL
                            You been motoring on them
                            slippery roads, sir?

        (CONTINUED)

(CONTINUED)

                                    THE STRANGER (without answering
                                                her question)
                                        You can take my overcoat,
                                        and dry it.

                                    MRS. HALL
                                        Very good, sir.

                                    THE STRANGER
                                        Leave the hat.

                                    MRS. HALL
                                        Yes, sir.

Mrs. Hall reaches forward and
puts down the mustard as if she
expects him to bite her - she
backs away from the table, turns
and leaves the room with alacrity.
THE CAMERA FOLLOWS her out, then
slowly returns to the stranger.
He is sitting quite rigidly, glanc-
ing over towards the door. CAMERA
MOVES UP to CLOSE SHOT. His gloved
hands rest on the table - the
handkerchief no longer covers his
mouth and chin. The bandages below his nose have been pulled down
to enable him to eat. And where
his mouth and chin should be there
is nothing - just an empty space.
The whole of his bandaged head
seems to be supported by the tiny
place where his hair comes down at
the back to meet his collar.
CUT TO:

A-42   INT. SALOON..FULL SHOT

          Mrs. Hall, breathless, comes running
          into car - and is quickly surrounded
          by the loungers at the bar - her hus-
          band stands by with his mouth open,
          she speaks tremulously and confidentially.

                                    MRS. HALL
                                        Bandages! - right up to
                                        the top of his head! All
                                        round his ears!

                                    FIRST CUSTOMER (in a hoarse
                                                    whisper)
                                        Any blood?

                                    MRS. HALL
                                        No - no blood. Looks like
                                        some kind of horrible ac-
                                        cident!

                                    SECOND CUSTOMER (dryly)
                                        Bumped his head on the
                                        prison wall, getting over.

He nods knowingly and spits
as we .....
                        FADE OUT

"INVISIBLE MAN"

SEQUENCE "B"

B-1   FADE IN:
        CRANLEY'S HOME.. LIBRARY
        LONG SHOT.. (DAY)

            A long comfortable furnished
            library.. at one end.. in large
            bow windows, there is fitted a
            small scientific laboratory, a
            bench with instruments and shelves
            lined with bottles. DR. CRANLEY,
            a distinguished looking man of
            middle age, is at work by the
            windows. He holds a test tube to
            the light.. shakes it, and holds
            it up again. He is too absorbed in
            his work to hear the door open
            at the library end of the room.

            CUT TO:

B-2   INT. LIBRARY.. MED. SHOT
        AT DOOR

            A girl has entered. She stands
            for a moment, watching the white-
            coated doctor busy at his work.
            FLORA CRANLEY is a beautiful girl..
            dressed in outdoor costume.
            She is quiet, but there is a
            burning anxiety beneath her outward
            control.
                                FLORA
                            Father!
            CUT TO:

B-3   INT. LIBRARY.. MED.
        CLOSE SHOT

            Dr. Cranley looks over his
            shoulder with a frown. He speaks
            with a mixture of kindness and
            severity.
                                DR. CRANBY
                            I wish you would leave me
                            alone, Flora, when I'm work-
                            ing.

                                FLORA   (Coming into shot)
                            I can't bear it. We've got
                            to do something.

                                DOCTOR   (Vaguely)
                            Do something.. what about?

                                FLORA
                            About Jack.

            Dr. Cranley patiently
            returns to his experiment.

                                DOCTOR
                            He'll come back.. don't you
                            worry.

        (CONTINUED)

Flora can scarcely
control herself.

                     FLORA
                        Father! --Put that horrid
                        thing down, and listen!

Dr. Cranley lowers the test
tube in surprise and comes
over to his daughter. She
is trembling.

CAMERA MOVES IN CLOSER.

                     FLORA   (continues)
                        It's nearly a month now..
                        without a word.

                    DOCTOR   (kindly)
                        But the note he left was
                        quite clear! He said we
                        might not hear for a while.
                        It's a good thing sometimes
                        to go right away by yourself
                        when you're finishing a
                        difficult experiment.

                     FLORA
                        What kind of experiment is
                        it, Father?

                    DOCTOR   (with a shrug)
                        Something of his own.

                     FLORA
                        I had a terrible feeling
                        last night. I felt he was
                        in desperate trouble.--

Flora starts in fear..
her nerves are on edge.

CUT TO:

B-4   INT. LIBRARY..
        AT FRENCH WINDOWS

        They have opened abruptly,
and a tall young man, in
the white coat of a scientist,
is standing on the threshold.
He comes in. He is good looking,
but there is an unpleasant harshness
about him. He stands looking off in
the direction of the Doctor and Flora.

                    FLO
                    DOCTOR   (offstage)
                        Hello, Kemp.
                          (pause)
                        Flora's worried about Grif-
                        fin.

CAMERA PANS WITH KEMP
as he comes and joins the
other two.

                    KEMP   (dryly)
                        I don't wonder. I should
                        have thought at least he
                        could drop a line.

                    DOCTOR
(CONTINUED)   It's a queer thing.

B-4   (CONTINUED)

                                    KEMP   (lighting a cigarette)
                                        It certainly is. Considering
                                        he was in your employ.

                                    DOCTOR
                                        He had my permission to
                                        carry out his own experiment
                                        in his spare time.

                                    KEMP
                                        And to clear off when he
                                        liked.. for as long as he
                                        liked?

                                    FLORA   (bursting in)
                                        What does it matter!-- if
                                        he's in trouble?

        Flora turns quickly and
        leaves the room; she is on the
        verge of tears. The old Doctor
        looks after her.. perplexed and
        unhappy.

        Kemp's eyes are following Flora..
        some where in the room beyond
        the library. He turns and goes after
        her. CAMERA FOLLOWS HIM.. Flora
        is seen a little ahead of him..
        they go into the lounge.
        A tastefully furnished, comfortable
        room with big windows, that look
        out over the country. Flora cannot
        rest; she wanders over to a window
        and gazes out.

        Kemp comes over to her and stands
        by her side.
        CUT TO:

B-5   INT.LOUNGE.. MED. CLOSE ON TWO

                                    KEMP
                                        I've got the car outside,
                                        Flora. It'll be a rest to
                                        come for a run.

        Flora does not reply to his
        invitation. It seems as if
        she has not heard.
                                    FLORA
                                        Do you think there are any
                                        papers in his room to help us?
                                        He must have arranged where
                                        he was going? There may be
                                        letters.

                                    KEMP
                                        He left a heap of burnt
                                        papers in the fireplace..
                                        that's all.

                    CUT TO:

B-6   (CONTINUED)

                                    KEMP   (continued)
                                    .. give me a chance, darl-
                                    ing.. to tell you what I
                                    feel! I can't work, or
                                    sleep till I know...

      CUT TO:

B-7   INT. LOUNGE.. CLOSE
       SHOT.. FLORA

       As she sinks down into a
       chair. She buries her face
       in her hands and cries.

                                    FLORA
                                    For God's sake leave me
                                    alone!-- How can you dare
                                    when...

       Her words are lost in
       convulsive sobbing. CAMERA
       PANS UP TO KEMP who stands
       looking down at her.. there is
       no sympathy in his face..
       only unpleasant, rather
       sinister anger.

       DISSOLVE TO:

B-8   THE SITTING ROOM AT THE
       VILLAGE INN.   FULL SHOT

       A remarkable change has taken
       place. The ornaments on the
       sideboard have given place to
       rows of bottles.. line upon line.
       Upon the table are other bottles,
       some scientific instruments of
       strange design and two large,
       open books.

       On a small table, in a corner
       beneath the lights, stands a
       delicate scientific balance of
       weights and scales and other
       instruments. Beside the table
       stands the stranger.. with his
       eerie, bandaged head and gloved
       hands. He is not wearing his
       greatcoat or hat, and the bandages
       can be seen to come right
       down, round his neck, till they
       disappear beneath his collar.
       He is very carefully stirring a
       mixture in a small glass container;
       observing its colour, and
       occasionally turning to note down
       his observations in one of the large
       books on the table behind him.
       CAMERA PANS WITH HIM as he goes
       to the window and back to the table.
       All the time he is muttering feverishly
       and incoherently to himself... only
       once are the words a little
       louder and understandable.

                                    (CONTINUED)

B-8   (CONTINUED)

                                        STRANGER
                                    There's a way back, you
                                    fool! -- there must be a
                                    way back!

There comes a knock at
the door.

CUT TO:

B-9   INT. SITTING ROOM
       MED. CLOSE SHOT STRANGER

He starts up with an oath.

                                    THE STRANGER
                                        What is it?

                                MRS. HALL (outside)
                                    Your luncheon.

                                    THE STRANGER (shouting)
                                        Take it away.

       CUT TO:

B-10   OUTSIDE SITTING ROOM DOOR
       MEDIUM SHOT

Mrs. Hall with a tray in her
hand stands listening.
                                MRS. HALL
                                    You don't want it cold, do
                                    you?

There is a marked difference
in Mrs. Hall's attitude. Her
politeness and fear of the
stranger have gone. She is
truculent and angry.

                                MRS. HALL
                                    D'you suppose I'm going to
                                    carry trays backwards and
                                    forwards all day! Luncheon's
                                    at one.. and it's one now!

She impatiently pushes
the door with the tray.. but
it opens reluctantly. A large
chair has been placed against
it inside the room. The stranger
comes forward in fury.

CUT TO:

B-11   OUTSIDE DOOR.. CLOSE TWO SHOT

                                    THS STRANGER
                                        Get out I tell you!

He viciously thrusts the
door back with his fist.
The tray crashes to the
floor outside. Mrs. Hall screams
and runs down the passage.

CUT TO:

B-12   INT. SITTING ROOM
        MEDIUM SHOT

            CAMERA PANS WITH STRANGER
            back to the table. He is
            quivering with fury.

                                    THE STRANGER
                                    My God! Why can't they
                                    leave me alone!

            He holds up the glass con-
            tainer he has been stirring;
            the mixture has gone cloudy.
            He holds it above him.
                                    ... and a day's work ruined by
                                    a damnable, ignorant woman!

            He crashes the container
            into a corner of the room
            and sinks into a chair with
            his hands clutching his head.

            CAMERA MOVES SWIFTLY UP TO A
            CLOSE UP
                                    ...there's a way back..
                                    God knows there's a way
                                    back.. if only they'd leave
                                    me alone!

            CUT TO:

B-13   INT. SALOON BAR
        FULL SHOT

            SHOOTING TOWARD THE BAR.
            Mrs. Hall, crimson with
            indignation, is pouring out her
            anger to a sympathetic circle
            of customers around her. Her
            husband stands by with his
            mouth open.
                                    MRS. HALL
                                    He's not goin' to stay
                                    under this roof another
                                    hour! Crashed the tray out
                                    of me hand and swore at me..
                                    turns my best sitting room
                                    into a chemist's shop..
                                    spills it on the carpets..
                                    and a week behind with his
                                    money!
                                        (she swings around on
                                        her husband)
                                    Go and tell him now. Tell
                                    'im if he isn't packed up
                                    and gone in half an hour
                                    we'll have the law in to
                                    turn him out.. and take 'is
                                    bill, too.. three pounds
                                    ten.. and see you get it
                                    before you come out!

            She thrusts the bill into
            Mr. Hall's nervous hands
            and gives him a shove to-
            wards the stranger's room.
            Mr. Hall proceeds anxiously
            for a few steps and suddenly
            turns with an appealing face.

            CUT TO:

B-14 INT. SALOON CLOSE
      TWO SHOT

    On Mr. and Mrs. Hall.

                        MR. HALL
                          Let's leave him a bit,
                          Janny... till he cools off.

                        MRS. HALL
                          Go on.. do it now! Him and
                          his goggles and his chemist
                          shop! If you don't kick
                          him out.. I'm clearing out
                          meself.. and that's the
                          truth!

Mr. Hall reluctantly goes on.
CAMERA FOLLOWS HIM THROUGH
DOOR AND UP THE STAIRS.
He pauses at the door and
timidly knocks. There is no
reply. Mr. Hall looks surprised,
then slowly pushes the door and goes
in.

    CUT TO:

B-15 INT. SITTING ROOM
      MEDIUM SHOT

    The stranger is sitting as we
left him.. his head in his hands..
a pathetic picture of despair.
Mr. Hall comes up to the table;
fidgets, clears his throat and
speaks..

                        MR. HALL
                          Look 'ere, Mister. We can't
                          'ave this no more. You've
                          broke the wife's best china
                          and you're a week behind in
                          the rent. You got to pack
                          up and go.

    CUT TO:

B-16 INT. SITTING ROOM.
      CLOSE UP

    The Stranger raises his head.
He is eyeing Mr. Hall queerly
and rigidly thru his great
blue goggles. There is something
pitiful, and broken about him...
his masterful manner has gone.

                        THE STRANGER
                          I'm expecting some money,
                          Mr. Hall. I'll pay you di-
                          rectly it comes.

                      MR. HALL (offstage)
                          You said that last week..
                          and it hasn't come.

    (CONTINUED)

76

B-16   CONTINUED

                                        THE STRANGER
                                            I came here for quiet -
                                            and secrecy. I'm carrying
                                            out a difficult experi-
                                            ment. I must be left
                                            alone. It's vital - it's
                                            life and death that I
                                            should be left alone. You
                                            don't understand!

B-17   INT SITTING ROOM. MED CLOSE
        TWO SHOT

        The quiet, pleading manner
        of the stranger makes Mr. Hall
        bolder.

                                        MR. HALL
                                            I understand all right!
                                            You don't pay and what's
                                            more, you're driving folks
                                            away from our house!

                                        THE STRANGER
                                            I've had a serious accident.
                                            It's disfigured me - affect-
                                            ed my eyes.

                                        MR. HALL
                                            I don't mean that. I mean
                                            the way you carry on -
                                            throwing stuff on the car-
                                            pets and swearing. It's no
                                            good, mister, you gotter
                                            go.

B-18   INT SITTING ROOM.
        CLOSEUP STRANGER

        Looking up at Mr. Hall
        pleadingly.

                                        THE STRANGER
                                            I implore you to let me
                                            stay! I beg of you! --

B-19   INT SITTING ROOM. CLOSE
        SHOT MR. HALL

                                        MR. HALL
                                            The wife says if you don't
                                            go she is, so it's gotter
                                            be you.

        CAMERA DRAWS BACK to a
        MED SHOT as he comes forward
        to collect the books and in-
        struments on the table.
                                            Come on. I'll help you
                                            get the stuff packed up.

        The stranger leaps from
        his chair in sudden fury.

                                        THE STRANGER
                                            Leave that alone!

        (CONTINUED)

B-19   CONTINUED

    Mr. Hall starts back,
    astonished.

                          THE STRANGER (Cont'd)
                              -- and get out of here!

                         MR. HALL   (blustering)
                              Look 'ere - is this my
                              house or yours?

    Mr. Hall proceeds to
    pick up the books; a mania-
    cal fury sweeps over the
    stranger. He rushes forward
    and strikes Mr. Hall a terrific
    blow that sends him reeling onto
    the floor in a corner.

B-20   INT SITTING ROOM. MED LONG SHOT

    HIGH CAMERA SHOOTING DOWN. He
    is over him in a second; he seizes
    the little struggling, shouting
    man by the waist and flings him
    brutally into the passage. He
    crashes the door to, and stands
    sobbing and groaning with his whole
    weight against it. Mr. Hall is heard
    shrieking outside.

B-21   INT PASSAGE. MED SHOT

    SHOOTING DOWN FROM STAIRS.
    Mr. Hall lies prostrate on the floor.
    Mrs. Hall is wailing and crying on
    her knees beside him. A crowd of
    gaping villagers is peering at the
    astonishing sight.

                         A VILLAGER
                              Gawd! He's a raving
                              lunatic!

    A tall, gaunt countryman
    has knelt down beside Mr.
    Hall.

B-22   INT PASSAGE. CLOSEUP MAN

    He raises his head to the
    crowd.

                         MAN
                              Go and get the policeman.

B-23   EXT INN. FULL SHOT

    A crowd of curious sight-
    seers has collected, attracted
    by Mrs. Hall's screams. A man
    comes out of the Inn and glances
    around.

                                  (CONTINUED)

B-23   CONTINUED

> THE MAN
> Here! Go and find Jaffers,
> and tell him to bring his
> handcuffs. There's a mad-
> man inside.

> A VOICE
> What! The bloke with
> goggles?

> ANOTHER VOICE
> I said he was off his nut!

> ANOTHER VOICE
> Here's Jaffers coming now.

B-24   EXT INN. MED CLOSE SHOT

A stout, solid policeman
pompously advancing down the
village street. He hears a
voice call - "Here, Jaffers!
Come along here!" Jaffers
advances and joins the crowd
outside the inn.

> JAFFERS   (officially)
> What's all this?

The gaunt man comes out
of the inn.

> GAUNT MAN
> That stranger with the
> goggles. He's gone mad.
> Assaulted Mrs. Hall and
> damn near killed her hus-
> band.

Jaffers looks perturbed.

> JAFFERS
> Where is he?

> GAUNT MAN
> In the sitting room.

Jaffers solidly enters
the inn - the crowd surge
in after him.

B-25   INT SALOON. FULL SHOT

Mr. Hall has been raised to
a chair; he is dazed, but con-
scious. There is a bad cut over,
his eye which his wife is dab-
bing with a handkerchief. Jaffers
comes in, pauses apprehensively.
Mrs. Hall turns excitedly and
points to the sitting room door.

> MRS. HALL
> He's in there -- in the
> sitting room! He's homi-
> cidal!

(CONTINUED)

B-25   (CONTINUED

       Jaffers looks still more
      -worried. He does not relish
      the job at all. CAMERA PANS
      ACROSS taking Jaffers thru
      the door towards the hall, as
      he slowly goes, followed by a
      little group of villagers.

B-26   INT PASSAGE. MED SHOT

      shooting over the backs of the
      people on Jaffers, as he goes
      up the stairs to the door of
      the sitting room.

B-27   INT PASSAGE. MED CLOSE SHOT

      on Jaffers as he takes the handle,
      slowly turns it, and goes in.

B-28   INT SITTING ROOM. MED CLOSE
        SHOT STRANGER

      The stranger is standing by
      the table. He is calm now, quiet
      and ominous.

B-29   INT SITTING ROOM. MED SHOT

      There is something so uncanny
      in the stranger's appearance
      that Jaffers pauses, irresolute.
      Numerous heads are peering into
      the room behind him.

                  JAFFERS
                    Here. What's all this?

                  THE STRANGER (commandingly)
                    Keep back there!

                  JAFFERS
                    Keep back! Who d'you
                    think you're talking to!

                  THE STRANGER
                    I give you a last chance -
                    to leave me alone!

B-30   INT SITTING ROOM. MED CLOSE

      on Jaffers and group at door.

                  JAFFERS
                    Give me a chance, eh!
                    You've committed assault--
                    that's what you've done! --
                    And you can just come
                    along with me to the
                    station.

                    (CONTINUED)

B-30   CONTINUED

As the stranger does
not move, Jaffers takes
a step forward.

                              JAFFERS
                                  Come on! Better come
                                  quietly - unless you want
                                  the handcuffs on.

B-31   INT SITTING ROOM
        MED SHOT LOW CAMERA

The stranger rises to his
full height - there is tremendous, ominous power in
him.

                              THE STRANGER
                                  Stop where you are! --
                                  You don't know what you're
                                  doing!

        CUT TO:

IH   B-32   INT. SITTING ROOM
                MED. LONG SHOT ON GROUP
                ─────────────────────

       Jaffers despite himself is
       awed. He shuffles.

                                                    JAFFERS
                                                        I know what I'm doing
                                                        all right -- come on.

                                                    VOICES FROM CROWD
                                                        Get hold of him!
                                                        Put him in gaol!

       They surge forward.

       CUT TO:

       B-33   INT. SITTING ROOM
                MED. CLOSE ON STRANGER
                ──────────────────────

                                                    THE STRANGER
                                                        All right, you fools!
                                                        You've brought it on
                                                        yourselves! Everything
                                                        would have come right
                                                        if you'd left me alone.
                                                        You've driven me near
                                                        madness with your
                                                        peering thru keyholes
                                                        and gaping thru the
                                                        curtains! And now
                                                        you'll suffer for it.

       He pauses.
       CUT TO:

       B-34   INT. SITTING ROOM
                MEDIUM SHOT (CLOSE)
                ───────────────────

       Jaffers, with the little group
       behind him, is rooted to the
       ground by the outburst. The
       stranger gives a fierce, de-
       risive laugh.

       CUT TO:

       B-35   MEDIUM SHOT STRANGER
                ────────────────────
                                                    THE STRANGER
                                                        You're crazy to know
                                                        who I am -- aren't you?
                                                        All right then! I'll
                                                        show you!

       CAMERA MOVES SWIFTLY IN and
       FOCUSES on his gloved hand as he
       raises it up to his nose -- CAMERA
       PANS UP TO HIS FACE - he lowers
       his hand with the nose between
       his fingers, and throws it at the
       feet of the policeman.

                                                        -- there's a souvenir
                                                        for you!

       CUT TO:

                                    82

B-36   MEDIUM SHOT ON GROUP

There is a gasp of horror
from the group. They stand
gazing in amazement at the
nose on the ground before and
slowly raise their heads to the
stranger.

CUT TO:

B-37   CLOSEUP ON STRANGER

He removes his glasses and
throws them in front of the man
beside the policeman.

                              THE STRANGER
                                   -- and one for you.

No eyes look out from be-
neath; a hideous cavity.

CUT TO:

B-38   INT. SITTING ROOM
        CLOSEUP .... MAN

There are gasps of horror;
someone whispers.

                              MAN
                                   Gawd! -- he's all eaten
                                   away!

CUT TO:

B-39   MED. SHOT ON ... STRANGER

The stranger's hands go to
his head and begin to unwind
the bandages - his voice sweeps
over the shivering group that
shrinks towards the door.

                              THE STRANGER
                                   I'll show you who I am -- .
                                   and what I am.

He tears off his matted wig,
then roll after roll of the
bandages fall away - revealing
emptiness beneath. At last
there is nothing but a headless
man beside the table - and a
loud diabolical laugh.

CUT TO:

B-40   INT. SITTING ROOM...MED. SHOT
        GROUP

There are shrieks from the crowd,
then panic and a mad rush to get
from the room

CUT TO:

B-41 FRONT DOOR OF THE INN
MED. LONG SHOT

of people rushing out - shouting
and crying.

CUT TO:

B-42 INT. SITTING ROOM...MED. CLOSE
STRANGER

of the headless stranger shaking
with mad laughter by the table.

CUT TO:

B-43 INT. SALOON...MED. SHOT

on Jaffers, the policeman who,
with two or three more courageous
villagers, stand in the saloon.

                    JAFFERS
               He's invisible! That's
               what's the matter with 'im.
               If he gets them other
               clothes off we'll never
               catch him in a thousand
               years! Come on!

The men rush towards the
sitting room.

CUT TO:

B-44 INT. SITTING ROOM...MED. SHOT
ON STRANGER

SHOW here, as far as can be
devised, the stranger undressing
himself. His coat should slip
to the ground - revealing a headless figure in shirt and trousers...

CUT TO:

B-45 CLOSE SHOT

...the trousers slip down onto
the floor revealing nothing re-
maining in the air, but a shirt.

(NOTE: I suggest that trick photography be employed here as far as
possible with the aid of invisible
wire frames minipulated by the
marionette method. Exact details
depend upon the extent to which
these methods - or other methods -
can be employed.)

CUT TO:

84

B-46   INT. SITTING ROOM
        MED. SHOT ON... (CLOSE)

        The policeman, with his two
        companions, burst into the room
        and stand transfixed at...

        CUT TO:

B-47   CLOSE SHOT ON...

        the sight of a shirt bobbing
        about behind the table, cutting
        fantastic capers.

        CUT BACK TO:

B-48   INT. SITTING ROOM
        MED. SHOT ON...:.(CLOSE)

        the three men.

                                    A VILLAGER
                                        Put the handcuffs on!

                                    JAFFERS (indignantly)
                                        How can I handcuff a bloomin'
                                        shirt?

                                    VILLAGER
                                        Quick! - Get hold of it!

        CAMERA DRAWS BACK as he
        darts forward. There is a
        hoarse laugh from the emptiness
        as the shirt moves away. The
        man grasps hold of the tail of
        the shirt; it writhes and falls
        to the floor as the Invisible
        Man slips out of it. The room
        is empty, save for the scattered
        clothing of the Invisible Man - the
        gasping policeman; the villagers
        standing round as if in a dream,
        and the men helplessly grasping
        the shirt tail. A calm, strong
        voice comes from the corner.

                                    THE VOICE
                                        Are you satisfied now, you
                                        fools?

        There is a moment of silence.
        The policeman and villagers do
        not move. The voice comes again
        as the CAMERA MOVES searching
        for the stranger - CAMERA   ---It's easy, really - if
        FOCUSES on corner as if finding   you're clever. A few
        him. A curtain moves as if   chemicals mixed to-
        brushed by someone; also a   gether - that's all.
        plant of flowers moves as   And flesh and blood
        stranger apparently passes by.   and bone just fade
                                             away.

        CUT TO:

                                    85

B-49   INT. SITTING ROOM
          MED. CLOSE SHOT ON....

A drawer opens and a bottle
rises from it - as it would
if a man were holding it.

                    THE VOICE
                    A little of this injected
                    under the skin of the arm -
                    every day for a month. Only
                    one man in the world was
                    clever enough to find it;
                    no one else ever knew.

The bottle falls and the
CAMERA PANS to the floor.

CUT TO:

B-50   SITTING ROOM...MED. SHOT ON

We see a chair move as if the
stranger is moving about.

                    THE VOICE
                    An Invisible Man can rule
                    the world; nobody will see
                    him come - and nobody will
                    see him go! He can hear
                    every secret - he can rob,
                    and wreck and kill -

CUT TO:

B-51   INT. SITTING ROOM
          MED. CLOSE ON...

the group of men; huddled
together - terrified.

                    JAFFERS
                    Not if he gets no further
                    than this room he won't!

He swings round to one of
the villagers.

                    Here! Shut that door!
                      (turns round and speaks
                        to the emptiness)
                    Now then, you come along
                    quietly!

There is no answer but a
derisive laugh. There is
silence - then suddenly...

CUT TO:

B-52   SITTING ROOM
          CLOSE SHOT ON....

the window shoots up. The
policeman dashes across.

                    JAFFERS
                    Look out! Mind that window!

(CONTINUED)

B-52   (CONTINUED)

          He swings round as a laugh
          comes from another corner
          of the room.

                                        THE INVISIBLE MAN
                                        You think I'd escape like
                                        a common criminal!

          The voice comes nearer -
          slowly and thoughtfully.

                                        You need a lesson. I think
                                        I'll throttle you.

          CUT TO:

B-53   SITTING ROOM..CLOSEUP ON...

          There is a moment of silence.
          The policeman stands bewildered
          by the window. Suddenly he
          raises his hands to his throat
          and screams. The voice of the
          Invisible Man comes close to the
          policeman's face.

                                        INVISIBLE MAN
                                        You must be made to under-
                                        stand what I can do.

          QUICK CUT TO:

B-54   MED. SHOT ON....

          one of the villagers at first
          too terrified to move - then he
          dashes forward and doubles up
          with a groan as he receives a
          kick in the stomach. The police-
          man's knees sag - he drops to the
          ground.

          QUICK CUT TO:

B-55   MED. SHOT ON....

          a villager by the door suddenly
          crashes back against it with a
          cry of terror and falls sideways,
          bringing down a table. The door
          flies open.

          QUICK CUT TO:

B-56   PASSAGE OUTSIDE OF SITTING ROOM

          Mrs. Hall and a shaky Mr. Hall
          are standing by - waiting for news.
          They see the door open, and then
          the coat rack crashes over as the
          Invisible Man rushes by. Mrs. Hall
          screams.

          CUT TO:

B-57   INT. SALOON...MED. SHOT

        of the bar as people are thrown
        back and glasses are swept from
        the bar with a crash.

        QUICK CUT TO:

B-58   EXT. INN...MED. LONG SHOT

        A crowd of gaping sightseers,
        standing by. The door of the
        Inn flies open. No one moves
        for a moment - then the whole
        crowd collapses outwards as the
        Invisible Man strikes a passage.
        between them. There are cries
        of terror.

        QUICK CUT TO:

B-59   EXT. STREET

        A woman with a pram. The pram
        suddenly flies sideways and
        collapses in the road.

        QUICK CUT TO:

B-60   EXT. ROAD

        An ancient villager; whose hat
        suddenly shoots off his head
        into a pond.

        QUICK CUT TO:

B-61   SHOT OF....

        A stone rising from the ground -
        and a window crashing.

        (NOTE: The following shots are
        taken with great rapidity to show
        vividly the spreading of a panic.)

        QUICK CUT TO:

B-62   EXT. STREET...LONG SHOT ON..

        a crowd of villagers racing panic-
        stricken down the street - shouting
        incoherently.
                                VOICES
                                    Look out!
                                    Get indoors!
        QUICK CUT TO:

B-63   SHOT OF....

        a woman snatching up a child
        and running into her house,
        slamming the door.

        QUICK CUT TO:

B-64   SHOT OF...

a man, in a small jeweller shop,
feverishly shovelling his goods -
(watches, rings, etc.) from their
show case into a safe. His wife
is helping him.

QUICK CUT TO:

B-65   SHOT OF....

a man standing against the
pavement with a bicycle.
Suddenly the bicycle is snatched
by invisible hands and peddles
off by itself down the road.

QUICK CUT TO:

B-66   EXT. STREET
        MED. SHOT ON.....

People staring in open-mouthed
wonderment as the bicycle goes
by. Someone shouts:

                          VOICE
                     It's him....the Invisible
                     Man!

There are shouts - some of
anger, some of terror. Some
people rush away - others more
courageous dash after the reced-
ing bicycle.

QUICK CUT TO:

B-67   STEEP HILL OUTSIDE VILLAGE

The bicycle comes in sight - runs
at the hill, then wobbles and
slows down. The men behind gain
upon it, shouting:

                          MEN
                     Come on! We've got him
                     now!

CUT TO:

B-68   EXT. HILL...MED. SHOT..

Suddenly the bicycle rises
from the ground and is flung
back into the midst of the pur-
suers. Some are thrown to the
ground, injured. The others
break and run, panic-stricken.

CUT TO:

B-69   INT. VILLAGE INN.
       CLOSE SHOT ON....

       Jaffe s, exhausted, but still
       game - telephoning from the Inn.

                                    JAFFERS
                               On the Gospel it's the
                               truth! -- Tried to strangle
                               me, sir!

       CUT TO:

B-70   INT. POLICE STATION CLOSE
       SHOT ON....

       Police Inspector Bird, a thick
       set mustached, stupid bully,
       sitting in the station, reply-
       ing to the telephone call.

                                    INSPECTOR BIRD
                               Where are you speaking from,
                               Jaffers? From the Lion's
                               Head Inn? Did you say an
                               'Invisible Man?' -- Well,
                               look here - you put more
                               water in it next time!

       CUT BACK TO:

B-71   INT. VILLAGE INN..CLOSE SHOT ON

       Jaffers, handing the telephone
       to Mr. Hall, the Innkeeper, in
       despair.

                                    JAFFERS
                               He won't believe me -- you
                               tell him!

       CUT TO:

B-72   A CITY STREET

       A newsboy - running - calling
       out:

                                    NEWSBOY
                               All about the Invisible Man-
                               Special! Invisible Maniac-
                               Special!

       People buy papers - and
       stand still - reading.

                      FADE OUT

SEQUENCE 'C'

FADE IN:

C-1   INT. LABORATORY
        LONG SHOT...LATE AFTERNOON

        HIGH CAMERA. A small labor-
        atory which belongs to Dr.
        Cranley and was used by Jack
        Griffin before his disappear-
        ance. It stands in the grounds
        of Dr. Cranley's house.

        Dr. Cranley and Dr. Kemp are
        searching through papers and
        books that lie scattered on a
        long table. Behind them down
        the center of the room runs a
        bench, fitted with the usual
        instruments of a scientist's
        work. CAMERA FOLLOWS THEM DOWN
        the long table as they search.

                        DR. CRANLEY
                    Not the slightest clue.

        As they reach the fire-
        place, we...
        CUT TO:

C-2   INT. LABORATORY
        MED. SHOT...SIDE ANGLE

        Dr. Cranley standing by the
        stove. - Kemp comes into shot
        - pokes the fireplace with his
        stick. It is filled with burnt
        papers.

                        KEMP   (dryly)
                    Didn't expect there would
                    be. That's where the
                    clues are - he wasn't
                    leaving anything to chance.

                        DR. CRANLEY
                    Griffin was never a man
                    for secrets. He came to
                    me with everything.

C-3   INT. LABORATORY
        MED. CLOSE SHOT ON...

        Kemp and including a large
        empty cupboard, which Kemp
        turns and points at...

                        KEMP
                    He kept a lot of stuff
                    locked in there. I came
                    in one evening - when
                    he didn't expect me...

        (CONTINUED)

g
h
r

C-3   (CONTINUED)

                                        KEMP   (continued)
                                             ...he was standing by this
                                             cupboard - it was full of
                                             instruments. When he saw
                                             me he slammed the door and
                                             turned the key.

        CUT TO:

C-4   INT. LABORATORY
        MED. SHOT ON...

        Dr. Cranley who has wandered
        away. He shakes his head; is
        restlessly searching amongst
        the instruments on the table.

                                        DR. CRANLEY
                                             You say he brought a pack-
                                             ing case up here in his
                                             car?

                                        KEMP   (coming into shot)
                                             The night before he dis-
                                             appeared. I heard him
                                             hammering - packing every-
                                             thing up.

        Dr. Cranley does not reply.
        CUT TO:

C-5   INT. LABORATORY
        MED. CLOSE ON...

        Dr. Cranley - he has
        come upon a fragment of
        papers beneath an earthen-
        ware jar on the laboratory
        bench, or high shelf.
                                        DR. CRANLEY
                                             (eagerly fumbling
                                              for his glasses)
                                        Here's something, Kemp!
                                             (he flicks some dust
                                              off with his fin-
                                              gers)

        CUT TO:

C-6   INT. LABORATORY
        CLOSE UP ON...

        Dr. Cranley, his glasses are
        on; he peers at the paper;
        slowly, as he reads, the eager-
        ness on his face changes to
        consternation and fear. He low-
        ers his hand to his side and
        looks up at Kemp in silence.
        CUT TO:

C-7   INT. LABORATORY
       CLOSE SHOT ON...

g
h
r

       Kemp and Dr. Cranley -
       as Cranley looks up at
       Kemp...

                                        KEMP
                                            What is it?

       Dr. Cranley does not
       reply.

                                            ...Bad news?

                                        DR. CRANLEY
                                              (slowly)
                                            It's only a rough note. A
                                            list of chemicals. The
                                            last on the list is -
                                            Monocane.

                                        KEMP
                                            Monocane? What is mono-
                                            cane?

                                        DR. CRANLEY
                                            Monocane's - a terrible
                                            drug.

                                        KEMP
                                            I've never heard of it.
                                              (his vanity as a
                                                scientist is hurt
                                                by his ignorance)

       CUT TO:

C-8   INT. LABORATORY
       MED. CLOSE ON...

       Kemp and Dr. Cranley.
       Dr. Cranley leans against
       bench, wearily.

                                        DR. CRANLEY
                                            You wouldn't, Kemp. It's
                                            never used now. I didn't
                                            know it was even made.
                                            It's a drug that comes
                                            from a flower that grows
                                            in India. It draws color
                                            from everything it touch-
                                            es. Years ago it was tried
                                            for bleaching cloth. They
                                            gave it up because it de-
                                            stroyed the material.

                                        KEMP
                                            That doesn't sound very
                                            terrible.

       CUT TO:

C-9   INT. LABORATORY
       CLOSE UP ON...

       Dr. Cranley -

                                        DR. CRANLEY
                                            I know. But it does some-
                                            thing else, Kemp. It was
                                            tried on some poor animal
                                            - a dog, I believe. It

       (CONTINUED)

C-9   (CONTINUED)

                                    DR. CRANLEY
                                        (continued)
                                    was injected under the
                                    skin; it turned the dog
                                    dead white, like a marble
                                    statue.

                            KEMP   (offscene)
                                    Is that so?

                                    DR. CRANLEY
                                    Yes. It also sent it
                                    raving mad.

            CUT TO:

C-10   INT. LABORATORY
        MED. SHOT

        There is a long silence.
        The two men stand facing
        one another. Kemp's jaunty
        manner has left him when
        he speaks again...
                            KEMP

        Dr. Cranley breaking in;   - You sure don't think? -
        his voice is level and
        controlled...
                                    DR. CRANLEY
                                    I only pray to God that
                                    Griffin hasn't been med-
                                    dling with this ghastly
                                    stuff.

                            KEMP

                                    He'd never touch a thing
                                    with madness in it.

        CAMERA PANS
        as Dr. Cranley walks
        over to the cupboard.
                                    DR. CRANLEY
                                    He might not know. I found
                                    that experiment in an old
                                    German book just by chance.
                                    The English books only
                                    describe the bleaching
                                    power; they were printed
                                    before the German exper-
                                    iment.

        Dr. Cranley is staring at
        the empty cupboard as if
        trying to read its secret.
        At last he turns abruptly as
        Kemp comes into the shot.

        (NOTE: Possibly bring them
        out here and have the follow-
        ing dialogue walking across
        the lawn.)
                            KEMP

                                    What are we going to do,
                                    Doctor?

        (CONTINUED)

C-10   (CONTINUED)

                                        DR. CRANLEY
                                    I think we must tell the
                                    police - that Griffin's
                                    disappeared - only that
                                    he's disappeared. I put
                                    you on your honour, Kemp,
                                    - not to breathe a word
                                    of this - to anyone.

        They go to the door.
        CUT TO:

C-11   INT. LABORATORY
        CLOSE SHOT ON...

        Dr. Cranley and Kemp stand-
        ing at the door. The old
        Doctor holds out the little
        fragment; then silently he
        drops it into his pocketbook.
        CAMERA PANS DOWN to pocket-
        book as he does so.
        CUT TO:

C-12   INT. LABORATORY
        MED. SHOT ON...

        Dr. Cranley and Kemp at
        door.

                                    KEMP
                                    Shall I come down to the
                                    station with you?

                                    DR. CRANLEY
                                    It's all right, Kemp,
                                    I'll go tonight - when
                                    Inspector Lane's on duty.

                                    KEMP
                                    I'll get along back home
                                    then. Goodnight.

                                    DR. CRANLEY
                                    Goodnight.

        Kemp goes out.
        Dr. Cranley stands
        thoughtfully gazing
        after him.

                        FADE OUT.

tw

"THE INVISIBLE MAN"

SEQUENCE "D"

FADE IN:

D-1   INT. SITTING ROOM IN DR. KAMP'S HOUSE..
        LONG SHOT..NIGHT

    A tastefully furnished old-
fashioned room with large French
windows opening on to a dark lawn.

    Kemp is sitting smoking by the fire,
reading a book by the light of a lamp
beside him. He has a **whiskey** and soda
by his side. The wireless is playing
soft, but cheerful music in the opposite
corner.
                                SOUND: MUSIC
    CUT TO:

D-2   INT. SITTING ROOM..AT WINDOWS

    Very slowly the French windows
are seen to open - scarcely more
than a foot. They remain open for
a moment, then softly close again.

    CUT TO:

D-3   INT. SITTING ROOM..MED. SHOT ON..

    Kemp seated with his back to the
windows - (unsuspecting) and does
not see the strange phenomenon,
but the draught slightly sways the
silk draping of the mantle-piece.
He looks up, puzzled - turns to the
windows that have closed again, and
after a moment settles down to his
book once more. The wireless music
has stopped. There is a short silence,
then the voice of the announces comes:

                   ANNOUNCER

    This is the National Station
broadcasting this evening's news.
Remarkable story from country
Village. The police amd doctors
are investigating an atonishing
story told this afternoon by the
people of the Village of Iping. It
appears that a mysterious disease
has broken out infecting a large
number of the inhabitants. It
takes the form of a delusion that
an Invisible Man is living among
them. Several people have been seriously injured, probably through
fighting among themselves in their
belief that their opponent is an
Invisible Man. The whole village
is in a state of panic and everyone --

CAMERA MOVES UP
UNTIL WE HOLD A
CLOSE UP on KEMP
during the an-
nouncing.

    CUT TO:

96

D-4   INT. SITTING ROOM...CLOSE UP
        ON WIRELESS

     The wireless set showing the
     dial, which is seen to turn
     softly over - and there is
     silence.
     CUT TO:

D-5   INT. SITTING ROOM...MED SHOT ON..

     Dr. Kemp looks across in surprise.
     He is about to rise when he is
     startled by a low, unpleasant laugh.
     Then a voice, the voice of the In-
     visible Man, takes up the story cut
     short by the silent radio.

                      INVISIBLE MAN
                       - and everyone deserves the
                       fate that's coming to
                       them. Panic - death -
                       things worse than death -

     CAMERA MOVES IN TO CLOSE
     SHOT as if the Invisible Man
     gets nearer. There is a low
     horrible chuckle. Then silence.
     Kemp sits rooted to his chair
     in astonishment. Then the
     voice comes again, softly:
                      - don't be afraid, Kemp.
                       It's me, Griffin, Jack
                       Griffin. How are you, my
                       friend.

     He thumps Kemp on shoulder or
     ruffles his hair, Kemp passes
     his hand across his forehead as
     if to clear a ghastly dream.
     Then the Invisible Man speaks
     again:
                      I'm frozen with cold - dead
                       tired. Thank God for a
                       fire.

     Kemp sits petrified as...we
     CUT TO:

D-6   INT. SITTING ROOM...MED CLOSE ON..

     ...the rocking armchair opposite
     trundles up to the fire. Then
     a dent appears in the soft back
     of the chair as the Invisible Man
     sits down.
     CUT TO:

D-7   INT. STUDY...MED CLOSE ON...KEMP

     A wave of horror sweeps over Kemp
     as the realization comes. With a
     hoarse cry he springs up and retreats
     to the opposite wall. He is panting
     for breath - speechless with fear.
     The voice rings out, harshly and
     impatiently.
                   INVISIBLE MAN
                   Sit down, you fool! - and
                   let's have a decent fire.
     CUT TO:

nn   D-8   INT. STUDY...MED SHOT ON..

        The rocking chair rocks as
        if a man had risen from it,
        then a log rises from the box by
        the fireplace, hovers in midair,
        then settles with a splutter on
        the fire. The voice barks out
        again - viciously.

                              INVISIBLE MAN
                    D'you hear me! - sit down!
                    Unless you want me to
                    knock your brains out.

        QUICK CUT TO:

D-9   INT. STUDY...CLOSE UP ON...

        Quick flash of Kemp too terror
        stricken to move. There is
        silence, then off-stage we
        hear:

                              Sit down! - or by God,
                              I'll --

        QUICK CUT TO:

D-10   CLOSE SHOT

        The heavy poker rises men-
        acingly from the hearth.
        CUT TO:

D-11   INT. STUDY...MED SHOT ON...
        KEMP

        He creeps back in terror to
        his chair. The Invisible Man
        speaks again - calmly, but
        ominously.

                              INVISIBLE MAN   (off-scene)
                    I want you to listen care-
                    fully, Kemp. I've been
                    through hell today. I
                    want food - and sleep.
                    But before we sleep there's
                    work to do.

        The voice dies away. Kemp
        is huddled in his chair.
        CUT TO:

D-12   INT. STUDY...CLOSE UP ON...
        KEMP

        He is far too panic stricken
        to do anything but stare with
        protruding eyes at the empty
        chair opposite him. We feel
        that Invisible eyes are upon
        him, considering him - weighing
        him up.
        CUT TO:

D-13   INT. STUDY...MED CLOSE ON...

        The rocking chair as Kemp sees.
        A cigarette lifts out of box -
        match is extended in mid-air,
        cigarette is lighted and smoke

        CONTINUED

D-13   CONTINUED

comes forth - all as if the
Invisible Man were smoking.
Then the voice comes again:

                              INVISIBLE MAN
                         You always were a dirty
                         little coward, Kemp.
                         You're frightened out of
                         your wits, aren't you.
                         It's no good talking like
                         this.

CUT TO:

D-14   INT. STUDY...TWO SHOT ON...

Kemp and the rocking chair -
Kemp makes no reply. The
chair leans forward.

                              INVISIBLE MAN
                         Have you got a good long
                         surgical bandage?

Kemp nods in a dazed
way.
                         - Good. And the dark
                         glasses you wear for X-Ray
                         work?

Kemp nods again.
                         All right. Go and get
                         them at once, and let me
                         have a dressing gown and
                         pajamas - and a pair of
                         gloves. You'll feel
                         better if you can see me -
                              (pause)
                         - won't you?

The chair opposite Kemp
is thrust back - CAMERA
PANS to the door, which opens,
and the voice barks out
again.
                         - Come on! We've no time
                         to waste!

CUT TO:

D-15   INT. STUDY...MED SHOT

SHOOTING THRU DOOR FROM
OUT SIDE...
Kemp tries to pull himself
together. He rises unsteadily
and creeps to the door. He
goes out, and the door closes
behind him.
WIPE OFF TO:

nn   D-16   INT. PASSAGE

        A small room or cupboard in a
        dark passage in Kemp's house
        used for medical stores. Kemp
        still dazed and trembling,
        takes a large roll of surgical
        bandages from a cupboard, and a
        pair of rubber gloves. Then he
        takes up a pair of dark glasses
        and leaves the room. We follow
        him down a short passage to the
        bedroom.
        CUT TO:

D-17   INT. BEDROOM...LONG SHOT

        CAMERA ENTERS with Kemp as he
        nervously opens the door and
        goes in. CAMERA PANS as he goes
        up to the bed to include the
        Invisible Man. He is sitting
        rigidly on the bed. He is clad
        in pajamas, slippers and dressing
        gown - emptiness where his head
        and hands should be.
        CUT TO:

D-18   INT. BEDROOM...MED CLOSE ON...

        The Invisible Man as he raises
        handless arm and points.

                        INVISIBLE MAN
                        Put them on the table.

        CUT TO:

D-19   INT. BEDROOM...MED. ON KEMP

        He comes forward and puts
        the gloves and glasses on the
        dressing table.

                    INVISIBLE MAN (off-scene)
                        Now go down and draw the
                        blinds in your sitting
                        room.

        As Kemp obediently turns
        to go we ....

        CUT TO:

CG   D-20   INT. BEDROOM...TWO SHOT

                        Kemp and the Invisible man.

                                        INVISIBLE MAN
                                            Are we alone in the house?

                                        KEMP
                                            Yes.

                                        INVISIBLE MAN
                                            Good
                                                (pause)
                                            All right. Go now. If you
                                            raise a finger against me
                                            you're a dead man. I'm
                                            strong, and I'll strangle
                                            you. You understand? Wait
                                            for me downstairs.

                        Kemp goes out and the door
                        closes.
                        CUT TOP

        D-21   INT. HALL..LONG SHOT.

                        Kemp, slowly and unsteadily
                        descending the stairs. At the
                        bottom he halts, hesitates and
                        takes a step towards the front
                        door. But even as he moves a
                        voice comes from above.
                        CUT TO:

        D-22   INT. HALL..SHOOTING UP THE STAIRS

                        On the half open door and the
                        Invisible Man empty clothes.

                                        INVISIBLE MAN
                                            The sitting room, I said,
                                            Kemp.

                        CUT BACK TO:

        D-23   INT. HALL..MED.SHOT ON...KEMP

                        He hastily turns, and makes his
                        way to the sitting room. The
                        voice follows him as he goes.

                                        INVISIBLE MAN
                                            -- and if you try and es-
                                            cape by the window I shall
                                            follow you - and no one in
                                            the world can save you!

                        Kemp goes into the sitting
                        room as we...
                        CUT TO:

        D-24   INT. SITTING ROOM

                        Kemp goes to the blinds, and
                        draws them, mechanically, as if
                        he is walking in his sleep. He
                        pauses by the telephone.
                        CUT TO:

CG   D-25   INT.SITTING ROOM.MED.CLOSE SHOT

           On Kemp by the telephone, looks
           at it longingly, then glances in
           fear towards the door. He dares
           not use the telephone. He stands
           there miserably waiting.
           DISSOLVE TO:

     D-26   EXT. VILLAGE STREET..LONG SHOT

           The main street of the village
           of Iping. A police car comes
           swiftly down the road and pulls
           up at the Inn. The villagers
           gaping.
           CUT TO:

     D-27   INT. VILLAGE INN...FULL SHOT

           A number of villagers are sitting
           around waiting. There is an at-
           mosphere of suspense. Mr. Hall,
           with a bandage around his head,
           still looks fuddled and shaken.
           A police sergeant is waiting
           anxiously b the windows, watch-
           ing out. Now he starts to at-
           tention and makes for the door,
           CAMERA PANS WITH HIM - speaking
           over his shoulder to the waiting
           people as he goes:
                              SERGEANT
                         Here's the Inspector!
           CUT TO:

     D-28   EXT. VILLAGE STREET. MED. SHOT

           The street outside. An important
           looking Police Inspector gets out
           of the car, followed by a smart
           assistant. They go up the steps
           into the Inn. The Inspector is
           Bird.
           CUT TO:

     D-29   INT. VILLAGE INN..MEDIUM SHOT

           The villagers have risen. The
           Inspector enters. The Sergeant
           salutes. The Inspector glares
           around, obviously annoyed.

                              INSPECTOR BIRD
                         Nice fool, you've made of
                         me! I've got reports from
                         ten miles round. Not a
                         sign of anything.
                              (he pauses)
                         I'll tell you what I think
                         of your Invisible Man.
                         It's a hoax..
           CUT TO:

CG   D-30   INT. VILLAGE INN..MEDIUM CLOSE
              SHOT

                    On Inspector Bird and his assist-
                    ant as Bird continues.

                                        INSPECTOR BIRD
                                   I'll have an enquiry right
                                   now!

                    He turns to his assistant:

                                   Bring in everybody who
                                   says they saw or heard
                                   anything. I'll get to the
                                   bottom of this before the
                                   night's out.

                    CUT TO:

      D-31   INT. VILLAGE INN...MED. LONG
              SHOT

                    The Sergeant salutes and goes
                    to the door. The Inspector
                    pulls a chair up to the saloon
                    table, produces a large note-
                    book and looks fiercely round
                    at the uneasy people standing
                    by the walls, Mrs. Hall among
                    them.

                    DISSOLVE TO:

      D-32   INT. KEMP'S HALL (NIGHT) PAN
              SHOT...ON

                    The door of the bedroom of
                    Kemp's house. It opens, and the
                    Invisible Man steps out. He
                    closes the door and walks stiffly
                    and erect downstairs. His head
                    is completely covered by the
                    bandages; he weaves the dark
                    glasses and the gloves. He looks
                    almost as he did when we first
                    saw him at the Inn -- except that
                    he wears no wig, and bandages
                    takes the place of the false nose.
                    CUT TO:

      D-33   INT. STAIRS...DOLLEY SHOT

                    The Invisible man coming down
                    the stairs. We follow him as
                    he reaches the bottom of the
                    stairs and turns along the
                    passage to the sitting room.
                    He goes in.

                    CUT TO:

                              103

CG   D-34   INT. SITTING ROOM...LONG SHOT

>HIGH CAMERA. The Invisible Man
closes the door. Kemp stands
waiting where we left him.

>>INVISIBLE MAN
>>Now then. We can talk
as man to man.

>He gives a low chuckle
and motions to a chair.

>>-- sit down.

>Kemp obediently goes to a
chair and sits down. The
Invisible Man takes a quick
glance round the room; at
the drawn curtains - at
the telephone. He goes to
the windows - cautiously
feels between the curtains
with his gloved hands and
thrusts up the bolt. He
goes to the door and turns
the key - Kemp watching apprehensively. There is a
restless, hunted look about
the strange figure. Then he
comes forward and draws up
a chair.
CUT TO:

D-35   INT. SITTING ROOM..EXTREME
        CLOSE ON

>The Invisible Man.

>>INVISIBLE MAN
>>One day I'll tell you
everything. There's no
time now. I began five
years ago - in secret.
Working - all night -
every night - right into
the dawn. A thousand
experiments - a thousand
failures -- and then at
last the great, wonderful
day!

>He pauses.

>CUT TO:

D-36   INT. SITTING ROOM
        CLOSE UP ON..KEMP

    At last Kemp finds a
    choking, hysterical voice:

                  KEMP
                  But - Griffin - it's -
                  ghastly!

CUT TO:

D-37   INT. SITTING ROOM
        MED. CLOSE...TWO-SHOT

    QUEER LOW ANGLE.
    The Invisible Man goes on
    as if he has not heard.

                  INVISIBLE MAN
                  - the great, wonderful
                  day! - the last little
                  mixture of drugs. I could
                  n't stay here any longer,
                  Kemp. I couldn't let you
                  see me slowly fading away.
                  I packed up and went to a
                  village for secrecy and
                  quiet - to finish the ex-
                  periment and complete the
                  antidote - the way back to
                  solid man again. I meant
                  to come back just as I was
                  when you saw me last - but
                  the fools wouldn't let me
                  work in peace. I had to
                  teach them a lesson.

    He pauses - and chuckles
    at the memory. There is a
    horrid, unearthliness in
    his laugh.
                  KEMP
                  But why! - why do it,
                  Griffin!

CUT TO:

D-38   INT. SITTING ROOM
        MED. SHOT ON...

    Vivid flash of the Invisible
    Man sitting up - but before
    he can speak...we...
    CUT TO:

D-39   INT. SITTING ROOM
        BIG CLOSE UP ON...

    The Invisible man.

                  INVISIBLE MAN
                  Just a scientific experi-
                  ment - at first. That's
                  all. To do something no
                  other man in the world had
                  done.
                      (he is quivering with
                      excitement - his
                      voice comes in a
                      hard, icy whisper)

          (CONTINUED)

gh
r

D-39   (CONTINUED)

                                    INVISIBLE MAN
                                       (continued)
                                    But there's more to it
                                    than that, Kemp - I know
                                    now - it came to me -
                                    suddenly - the drugs I
                                    took seemed to light up
                                    my brain. Suddenly I saw
                                    the power I held - the
                                    power to rule! To make
                                    the whole world grovel at
                                    my feet.
                                       (he laughs)
                                    We'll soon put the world
                                    right now, Kemp! You and
                                    I!

         CUT TO:

D-40   INT. SITTING ROOM
         CLOSE UP ON..KEMP

                                    KEMP   (appalled)
                                       I! You mean? -

         CUT TO:

D-41   INT. SITTING ROOM
         TWO-SHOT...MEDIUM

         On Kemp and the Invisible
         Man.
                                    INVISIBLE MAN
                                    I must have a partner: a
                                    visible partner - to help
                                    me in the little things -
                                    you're my partner - Kemp!

         CUT TO:

D-42   INT. SITTING ROOM
         MED. CLOSE ON...

         The Invisible Man as he
         points with finger
         (gloves?) at Kemp.
                                    INVISIBLE MAN
                                    We'll begin with a reign
                                    of terror - a few murders
                                    - here and there - murders
                                    of great men - and little
                                    men - to show we make no
                                    distinction: we may wreck
                                    a train or two -

         CUT TO:

D-43   INT. SITTING ROOM
         CLOSE SHOT ON...

         The Invisible Man as he
         leans forward - thrusts
         out his gloved hands and
         goes through the imaginary
         motions of strangling.
                                    INVISIBLE MAN
                                    Just these fingers - round
                                    a signal-man's throat,
                                    that's all.
         He laughs.
         CUT TO:

106

D-44   INT. SITTING ROOM
         MED. SHOT ON THE TWO

         Kemp springs from his
         chair with a cry:

                             KEMP
                        Griffin! For God's sake!

         The Invisible Man rises
         slowly and takes hold of
         the buttons of his dressing
         gown.

                       INVISIBLE MAN
                      You want me to - throw
                      these off?

                       KEMP
                      No! - no!
                        (in agony)

         CUT TO:

D-45   INT. SITTING ROOM
         CLOSER TWO-SHOT

         Favoring the Invisible Man.
         He chuckles and resumes
         his seat.

                       INVISIBLE MAN
                      Very well, then. We shall
                      make our plans tomorrow.
                      Tonight there's a small
                      job to do. Go and get your
                      car out, Kemp.

                     KEMP
                      Why? Where are we going?

                       INVISIBLE MAN
                      Back to the village I left
                      this morning. I came away
                      without my notebooks. They
                      contain all the results of
                      my experiments. I must
                      have them here.

                     KEMP
                      But - it's past eight
                      o'clock.

                     INVISIBLE MAN
                      It's only fifteen miles.
                      Go now - quickly, and
                      take a bag with you - for
                      the books.

         CUT TO:

D-46   INT. SITTING ROOM
         LONG SHOT

         Keeping Kemp in the fore-
         ground - as he gets up and
         goes to the door. He seems
         completely under the spell of
         Invisible Man now - he moves
         as though hypnotized. The
         Invisible Man throws a final
         command as Kemp goes.

         (CONTINUED)

D-46   (CONTINUED)

                                        INVISIBLE MAN
                                    Put a warm rug in the car.
                                    It's cold outside - when
                                    you've got to go about
                                    naked.

        The Invisible Man rises
        as we...
        CUT TO:

D-47   MED. CLOSE ON...

        The Invisible Man begins
        to unwind the bandages off
        his head as the picture...

        DISSOLVES TO:

D-48   EXT. KEMP'S HOUSE
        LONG SHOT

        Kemp draws up in his car,
        gets out and goes up the
        steps to the front door -
        CAMERA PANS WITH HIM. - He
        opens the door and a voice
        says:

                                    INVISIBLE MAN
                                    All ready?

                                KEMP
                                    Yes.

        Kemp turns and goes back
        to the car. He has a rug
        under his arm - he looks
        vaguely round - wondering
        where his invisible companion
        is, until suddenly he is star-
        tled by a voice that raps out
        beside the car...

                                INVISIBLE MAN
                                    Come on ! - Get in.

        CUT TO:

D-49   EXT. HOUSE....AT CAR

        CLOSER SHOT OF DOOR.
        The door of the car jerks
        open; Kemp clambers hastily
        in - and the door slams behind
        him. The car starts and glides
        off into the night.
        CUT TO:

D-50   SHOT INSIDE THE CAR

        Kemp sits rigidly at the driv-
        ing wheel. Beside him sits the
        Invisible Man - only a blanket
        can be seen - wrapped round his
        shoulders.

        (CONTINUED)

D-50   (CONTINUED)

                                        INVISIBLE MAN
                                            We'll stop in a lane - a
                                            hundred yards from the Inn.
                                            I'll go in and give you the
                                            books through the window.

                                        KEMP
                                            But they'll have a guard!

                                        INVISIBLE MAN
                                                (with a laugh)
                                            A guard! - what can a guard
                                            do - you fool!
                                                (there is a pause)
                                            I must have those books,
                                            Kemp. I'll work in your
                                            laboratory till I've found
                                            the antidote. Then sometimes
                                            I'll make you invisible - to
                                            give me a rest.

            Kemp stares at the huddled
            blanket - shudders - but
            makes no reply.

            DISSOLVE TO:

D-51   INT. VILLAGE INN
        FULL SHOT...

            The Bar is arranged rather
            like a court. The enquiry
            is in full progress. Witnesses
            sit round on the benches. The
            Inspector, with his assistant
            beside him, is questioning the
            old man whose hat was thrown
            into the pond. (The old man -
            a farmer type; bald - with a
            beard and wearing a smock.)

                                        THE OLD MAN
                                            I was walking home to my
                                            lunch, sir - when all of a
                                            sudden something takes hold
                                            of my hat and throws it in
                                            the pond!

            CUT TO:

D-52   INT. SALOON
        MED. CLOSE TWO-SHOT

            On Inspector Bird and the
            old man.

                                        INSPECTOR BIRD
                                            How many drinks did you
                                            have on your way home?

                                        THE OLD MAN
                                            Only a couple - that's all,
                                            sir.

            (CONTINUED)

D-52   (CONTINUED)

                                    INSPECTOR BIRD
                                        A couple of drinks and a
                                        gust of wind - so much for
                                        you.
                                            (he glares round)
                                        Now then - about the bi-
                                        cycle. Where's the owner
                                        of the bicycle?

        CUT TO:

D-53   INT. SALOON
        CLOSE SHOT ON...

        A man - another type.

                                    THE MAN
                                        Here, sir!

        CUT TO:

D-54   EXT. LANE...
        MED. LONG SHOT

        A lane - with high hedges.
        Kemp's car, travelling slowly,
        draws up in the shadows.
        CUT TO:

D-55   INT. CAR
        CLOSE SHOT

                                    INVISIBLE MAN
                                        Take your bag and walk
                                        straight down the street.
                                        I'll guide you. Wait out-
                                        side the window till the
                                        books come out. Put them
                                        in your bag and come back
                                        to the car. Then wait for
                                        me.

        CAMERA PANS as the blanket
        drops over the seat and the
        door of the car opens. Kemp
        takes his bag and gets out.
        CUT TO:

D-56   EXT. LANE
        FOLLOW SHOT ON...

        Kemp - he sets off down the
        lane - fearfully gazing to
        his side.

                                    INVISIBLE MAN
                                        Don't stare at me, you
                                        fool! Look in front of
                                        you.

        CUT TO:

                                110

D-57   EXT. LANE
        CLOSE SHOT ON KEMP

        He jerks his head round
        and looks straight in front
        of him with a fixed stare.
        CUT TO:

D-58   EXT. VILLAGE INN
        FULL SHOT

        Kemp comes down the street,
        carrying his bag. A man
        passes by, unconcerned. Kemp
        turns suddenly as if pushed,
        down a lane beside the Inn,
        until he comes beneath a win-
        dow.
        CUT TO:

D-59   EXT. VILLAGE INN
        MED. SHOT

        Kemp - under window.

                                    INVISIBLE MAN
                                        Here you are. Stroll up
                                        and down - as though you
                                        were waiting for someone.
                                        Watch for the window to
                                        open.

        Kemp stands still -
        rigidly. Then he whis-
        pers:

                                    KEMP
                                        Griffin ! - Are you there !

        There is no reply.
        Kemp looks fearfully
        round.

        CUT TO:

CG D-60   EXT. VILLAGE INN.MOVING SHOT

          THE CAMERA moves slowly round
          the Inn, as if following the
          Invisible Man. It comes to the
          front door. A few small boys,on
          tiptoe, are trying to look into
          the window, thru which the witnesses
          can be seen standing. The Inn door
          is seen.
          CUT TO:

D-61   EXT. VILLAGE INN. CLOSE SHOT ON

          The Inn door as it slowly opens.
          CUT TO:

D-62   INT. SALOON..MED. LONG SHOT

          Shooting towards the door. The
          owner of the bicycle is still
          giving his evidence.

                                    THE BICYCLE OWNER
                                    It was pulled clean out of
                                    my hand, sir! Then it
                                    went peddling offdown the
                                    street all by itself!

          The door opens, papers blow
          off the table.
                                    INSPECTOR BIRD (seeing this)
                                    Who's that -- opened the
                                    door?

                              MRS. HALL
                                    It's them boys again.

          CAMERA PANS with her as she
          goes to the door.
          CUT TO:

D-63   EXT. VILLAGE INN. MEDIUM SHOT

          Mrs. Hall peers angrily out
          at the boys by the window.

                              MRS. HALL
                                    Look 'ere - you leave this
                                    door alone - it's private
                                    see?

                              A BOY
                                    We never touched it!

                              MRS. HALL
                                    Yes you did! Go on! Hop it!

          She makes a threatening
          gesture and the boys run
          away.

          CUT TO:

                              112

CG D-64   PASSAGE OUTSIDE THE SITTING
           ROOM

           Shot of door opening to passage
           as they are all looking at the
           other door.
           CUT TO:

D-65   INT. SITTING ROOM...MEDIUM SHOT

           The door opens - CAMERA PANS to
           shefl, the notebooks lie on a
           shelf of the sideboard. After a
           moment they rise from the shelf
           and travel across to the table
           by the window.

           (NOTE: Invisible hands might
           tear up some obnoxious calender
           or smash a hideous ornament -
           or put portrait of landlady up-
           side down, or back to front.)

           CAMERA PANS to window - it slowly
           and softly opens; the books rise
           from the table and travel thru.
           They hover in mid-air.
           CUT TO:

D-66   EXT. VILLAGE INN..AT WINDOW...
           MEDIUM CLOSE

           Kemp standing on box or old cart,
           we see him look up and to the books
           in mid-air - CAMERA PANS - he
           feverishly grabs the books and drops
           them into his case. He closes the
           case, and with a fearful glance
           round, makes for the main road.
           CUT TO:

D-67   INT. SALOON..MEDIUM LONG SHOT

           HIGH CAMERA. The enquiry is over.
           The Inspector is sitting back,
           speaking to the villagers.

                                    INSPECTOR BIRD
                                    Lies, that's all. Lies
                                    from beginning to end. I've
                                    a good mind to prosecute
                                    the lot of you for con-
                                    spiracy.
           CUT TO:

D-68   INT. SALOON..CLOSER SHOT ON

           Inspector Bird continuing.

                                    I shall announce this eve-
                                    ning that the whole thing's
                                    a hoax - and you'll be the
                                    laughing stock of the whole
                                    country.

           He takes a last scowl round,
           and picks up his pen to sign
           his report.
           CUT TO:

D-69   INT. SALOON..CLOSE SHOT ON

      The Inkpot -- as Inspector Bird's
      hand reaches forward to dip the
      pen into the ink - but as he does
      so the inkpot gently moves away
      from him. He tries again and the
      inkpot dodges his pen. Then,slowly
      the inkpot rises from the table-
      hoves in mid-air and jerks the ink
      full into the Inspector's face.
      CAMERA PANS up to the Inspector as
      this happens.
      CUT TO:

D-70   INT. SALOON..LONG SHOT

      On the people. There is a moment
      of deathly stillness; everyone is
      hypnotized -- then comes a low,
      maniacal laugh -- and panic is let
      loose. There are shrieks and hoarse
      cries: Mrs. Hall screams.

                    MRS. HALL
                  He's here! The Invisible
                  Man!
      CUT TO:

D-71   INT. SALOON...SHOT OF BAR

      One after another a row pewter
      beer mugs rise from their places
      on the shelf and fly into the
      panic stricken crowd.
      CUT TO:

D-72   INT. SALOON...MEDIUM SHOT

      Someone smashes a window and
      leaps out - others dash for the
      door (old farmer man)
      CUT TO:

D-73   INT. SALOON....LONG SHOT

      Everyone rushing panic stricken
      out of the saloon. After a short,
      frantic struggle, everyone has gone,
      save the Inspector who lies on the
      floor, struggling with an invisible
      opponent who has him by the throat.
      CUT TO:

D-74   INT. SALOON..MED.CLOSE SHOT

      A horase, brutal voice breathes
      over the helpless Inspector.
                 INVISIBLE MAN
                A hoax is it? -- all a hoax
                all -- a -- hoax...!

               (CONTINUED)

D-74   (CONTINUED)

> The last three words are timed
> to the rise of a heavy stool--
> that hovers - and crashes into
> the Inspector's face on the last
> word - "hoax".
> CUT TO:

D-75   INT. SALOON..FULL SHOT

> The saloon bar is in silence.
> The Inspector lies crushed on
> the floor amidst indescribable
> wreckage left by the panic
> stricken crowd. Distant shout-
> ing can be heard from the streets
> outside.
> CUT TO:

D-76   EXT. LANE...PAN SHOT

> The corner of the land where
> the car stands. THE CAMERA picks
> up an empty scene, but there is
> the sound of padding, running
> feet and heavy breathing. CAMERA
> PANS past trees - dust, etc.
> FOLLOWING the sounds along the
> lane to the car, Kemp sits tensely
> inside. He starts as the door
> flies open and slams too.

                    INVISIBLE MAN
                         All right. Off you go!

> CUT TO:

D-77   EXT. LANE..MEDIUM SHOT

> Kemp obediently starts up and
> the car moves off.
                    INVISIBLE MAN
                         Go for your life too!

> The engine roars and the car
> jumps forward.
> CUT TO:

D-78   INT. CAR..MED. CLOSE SHOT...

> Kemp and the blanket, as the
> car sways and jolts on its
> journey thru the night.
>
> (NOTE: shoot so as to be able
> to cut this if necessary)

                    INVISIBLE MAN
                         Did you hear some shout-
                         ing and screaming?

                    KEMP
                         What was that screaming?

> (CONTINUED)

"THE INVISIBLE MAN"

SEQUENCE "E"

FADE IN:

E-1   EXT. STREET - PORT STOWE
        LONG SHOT.

        The main street of a small
        town.- It is practically
        deserted. The street lamps
        throw pools of light on the
        pavement. Dr. Cranley comes
        down the road, obviously not
        relishing the call he is about
        to make at the police station.
        He passes a policeman, who gives
        him a cheerful salute.

        CUT TO:

E-2   EXT. STREET
        MEDIUM SHOT.

                            POLICEMAN
                      Good evening, Doctor.

                         DR. CRANLEY
                      Good evening.
                        (he pauses)
                      Is Inspector Lane at the
                      station? I want a word with
                      him.

                         POLICEMAN
                      Yes, sir. He's on duty now.

        Dr. Cranley nods, and
        passes on. He comes
        to the station: looks
        reluctantly at the for-
        bidding doors and is
        about to enter when a
        newspaper boy comes
        running up. CAMERA PANS
        TO newsboy.
                            BOY
                      Late Special! - Invisible Man
                      kills policeman! - Special!

        People pour out of nearby
        door, dressed in night clothes
        etc - a few people in the
        street - all gather round
        the boy and eagerly buy copies.
        Gradually the significance of
        the boy's cry dawns upon
        the old Doctor's slow think-
        ing brain. His hand gropes
        for a coin in his pocket.
        The Doctor buys a paper; the
        boy runs excitedly on.

                          BOY
                      Late night special! Amazing
                      story of invisible maniac-
                      Special!

        CUT TO:

E-3   EXT. STREET
           CLOSEUP ON..DR. CRANLEY

              The Doctor reads the
              great black headlines.
              The dreadful truth flashes
              to his brain. He stands
              for a moment rigid -
              horrified - the papers
              gripped stiffly beside
              him. The crowd around
              him are too absorbed in
              their papers to notice him.

              CUT TO:

E-4   EXT. STREET
           MED. CLOSE ON..

              Two men - a big man and a
              little man - exchanging
              opinions.

                             BIG MAN
                                Nasty business, this.

                             LITTLE MAN
                                It's a conjuring trick;
                                that's what it is. I aaw
                                a feller make a peanut
                                disappear once.

              THE CAMERA PANS TO
              Dr. Cranley - we see
              people reading the news-
              papers. The Doctor gazes
              up the steps of the police
              station - shudders, and
              turns away. He makes
              blindly for his home.

              DISSOLVE TO:

E-5   INT. BEDROOM - KEMPS' HOUSE
           MEDIUM SHOT. (NIGHT)

              The Invisible Man is sitting
              at a small table. Thrust to
              one side is a tray containing
              the remains of a meal. His
              hands lay palm downwards upon
              the two big notebooks which he
              rescued from the Inn. He is
              dressed as he was before
              leaving the house. Kemp stands
              opposite him. The first acute-
              ness of Kemp's fear has passed
              away. He looks utterly dejected
              and cowed. He carries out his
              orders as if under hypnotic
              influence.

                             INVISIBLE MAN
                                There are one or two things
                                you must understand, Kemp.
                                I must always remain in
                                hiding for an hour after
                                meals.

              CUT TO:

E-6   INT. KEMP'S BEDROOM
       CLOSE SHOT OF...

          Head drinking - and we
          hear -.....

--/The food is visible inside me until it is digested. I can only work on fine, clear days.

          NOTE: During this scene he could eat or walk about - The business of eating will have to keep this scene going as suggested in the following cuts:

E-7   INT. BEDROOM
       CLOSE SHOT OF..

          Gloved hands dealing with food.

          CUT TO:

E-8   INT. BEDROOM
       CLOSE SHOT OF...

          Hands breaking bread.

          CUT TO:

E-9   INT. BEDROOM
       CLOSEUP OF...

          The Invisible Man eating.

          CUT TO:

E-10   INT. BEDROOM
       CLOSE ON KEMP...

          Watching him - and listening. (He might smoke comfortably here)

          NOTE: (During the above cuts we hear:-

          INVISIBLE MAN
          If I work in the rain - the water can be seen on my head and shoulders. In a fog you can see me like a bubble. In smoky cities the soot settles on me until you can see a dark outline. You must always be near at hand to wipe off my feet. Even dirt between my fingernails would give me away.

          (Shoot CLOSEUP in case of cutting here.)

          It is difficult at first to walk downstairs. We are so accustomed to watching our feet. But they're trivial difficulties - we shall find ways of defeating everything.

          CUT TO

```
E-11     INT. BEDROOM
         LONG SHOT...

                                        INVISIBLE MAN
                                        You will sleep in the room
                                        opposite and bring me some
                                        more food at eight o'clock.
                                        Good night.

         Kemp leaves the room
         without a word. The
         Invisible Man goes to
         the door and locks it.

         CUT TO:

E-12     INT. BEDROOM
         CLOSER PAN SHOT...

         The Invisible Man moves
         across to the dressing
         table and unwraps the
         bandages from his head.
         Then he takes off his
         dressing gown and gloves,
         and stands before the
         mirror - a headless,
         handless figure in
         pajamas. He goes to the
         bed and sits down.

         CUT TO:

E-13     INT. BEDROOM
         CLOSE SHOT....

         Of the Invisible Man's
         slippers being kicked off.

         CUT TO:

E-14     INT. BEDROOM
         MED. SHOT...

         He turns the covers of
         the bed down, - then
         gets into bed. Then,
         very wearily he pulls
         the clothes over him -
         switches off the light
         and lies still. The
         moon shines in upon
         the strange headless
         figure in bed.

         DISSOLVE TO:

E-15     INT. SALOON - IPING
         MED. SHOT (NIGHT)

         Two policemen stoop to
         a covered stretcher,
         raise it from the ground
         and bear the body of the
         dead Inspector from the
         room.

         CUT TO:
```

E-16   INT. SALOON
        FULL SHOT...

                High Camera. A group
                of Police Detectives
                watching in silence
                as the stretcher is
                borne away. Then the
                Chief Detective strides
                to the table where a
                large map is spread out.
                He gives orders to his
                staff like an Army Commander
                upon the eve of a battle.
                The others have gathered
                round the table.

                                        CHIEF DETECTIVE
                                        You understand my plan?
                                        You are in charge of all
                                        country east of here,
                                        Thompson, for twenty
                                        miles to the north of
                                        the main road.

        QUICK CUT TO:

E-17   INT. SALOON
        CLOSE UP ON....

                Neville. Over this we
                hear the Chief Detective:

                                        CHIEF DETECTIVE (off scene)
                                        Neville takes the opposite
                                        section to the south.

        CUT TO:

E-18   CLOSE UP ON..

                Stoddart - over this we
                hear the Chief Detective.

                                        Stoddard takes charge of
                                        the search in the hills and-

        QUICK CUT TO:

E-19   CLOSE UP ON...

                Hogan - we hear Detective
                off:

                                        --Hogan takes all the
                                        villages out to the river.

        CUT TO:

E-20   INT. SALOON
        MED. SHOT ON...

                The Chief Detective:

                                        We shall comb the country
                                        for twenty miles round.
                                        We've got a terrible
                                        responsibility. He's mad
                                        and he's invisible. He
                                        may be standing beside us
        (CONTINUED)   now.

                                    120

E-20   (CONTINUED)

            The Detectives shift
            uneasily.

                                        -- But he's human - and we shall
                                        get him....

            The scene darkens as the
            Detective goes on with
            his orders: and there comes
            a series of scenes, dissolv-
            ing quickly into each other -
            revealing the great man-hunt
            spreading throughout the
            country; silent pictures,
            over which comes the firm,
            incisive voice of the
            Detective.

            CUT TO:

E-21   POLICE STATION
            LONG SHOT - HIGH CAMERA

            A posse of motor cyclist
            police sweep out of a
            station yard and make in
            different directions.   DETECTIVE
                                        ...We shall have a thousand
                                        men out tonight: tomorrow
                                        we shall have ten thousand
                                        volunteers to help them.

            CUT TO:

E-22   EXT. ROAD
            LONG SHOT - LOW CAMERA

            An open line of uniformed   There's a broadcast warn-
            men - advancing stealth-   ing going out at ten o'
            ily abreast of a road -   clock. At all costs we must
            the line crosses the road,   avoid a panic spreading.
            taking in a wide section   Get away to your districts
            of the fields to either   at once and send me a note
            side.   of your headquarters. Re-
                                        member he will leave tracks -
            CUT TO: even if he's invisible...

E-23   SHOT OF...

            A giant wireless mast
            crackling its message
            out into the night.

            CUT TO:

E-24   SHOT OF

            A fast police car - racing
            down a main road.

            CUT TO:

E-25   SHOT ON...

            A part of police, beating
            their way through a thick
            copse of trees.
            CUT TO:

E-26   SHOT ON...

        There comes a faint,
        darkened picture of
        the Invisible Man -
        asleep, aswe left him
        in the bed in Kemp's
        room.

        THE PICTURE DISSOLVES TO:

E-27   INT. DANCE HALL
        LONG SHOT....

        A gay, brightly lit
        dancing hall. Couples
        glide round the room
        to the music of a large
        radio in a corner.
        Suddenly - without
        warning, the music fades.
        The dancers pause in
        surprise and look across
        at the radio.

        The voice of the Announcer
        comes clearly to the room.

                                        ANNOUNCER
                                    I must interrupt the dance
                                    music for a moment. I have
                                    an urgent message from
                                    Police Headquarters. Earlier
                                    this evening we broadcast
                                    a report of an Invisible
                                    Man.

        CUT TO:

E-28   INT. DANCE HALL
        PAN SHOT...ON DOLLEY

        On the dancers reactions
        as this comes across -
        they instinctively be-
        come tense and anxious.
        CAMERA TRAVELS THRU THE
        dancers as the voice of
        the Announcer is heard:

                                        ANNOUNCER
                                    The report has now been
                                    confirmed. It appears that
                                    an Unknown Man - by
                                     scientific means, has made
                                    himself invisible. He has
                                    attacked and killed a
                                    Police Inspector and is now
                                    at large...

        CAMERA ON DOLLEY has now
        reached the mouth of the
        radio, which is of the
        old-fashioned type horn,
        and it fills the screen-
        speaking directly out
        at the audience, as if
        appealing to them for
        their co-operation.
        (CONTINUED)

E-28   (CONTINUED)

        -- The Chief of Police appeals to the public for help and assistance...Those willing to co-operate in the search are requested to report tomorrow morning to their local station.

Out of the dark mouth of the radio, there comes a picture of...

        --The Invisible Man works without clothing. He will have to seek shelter ...

An old man and woman in a country cottage, listening from a small, primitive set - with earphones to their heads.

    DISSOLVE TO:

E-29   INT. ORPHANAGE
    MED. SHOT ON...

A room in an Orphanage. The children, in uniform, grouped round, listening to a radio - excited and awed. An older girl is in charge.

        ..You are requested to look every door and window - and every out-building he may use to hide in...

    DISSOLVE TO:

E-30   INT. OFFICE

A vacant, open-mouthed night watchman in an office, also listening in.

        ...The police will be glad to receive any suggestions that will help in capturing the fugitive. Remember he is solid - but cannot be seen...

    DISSOLVE TO:

E-31   SHOT OF...

        ...A reward of $5000.00 will be given to any person whose information leads to his capture...

A stout farmer, who rises upon news of the reward - picks up his hat and a large stick and makes for the door.

    DISSOLVE TO:

E-32   INT. DANCE HALL
    DOLLEY SHOT...

CAMERA STARTS ON CLOSE SHOT as the last words come from the full, open mouth of the original amplifier...

        ANNOUNCER
    .....The police appeal to the public to keep calm and to admit uniformed search parties to all property.

(CONTINUED)

E-32   (continued)

THE CAMERA PULLS BACK
as the words of the
Announcer die away -
and after a moment of
silence the dance music
returns. A few couples
begin to dance again-
half-heartedly: others
help their women on
with their coats and
go away quietly.

A SERIES OF DISSOLVES.

E-33   TRICK SHOT...OF

Hands shooting bolts -
turning window clasps,
locking doors - slamming
down windows - anxious,
fumbling hands super-
imposed one upon the
other.

DISSOLVE TO:

E-34   INT. KEMP'S BEDROOM
        CLOSE SHOT ON...

The Invisible Man -
sleeping in his bed -
the moon shining upon
the round dent in the
pillow where his head
lies - the armless
sleeve of his pajamas
outside the blankets.

The CAMERA MOVES across
the room and past the
locked door. It re-
veals Kemp, standing in
his dressing gown -
listening with bated
breath for any sound
that might come to him
from the room beyond.
Very slowly he turns -
and tiptoes downstairs.

CUT TO:

E-35   CLOSE SHOT ON...

Kemp going downstairs -
several times he looks
back and listens. His
face is contorted in
an agony of suspense
and fear.

CUT TO:

E-36   INT. PASSAGE
        MED. SHOT..

We follow him, as swiftly and
(CONTINUED)

124

E-36   (CONTINUED)

   silently he passes
   down the passage and
   enters his sitting
   room.

   CUT TO:

E-37   INT. SITTING ROOM
   MEDIUM SHOT...

   Kemp locks the door. He
   sways back against the
   door, half fainting:
   recovers himself and goes
   to the telephone. He
   feverishly fumbles with
   it, removes the receiver
   and dials a number.

   CUT TO:

E-38   INT. LIBRARY-
   CRANLEY'S HOME - FULL SHOT

   Dr. Cranley is pacing to and
   fro. The 'phone bell rings
   and he crosses to it.

   CUT TO:

E-39   INT. SITTING ROOM
   CLOSE SHOT ON..

   Kemp - waiting - his
   eyes fixed on the door.
   He quickly turns and
   speaks in a fast, breath-
   less undertone.

          KEMP
          Doctor! - listen! - it's
          something - ghastly - it's
          Griffin - he's come back-
          he's asleep in my room!
          He's the Invisible Man!
          he's mad - a raving lunatic-
          he killed a man tonight...

   His voice dies away;
   he sits listening - his
   eyes protrude his teeth
   are chattering - an
   abject picture of
   terror.

   CUT TO:

E-40   INT. LIBRARY
   CLOSE SHOT ON.

   Dr. Cranley. The old
   man is calm; he has only
   heard what he had feared.
         DR. CRANLEY
         Listen to me, Kemp. No one
         but you and I know that it's
         Griffin. I shall come in
         the morning.

   CUT QUICKLY TO

E-41   INT. SITTING ROOM
        CLOSEUP ON...

        Komp; very nervous.

                                    KEMP
                                    You must come now - I can't
                                    bear it!

        CUT BACK TO:

E-42   INT. CRANLEY'S LIBRARY
        MED. CLOSE SHOT ON...

        Dr. Cranley speaking into
        phone;

                                    DR. CRANLEY (firmly)
                                    I shall come in the morning-
                                    If I come now he'll be
                                    suspicious and escape. I
                                    shall come as though I know
                                    nothing; you must keep him
                                    calm and quiet till nine
                                    o'clock - we must take him
                                    together and bind him -
                                    it's our only hope - then
                                    we must work to find the
                                    antidote. I trust you,
                                    Kemp - that's all.

        Dr. Cranley replaces the
        receiver - and looks
        toward the door with
        a start of surprise.

        CUT TO:

E-43   INT. CRANLEY'S LIBRARY
        MED. LONG SHOT

        Flora is discovered stand-
        ing in the doorway - in
        her dressing gown.

                                    FLORA
                                    Who was that, father?

                                    DR. CRANLEY
                                    It was Kemp.

                                    FLORA   (coming down to him)
                                    It was about Jack - I know.
                                    What is it - tell me!

        Dr. Cranley sits in
        chair and covers his face
        with his hands.

                                    DR. CRANLEY
                                    Leave me alone, Flora -
                                    please!

        Flora comes slowly forward,
        conscious of tragedy, but
        fighting to keep calm as
        we...

        CUT TO:

E-44   INT. CRANLEY'S LIBRARY
        MED. CLOSE TWO SHOT.

        Flora sits on arm of
        chair by her father's
        side - quite resolute.

                FLORA
              I'm not afraid. Tell me.

        The old man looks up
        at his daughter. It is
        useless to conceal the
        news from her.

                DR. CRANLEY
              Jack Griffin's come back,
              Flora. He's at Dr. Kemp's
              house..Jack Griffin is
              the Invisible Man.

        CUT TO:

E-45   INT. LIBRARY
        CLOSE UP ON .. FLORA

        She sits quite rigidly
        as the picture...

        DISSOLVES TO:

E-46   INT. PHONE BOOTH
        MEDIUM SHOT ON...

        A cranky, excited looking
        man 'phoning.

                THE MAN
              Say! - that the police?
              Is that $5000. O. K.? Well
              listen! I got a way to
              catch him! The paper says
              he threw some ink at the
              man he killed.

        CUT TO:

E-47   INT. PHONE BOOTH
        CLOSEUP ON.....

                THE MAN   (continuing)
              Well, you get your own
              back and squirt ink about
              with a hose pipe till you
               hit him. The ink'll stick
              on him, see? - then you
              can shoot him!

        CUT TO:

E-48   SHOT OF...

Another mild little man
phoning the police.

                                        THE MAN
                                            Is that the police? I want
                                            to tell you how to catch
                                            the Invisible Man! The
                                            paper says it's going to be
                                            frosty in a day or two. Well,
                                            you watch out when it's
                                            frosty and you'll see his
                                            breath.

        CUT TO:

E-49   INT. SITTING ROOM (KEMP'S)
        FULL SHOT...

        Kemp is sitting as we left
        him - beside the telephone -
        in blank despair and misery.
        He rises - paces the room,
        turns and looks over at
        the telephone. It seems to
        be drawing him to it.
        Finally he makes up his mind.
        He comes forward into CAMERA
        to the telephone and takes
        off the receiver.

                                        KEMP (in a low, stifled voice)

                                            Police! Quickly!
                                            (he pauses a moment)

                                            Is that the police? This
                                            is Dr. Kemp. The Invisible
                                            Man is in my house -
                                            asleep upstairs. For
                                            God's sake come at once!

        CUT TO:

E-50   INT. LOCAL POLICE STATION
        AT PORT STOWE

        A sergeant is at the telephone,
        sitting with his feet up on the
        table. He is very happy - and
        slow. An Inspector is standing
        beside him. The sergeant looks
        up.
                                        SERGEANT
                                            It's Dr. Kemp. He's a
                                            sensible chap. He's not
                                            likely to imagine things.

                                        INSPECTOR
                                            Ask for particulars.

                                        SERGEANT (officiously)
                                            Are you there, Dr. Kemp?
                                            Can you tell me some
                                            particulars? What?
                                                (he looks up at the
                                                Inspector)
                                            He says he can't say any
                                            more - his life's in
        CUT TO: danger.

nn E-51 INT POLICE STATION
MED CLOSE ONL..

.The Inspector as he sprawls
over the table andtakes the
receiver. - CAMERA PANNING
with him.

                    INSPECTOR (lying on table)
                    Listen, Doctor. There's
                    only five men here. We
                    want a hundred to sur-
                    round the house. I'll
                    get them down as soon as
                    possible.

He puts on the receiver
and turns to the sergeant.

                    INSPECTOR
                    Call up Headquarters at
                    once.

He rolls off the table.

CUT TO:

E-52 INT. CRANLEY'S LIBRARY
MED CLOSE SHOT

The Doctor is sitting at the
table. Flora is sitting
opposite him. Both are calm
and thoughtful.

                    DR. CRANLEY
                    That's all there is to
                    tell, Flora.

She lowers her head,
and makes no reply.
He continues:

                    You know everything now.
                    You must leave it to me
                    and Dr. Kemp. We shall
                    take means to keep him
                    in the house. We shall
                    work day and night to
                    undo this terrible ex-
                    periment.

Flora raises her head.

CUT TO:

E-53 INT. CRANLEY'S LIBRARY
CLOSE SHOT ON...

Flora - SHOOTING OVER
Dr. Cranley's shoulder.

CONTINUED

                                        FLORA
                                            You must let me go to
                                            him!

                                        DR. CRANLEY (in sudden fear)
                                            Only when he's well again.

                                        FLORA   (rising)
                                            No! Now! - I can do far
                                            more with Jack than you or
                                            Dr. Kemp!

                                        DR. CRANLEY
                                            But, Flora - he's not
                                            normal! His mind's un-
                                            hinged - at present he's
                                            mad!

            CUT TO:

E-54   INT. CRANLEY'S LIBRARY
        FULL SHOT

        Flora and Dr. Cranley in
        foreground.

                                        FLORA
                                            I can persuade him to help
                                            you! You're powerless
                                            unless he helps you! Get
                                            your coat,father! I'll
                                            be ready in five minutes.

                                        DR. CRANLEY
                                            But it's gone midnight! -
                                            wait till the morning.

                                        FLORA
                                            It's life or death, father!
                                            You know it! - I'll go
                                            alone, then! -

                                        DR. CRANLEY
                                            Flora! - wait! -

        He leaps up - but
        Flora has gone.

        CUT TO:

INT. KEM.. ....
FULL SHOT

    Kemp, lying in his chair in the
sitting room, waiting in agony
for the police. He rises -goes
stealthily to the window and
peers between the blinds. Suddenly he wheels round with a
choking cry. A soft knock has
come at the sitting room door.
CUT TO:

E-56   INT. SITTING ROOM..CLOSE SHOT
    ON...

                    KEMP
                      Who's that!!

There is no answer. Kemp
screams hysterically.

                    Who's that?

The voice of the Invisible
Man comes from outside.

                INVISIBLE MAN (offscene)
                    Unlock the door, Kemp.
                    Let me in.

CUT TO:

E-57   INT. SITTING ROOM..CLOSE SHOT
    ON...

    The door handle rattling.
    CUT TO:

E-58   INT. SITTING ROOM...?MEDIUM
    LONG SHOT

    Kemp is powerless, hypnotized.
He goes slowly to the door,
unlocks it, and throws it open.
The Invisible Man stands on the
threshold, in his dressing gown
and pajamas. He has thrown the
bandages round his head once
more, and wears the great blue
goggles. He stands in the door.

                INVISIBLE MAN
                  What are you doing here,
                  Kemp?

    CUT TO:

E-59   INT. SITTING ROOM..AT DOOR.
    MEDIUM SHOT..HIGH CAMERA

                KEMP
                  I - I couldn't sleep -- I-
                  I had to get up and come
                  down.
              INVISIBLE MAN
                  Why did you lock the door?

    (CONTINUED)

                                KEMP
                        I - I was afraid.
                            (he pauses, then
                             feebly blusters)
                        Wouldn't you be afraid -
                        if I were - invisible
                        like you?

    The Invisible Man gives a
    soft laugh - he is flattered.
    CUT TO:

E-60   INT. SITTING ROOM...CLOSE TWO
        SHOT

                                INVISIBLE MAN
                        There's no need to be
                        afraid, Kemp -- we're
                        partners -bosom friends.

    He stretches out his hand and
    lays it on Kemp's shoulders.
    Kemp shudders away. The In-
    visible man laughs again.

                        We've a busy day ahead -
                        you must sleep.

    CU T TO:

E-61   INT. HALL...FULL SHOT

    The Invisible Man is standing
    by the door. Kemp meekly comes
    out of the sitting room, and the
    Invisible man follows him upstairs.
    CUT TO:

E-62   INT. LANDING ... MEDIUM SHOT

    The landing outside the bedroom
    doors; the two men are passing
    a large moonlit window that looks
    out upon the drive. Suddenly
    the Invisible Man becomes tense
    and watchful; his eyes are star-
    ing out into the night. Kemp,
    fascinated, stands beside him.
    THE CAMERA MOVES FORWARD - to
    shoot out of the window - a
    small car swings into the drive
    and comes to a halt beside the
    front door.
    CUT TO:

E-63   AT LANDING CLOSE TWO SHOT

    LOW CAMERA. The Invisible Man
    turns slowly to Kemp and speaks
    in a low icy voice.

                    (CONTINUED)

                                        INVISIBLE MAN
                                            I see, Kemp. You've told
                                            the police -- that was why
                                            you went downstairs?

    For a moment the Invisible
    Man towers over his abject
    companion; it seems as if
    he is about to spring and
    wring the life out of him,
    when Kem suddenly shouts
    hysterically.
                                        KEMP
                                            No, I didn't -- I swear
                                            I didn't ! Look! It's
                                            not the police -- it's
                                            Dr. Cranley - and Flora!

    CUT TO:

    E-64   LANDING...CLOSEUP ON...

    Slowly the Invisible Man
    draws back; he seems to
    relax, and soften -- his
    eyes are thoughtfully
    upon the window. Kemp's
    words have sent something
    echoing back into the
    mind of the Invisible Man;
    they awaken a forgotten
    memory. He looks down at
    Dr. Cranley and Flora as
    they come slowly up the
    steps to the door, as if
    they are two biological
    specimens to be analyzed.
    He speaks very softly
    in a wakened surprise.

                                        INVISIBLE MAN
                                            Why, yes - of course-
                                            Flora -
                                                (he repeats the word
                                                slowly as if it
                                                vaguely pleases him)
                                            Flora --

    CUT TO:

E- 65   ON LANDEND..CLOSE SHOT

        Kem- quickly notices the change that
        has come over the Invisible Man and seizes
        his chance.
                                    KEMP
                        I had to tell them you were
                        back, Griffin! Flora was
                        nearly mad with anxiety.
                        You must let them join us!
                        Let them help us!

        CUT TO:

E-66   ON LANDING..TWO SHOT

        The Invisible Man nods quietly to
        himself. There is almost a
        tenderness in his voice.
                                    INVISIBLE MAN
                        Flora. How could I forget?

        He looks puzzled and unhappy.
        The front door bell rings--
        very quietly. Kemp looks up
        at the Invisible Man.
                                    KEMP
                        Shall I--let them in?

        CUT TO:

E-67   ON LANDING..BIG C.U. ON

        The Invisible Man.

                                    INVISIBLE MAN (speaking as if
                                            in a dream)
                        Yes, of course you must let
                        them in. I shall go and
                        prepare myself--in my room.
                        I shall see Flora--alone.

        CUT TO:

E-68   ON LANDING..FULL SHOT

        The Invisible Man turns and goes
        silently into his room. Kemp looks
        wonderingly after him, then turns
        and goes down stairs. SWIFT PAN ON
        stairs with Kemp.

        CUT TO:

E-69   INT. HALL..MEDIUM SHOT

        Kemp opens the door. Dr. Cranley
        and Flora step into the hall. No
        word is spoken for a moment. Then
        Kemp speaks quickly in a whisper.

                                    KEMP
                        He knows you are here--

                                    DR. CRANLEY (with a start)
                        You said he was asleep.

                                    KEMP
                        He saw you from the window.
                        He wants to see Flora--alone.

        CUT TO:

                                    134

E-70   INT. HALL..CLOSE SHOT ON FLORA

    Flora steps eagerly forward.
    Dr. Cranley restrains her.

                      DR. CRANLEY   (offscene)
                        No, Flora! -- Don't--

                      KEMP   (off scene)
                        He's calm now--and quiet.

                      FLORA   (with a trace of scorn)
                        Do you think Jack would do
                        me any harm?

    CUT TO:

E-71   INT. HALL..THREE SHOT..ON

    Dr. Cranley, Kemp and Flora.

                      DR. CRANLEY   (in agony)
                        I tell you--he's insane--
                        It's for us to cure him--
                        Kemp and I--keep away, Flora.

                      FLORA
                        I must go to him!--leave me
                        alone!

    She shakes off her father's
    restraining hand and goes to
    the stairs--CAMERA PANS as
    Dr. Cranley and Kemp follow her
    over.

    CUT TO:

E-72   ON STAIRS..LONG SHOT

    Flora goes up to the dark staircase.

    CUT TO:

E-73   INT. HALL.MEDIUM CLOSE TWO SHOT

    HIGH CAMERA. Dr. Cranley looks
    helplessly after her. Kemp takes
    his arm and speaks with passionate
    anxiety.

                      KEMP
                        Listen, Doctor! He was a
                        different man when he saw
                        Flora leave the car. He
                        won't hurt her!--we must
                        play for time.

                      DR. CRANLEY (suddenly suspicious)
                        Why for time?

                      KEMP   (floundering)
                        We--we must prepare things--
                        if we try and bind him he'll
                        throw us off--and escape.
                        We must take him when he's
                        asleep and chloroform him!

        (CONTINUED)

E-73   CONTINUED

                                        DR. CRANLEY
                                   We must be near Flora--
                                   come on!

        CUT TO:

E-74   ON STAIRS..PAN SHOT OF FLORA

        Flora, ascending the stairs. She
        is wearing an old mackintosh coat
        over a tweed walking suit. Outwardly
        she is calm and composed: only by the
        way her knuckles whiten as she grips
        the balustrade and by her tense,
        determined face can we detect the
        terrible call she is making upon her
        will power. She reaches the landing--
        hesitates before the several doors and
        turns to Kemp for guidance.

        CUT TO:

E-75   ON STAIRS. MEDIUM SHOT

        Kemp, halfway up the stairs, indicates
        the door behind which the Invisible
        Man is waiting.

        CUT TO:

E-76   ON LANDING..CLOSE SHOT ON FLORA

        Watching Kemp--she then turns the
        handle of the door and goes in--
        CAMERA FOLLOWS HER IN. She stands
        by the door and looks.

        CUT TO:

E-77   INT. BEDROOM..MED. SHOT ON

        The Invisible Man--he is seated at the
        small table near his bed. His hands
        lying downwards upon the two thick note-
        books. He slowly rises as the girl
        appears on the threshold. He is in
        pajamas and dressing gown, slippers, and
        the thin, skin-tight scientists' gloves.
        His bulbous, band aged head and great
        staring goggles are even more terrible
        in calmness than in his moments of
        maniacal anger.

        CUT TO:

E- 78   INT. BEDROOM..CLOSEUP ON FLORA

        For one moment the girl's nerve almost
        breaks: she struggles for control--and
        to aid her struggle comes a voice--not
        of the Invisible Man--but of her lover
        of happier days. A strong voice, but
        soft and very tender, the voice of a
        man of culture--of humanity and charm.

                                        (CONTINUED)

E-78   CONTINUED

        -A voice that brings infinite pathos:

                                INVISIBLE MAN
                                    Flora--my darling--
        CUT TO:

E-79   INT. BEDROOM..MED. CLOSE ON

        The Invisible Man--a repulsive,
        unearthly figure by the table, as
        it slowly and gropingly advances
        towards the girl. Timidly, almost
        he stretches forward his gloved hands.

        CAMERA PANS TO INCLUDE flora--as she
        fights down the shudder that comes to
        her, and gently places her hands in his.

                                FLORA
                                    Thank God you are home, Jack.

        The Invisible Man seems to smile.

                                INVISIBLE MAN
                                    I would have come to you
                                    at once, Flora--but--for
                                    this.

        He raises his gloved hand to his
        head with a little awkward laugh.
        For a moment he seems just a big,
        confused boy, apologizing for some
        trivial graze that has disfigured
        him.

        CAMERA PULLS BACK as he leads her to
        a couch under the window, and sinks
        down beside her.
                                INVISIBLE MAN
                                    How wonderful it is to see
                                    you.

        The little bedside lamp illuminates
        part of the room--the moon shines
        brilliantly upon the strange couple
        by the window.

        CUT TO:

E-80   INT. BEDROOM..CLOSE SHOT ON..FLORA

        Flora sitting in the window seat.
        (Note: Romantic light)
                                INVISIBLE MAN´ (offscene)
                                    How beautiful you look.
                                        (he is silent for a
                                         moment then softly l
                                         laughs)
                                    That funny little hat I
                                    always liked...you've been
                                    crying, Flora.

        The girl looks quickly away--
        then up at him imploringly.

                                        (CONTINUED)

E-80   CONTINUED

                                        FLORA
                                    Jack!--I want to help you!
                                        (she struggles to find
                                        words)
                                    Why did you--do this?

                                        INVISIBLE MAN (offscene)
                                    For you, Flora.

                                        FLORA (scarcely above a whisper)
                                    For--me?

         CUT TO:

E-81   INT. BEDROOM..MED. CLOSE ON

         The Invisible Man.

                                        INVISIBLE MAN
                                    Yes--for you--my darling.
                                    I wanted to do something--
                                    tremendous--to achieve
                                    what men of science have
                                    dreamt of since the world
                                    began--to gain wealth and
                                    fame--and honor--to write
                                    my name above the greatest
                                    scientists of all time--
                                        (he lowers his head)
                                    I was so pitifully poor--I
                                    had nothing to offer you,
                                    Flora. Iwas just a poor,
                                    struggling chemist.

         He pauses as he sees:

         CUT TO:

E-82   INT. BEDROOM..CLOSE TWO SHOT

         ...how her eyes rove over his
         featureless head, white and ghastly
         in the light of the moon. He goes
         quickly on.

                                        INVISIBLE MAN
                                    ...I shall come back to you,
                                    Flora...very soon now. The
                                    secret of invisibility lies
                                    there in my books. I shall
                                    work in Kemp's laboratory
                                    till I find the way back--
                                        (fiercely)
                                    There is a way back, Flora.
                                        (softly)
                                    --and then I shall come to
                                    you--I shall offer my secret
                                    to the world--with all its
                                    terrible power--the Nations
                                    of the world will bid for it
                                    --thousands--millions--the
                                    Nation that wins my secret
                                    can sweep the world with
                                    invisible armies!

         Suddenly a terrible change begins
         to work upon his calmness and control.

         CUT TO:

138

E-83   INT. BEDROOM..BIG CLOSEUP ON

    The Invisible Man--the drug of madness--
    the Monocane is fighting to regain its
    power. His hands begin to twitch and
    tremble; his mouth falls open--a horrible,
    empty hole amidst the bandages that cover
    his head. Again and again he passes his
    gloved hand across his face--he clutches
    at it--he struggles to keep the sanity
    that has come to him for a fleeting moment.

    CUT TO:

E-84   INT. BEDROOM..MED. CLOSE ON FLORA

    The girl watches--helpless and dismayed..
    She takes hold of both his hands, and
    presses them.

                     FLORA
                Jack!--I want you to let my
                father help you. You know
                how clever he is. He'll
                work with you, night and
                day--until you find the
                second secret--the one
                that'll bring you back to us.
                Then we shall have those
                lovely, peaceful days again
                --out under those trees--
                after your work--in the
                evenings.
    CUT TO:

E-85   INT. BEDROOM..MED. CLOSE ON

    LOW CAMERA. The Invisible Man.
    The change has come: the drug has
    won its victory. The Invisible Man
    sits bolt upright--stiff and rigid:
    he is no longer a human being. He
    stares at the girl before him. His
    voice comes, sharp and gratingly.

                     INVISIBLE MAN
                Your father? -- clever!
                    (his head goes back
                    with a stiff jerk and
                    a high pitched, jagged
                    laugh)
                You think he can help me!
                He's got the brain of a
                tapeworm!--a maggot! beside
                mine! Don't you see what
                it means--Power!--power to
                rule--to make the world
                grovel at my feet!
    CUT TO:

E-86   INT. BEDROOM..MED. TWO SHOT

    The girl grips hold of his restless,
    struggling hands.
                     FLORA
                Jack! Listen to me! Listen!

    (CONTINUED)

E-86   CONTINUED

   The fierceness of her appeal for the
   moment silences him. He stares at
   her dumbly. He draws himself slowly
   and stiffly up, but does not speak.

   CUT TO:

E-87   INT. BEDROOM..CLOSE SHOT ON

   Flora, pleading earnestly.

                              FLORA
                     My father found a note in
                     your room! He knows some-
                     thing about Monocane that
                     even you don't know. It
                     alters you--changes you,
                     Jack--makes you feel
                     differently. Father be-
                     lieves the power of it will
                     go if you know what you're
                     fighting. Come and stay
                     with us--let's fight it out
                     together--
   CUT TO:

E-88   INT. BEDROOM..MED. SHOT

   The Invisible Man releases his
   hands from the girl's grasp, and
   rises to his feet. Her imploring
   eyes follow him. It is clear that
   he has neither heard nor understood.

   CUT TO:

E-89   INT. BEDROOM..CLOSE SHOT ON INVISIBLE MAN

   LOW CAMERA. He looks down at her and
   speaks in a low, trembling voice that
   is bursting with exultation and
   excitement.

                              INVISIBLE MAN
                     Power, I said--power to walk
                     into the gold vaults of the
                     Nations--into the secrets of
                     Kings--into the Holy of
                     Holies. Power to make
                     multitudes run squealing in
                     terror at the touch of my
                     little, invisible finger!
                          (he raises his head to
                           the window)
                     Even the moon's frightened
                     of me--frightened to death!
                     --the whole world's frighten-
                     ed to death!
   CUT TO:

E-90   INT. BEDROOM..MED. SHOT

 - He lowers his eyes from the sky and
 gloats over the silver-lit garden of
 lawns and trees beneath him. The
 CAMERA MOVES to take in what he sees
 below.

 Stealthy figures are gathering in dark
 groups amongst the shrubberies; uniformed
 men who come creeping forward from the
 fences they are scaling--creeping into
 the shelter of the trees.

 CUT TO:

E-91   INT. BEDROOM..MED. LONG SHOT

 CAMERA PANS ACROSS ROOM as swiftly
 and silently the Invisible Man crosses
 to a small window that looks out upon
 another side of the garden. The same
 scene greets his eyes:

 CUT TO:

E-92   EXT. GARDEN..LONG SHOT

 As the Invisible Man sees. Dark
 figures are forming into line in a
 flecked shadow of a rose pergola.
 A wall of men is steadily, relentlessly
 surrounding the house.

 CUT BACK TO:

E-93   INT. BEDROOM..MED. SHOT

 For a moment the Invisible Man stands
 watching--calmly, almost thoughtfully.
 Then he turns, and with his hands behind
 him, walks slowly to the little table.
 There is dignity in his bearing as he comes
 to a halt beside it. He looks across at
 the girl.

 CUT TO:

E-94   INT. BEDROOM..MED.CLOSE ON.INVISIBLE MAN

        INVISIBLE MAN
      So. I see. Kemp couldn't
      sleep. He had to go down-
      stairs. He was frightened.
      I put my trust in Kemp: I
      told him my secret and he
      gave me his word of honor.
       (he pauses for a moment)
      You must go now, Flora.

 CUT TO:

E-95   INT. BEDROOM..MED. SHOT

    Flora rises and crosses to him.
    CAMERA PANS with her. She too,
    - has seen the encroaching men below.

                    FLORA
              I want to help you, Jack!
              Tell me what I can do!

    The impending peril has brought
    a shadow of sanity to the
    Invisible Man. He speaks to the
    girl almost as softly as when she
    first came to him.
                  INVISIBLE MAN
              There's nothing for you to
              do,my dear--except to go.
              I shall come back to you--
              I swear I shall come back--
              because I shall defeat them.

    He is standing close by her.
    He tenderly takes her hand and
    kisses it.
                  INVISIBLE MAN
              Go now--my dear--

                  FLORA
              No! I want to stay! You
              must hide, Jack!

    He shyly lays his hand upon her
    shoulder and gives a soft laugh.

                  INVISIBLE MAN
              Don't worry! The whole
              world's my hiding place.
              I can stand out there
              amongst them--in the day
              or night--and laugh at them.

    CAMERA FOLLOWS THEM as gently
    but firmly he turns her to the
    door. He closes it, and with a
    lightning movement tears at the
    belt of his dressing gown as the
    scene darkens.

    CUT TO:

E-96   EXT. GARDENT.FULL SHOT

    A corner of the moonlit garden. A
    police Inspector is giving orders
    in a quiet, urgent undertone.

                  INSPECTOR LANE
              Pass down word to link hands
              -- all round the house!

    The stolid men in front of him
    raise their arms and take each
    other's hands.
                  VOICES
              Link hands !--lind hands !

    (CONTINUED)

                                    INSPECTOR LANE
                                         Keep close together--or
                                         he'll slip under your arm.!

     - CUT TO:

E-97   EXT. GARDEN..CLOSEUPS

        There is a fantastic series of
        trick shots of big hands linking
        one with the other, and then:

        CUT TO:

E-98   EXT. GARDEN..LONG SHOT

        HIGH CRANE SHOT. Of the men slowly
        advancing in a ring towards the house.

        CUT TO:

E-99   INT. HALL..KEMP'S MED.LONG SHOT

        The hall of the house, at the bottom
        of the stairs; Dr. Cranley and Kemp
        stand eagerly looking up as Flora comes
        down. The strain has done its work.
        The reaction has come--Flora sways and
        falls sobbing into her father's arms.

        CUT TO:

E-100   INT. HALL..MED. CLOSE ON FLORA

                                    FLORA
                                       Father! Save him!

        Her body becomes limp; she has
        fainted. CAMERA PULLS BACK as
        Dr. Cranley gently carries her to
        a chair. Kemp has turned.

        CUT TO:

E-101   INT. HALL..LONG SHOT

        CAMERA ON DOLLEY RECEDES Kemp as he
        gropes with staring eyes down the
        passage into the sitting room. He swiftly
        crosses to the window--throws back the
        curtains and feverishly fumbles with the
        latch. He throws open the doors and
        stands panting--gazing out onto the
        moonlit lawn. Some fifty yards away can
        be seen the line of policemen--very slowly
        and hesitantly advancing.

        CUT TO:

E-102   INT. SITTING ROOM..MEDIUM SHOT

        But as Kemp stands gazing out--a low
        chuckle comes close to his shoulder--
        and then the voice of the Invisible Man.

                                              (CONTINUED)

                              143

E- 102 CONTINUED

                                    INVISIBLE MAN
                                Thank you, Kemp--for
                                opening the windows.

        Kemp starts back with a low gasp
        of horror. The voice goes calmly on,
        gently chiding.

                                    . . . You were a true friend,
                                Kemp; a man to trust. I've
                                no time now, but, believe
                                me, Kemp--as surely as the
                                moon will set and the sun
                                will rise--I shall kill you
                                tomorrow night. I shall
                                kill you even if you hide
                                in the deepest cave of the
                                earth--at ten o'clock
                                tomorrow night I shall kill
                                you.

        The voice dies away. Kemp stands
        paralysed; his mouth is working--
        his eyes staring.

        CUT TO:

E-103   INT. SITTING ROOM..SHOT OF

        The curtains of the window moves with
        a little rustle. The door opens a
        little wider.

        CUT TO:

E-104   INT. SITTING ROOM..MED CLOSE ON KEMP

        There is a moment of silence before
        Kemp gives a piercing scream.

                                    KEMP K
                                Help!--help!--he's here L
                                --he's here!

        He shrinks back against the wall,
        gasping for breath.

        CUT TO:

E-105   EXT. GARDEN..MED. CLOSE ON

        Inspector Lane standing on the lawn--
        shouting to his men. Several other
        policemen included in this shot.

                                    INSPECTOR LANE
                                Steady there! Stand where
                                you are!--Keep your arms
                                down!
        CUT TO:

E-106   EXT. GARDEN..LONG SHOT

>   VERY HIGH SHOT ON CRANE of the
      policemen who have circled the house--
      standing rigidly still. Showing the
      almost superstitious dread and tension
      on their faces--roving eyes--drawn
      features in the brilliant moonlight.

      QUICK TO:

E-107   MEDIUM SHOT..FLASH OF

      A policeman--very nervous and frightened.

      QICK CUT TO:

E-108   EXT. GARDEN..CLOSEUP OF

      Another policeman--very tense--waiting.
      CAMERA PULLSBACK A LITTLE GETTING MED.
      CLOSE SHOT# - PANS along with the police-
      men--there comes a sharp smack and one of
      the men jerks back his head with a cry.

                              INSEECTOR LANE   (hurrying forward)
                                 What is it?

                              THE MAN   (in a terrified voice)
                                 Something--smacked my face!

      There comes a low laugh from the
      air. The Inspector wheels round
      as the voice of the Invisible Man
      says:
                              INVISIBLE MAN
                                 Naughty boy!

      CUT TO:

E-109   EXT. GARDEN..CLOSE SHOT OF

      Another policeman in a different part
      of the ring. His face is suddenly
      pulled forward: his eyes roll as he
      lets out a howl.
                              POLICEMAN
                                 Ow !--Ow !--

      CUT TO:

E-110   EXT. GARDEN.MED. PAN SHOT

      The flurried Inspector comes running
      forward. CAMERA MOVES INTO MED. CLOSE
      as he reaches the policeman.
                              INSPECTOR LANE
                                 What's the matter?

                              POLICEMAN
                                 He-he twisted my nose!

                              INSPECTOR
                                 Keep steady,boys ! Keep
                                 closed tightly up ! We've
      (CONTINUED)   got him all right this time !

                              145

E-110   CONTINUED)

>   As he speaks his helmet shoots sideways
>   off his head onto the ground. CAMERA
>   PANS DOWN as he darts to pick it up, but
>   with a thud it soars away over the heads
>   of the policemen--CAMERA PANNING WITH IT.
>   The Invisible Man's laugh bursts out nearby.

                    INVISIBLE MAN
                         Good shot ! Goal to me !
                         One nil !

>   CUT TO:

E-111   EXT. GARDEN..MEDIUM SHOT

>   There is a quick shot of the
>   Inspector as an invisible foot
>   smartly kicks him backside,

                    INSPECTOR LANE
                         Now then, boys--advance
                         slowly--it's all right.
                         He's unarmed ! You've got
                         him easily !

>   The policemen begin stealthily
>   to advance once more. There are
>   several shots of the slowly
>   contracting circle.

>   CUT TO:

E-112   EXT. GARDEN..LONG SHOT

>   HIGH CAMERA ON CRANE...of the
>   different parts of the garden
>   showing the contracting circle.
>   Then the CAMERA CONCENTRATES upon
>   a part of the line where a police-
>   man smaller than the rest is stationed.
>   Suddenly with a cry, his legs disappear
>   from beneath him and he hangs in mid-air.

>   CUT TO:

E-113   EXT. GARDEN..MEDIUM SHOT

>   The policemen to either side grasping his
>   out-stretched hands, his legs floating
>   helplessly out behind him where they are
>   help by the Invisible Man, who has run
>   between the little man's legs and picked
>   up his feet.

>   CUT TO:

E-114   EXT. GARDEN..CLOSE SHOT OF

>   The three heads. The policemen are too
>   bewildered and amazed to do anything but
>   stare openmouthed at their floating
>   companion.

>   CUT TO:

E-115 EXT. GARDEN..CRANE SHOT

        The men to either side hang grimly
        onto his hands, but the little
        policeman is pulled outwards and out-
        wards, kicking and squealing until the
        line breaks--the policemen to either
        side of him leave go of his hands; he
        falls to the ground with a thud and goes
        sliding and bumping away from them
        across the lawn, on his chest.

        CUT TO:

E-116 EXT. GARDEN (ON DOLLEY) MED. CLOSE
        SHOT..POLICEMAN

        His outstretched hands grasping at the
        grass--his face looking beseechingly
        at his receding companions, his feet in
        the air, where they are firmly held and
        drawn along by the Invisible Man.

        He proceeds a considerable distance in
        this remarkable manner--squealing and
        gibbering with terror.

        CUT TO:

E-117 EXT. GARDEN..FULL SHOT

        Of the gap in the line. The policemen--
        stolid, slow thinking, unimaginative men--
        are completely bewildered; they stand looking
        after the little man in helpless amazement.

        CUT TO:

E-118 EXT. GARDEN..CLOSEUP ON

        Two large astonished faces looking
        at each other.
                                POLICEMAN
                        Who taught him to do that?

        CUT TO:

E-119 EXT. GARDEN..MED. SHOT..LONG

        Inspector Lane recovers from his
        astonishment and springs to activity.

                                INSPECTOR LANE
                        It's the Invisible Man--got
                        him by the feet! After him,
                        boys, quick!

        The policemen pelt after their
        unfortunate comrade, who has now reached
        a further side of the lawn.

        But before they reach him a still more
        remarkable thing occurs. The little man
        stops sliding, and executes a strange
        circular swing on the grass.

        CUT TO:

E-120   EXT. GARDEN..MED. SHOT OF

    The whirlwind policeman. The Invisible
    Man--in the manner of an acrobatic dancer
    begins to swing the little policeman in a
    circle; the policeman leaves the ground
    and swings round, head outwards, feet
    inwards, a foot or two from the ground.
    Once, twice, three times he circles--and
    then there is the sound of bursting braces.
    The little policeman flies out of his
    trousers.

    CUT TO:

E-121   EXT. GARDEN.. SHOT OF

    The policeman's trousers which remain in
    the hands of the Invisible Man.

    CUT TO:

E-122   EXT. GARDEN..MED. SHOT OF GROUP

    The trousers describes a circle in the
    air and lands with a thud, full in the
    midst of the pursuing policemen. They
    collapse in a heap on the lawn: the little
    man, in tunic and wollen pants, on top.
    There are cries of anger, groans of pain,
    and chaos.

    CUT TO:

E-123   EXT. COUNTRY LANE..MED. SHOT

    An old woman, dashing headlong down a
    lane, shrieking for help.

    A moment later the policeman's trousers come
    into view, walking griskly and jauntily along
    the lane behind her. A cheerful tune is being
    whistled from the emptiness above the
    marching trousers.

    THE PICTURE FADES.

                 END OF SEQUENCE "E"

"THE INVISIBLE MAN"

SEQUENCE "F"

FADE IN:

F-1   INT. KEMP'S SITTING ROOM
       FULL SHOT (DAY)

       Converted by the Police
       into an informal Court of
       Inquiry. The Chief of Police
       is seated at the table. Dr.
       Kemp, Dr. Cranley and Flora
       are present. A strong police
       guard is stationed at the doors
       and windows. Kemp is leaning
       forward, begging for protection.
       CUT TO:

F-2   INT. SITTING ROOM
       MED. CLOSE ON...KEMP

                                        KEMP
                                    He threatened to kill me! -
                                    at ten o'clock tonight! - You
                                    must lock me up! - put me in
                                    prison! -

       CUT TO:

F-3   INT. SITTING ROOM
       MEDIUM SHOT OF...

       The group. The Chief of
       Police thinly disguising
       his contempt.
                                        CHIEF OF POLICE
                                    You are not the only one in
                                    danger, Dr. Kemp. I'll see
                                    that you have protection.
                                        (he turns to Dr. Cranley)
                                    Now, Dr. Cranley:
                                        (he pauses, and looks very
                                         keenly at the old doctor)
                                    You are concealing something
                                    from me.

       CUT TO:

F-4   INT. SITTING ROOM
       CLOSEUP ON...

       The unhappy old Doctor makes
       a gesture to speak, but the
       Officer curtly silences him.
       CUT TO:

F-5   INT. SITTING ROOM
       MED. SHOT...GROUP

                                        CHIEF OF POLICE
                                    .....One moment! I want you
                                    to explain why you and your
                                    daughter were in this house
                                    at two o'clock this morning.

       (continued)

149

F-5   (CONTINUED)

                              DR. CRANLEY
                                   Dr. Kemp rang me up. He told
                                   me the man was here. He wanted
                                   my help.

                              CHIEF OF POLICE
                                   Why did he ring you before the
                                   police? Why did your daughter
                                   come, too?

                              DR. CRANLEY
                                   She came to - to drive the
                                   car.

              There is a pause. The
              Chief of Police looks
              very sternly at the
              old Doctor.   CHIEF OF POLICE
                                   You know who the Invisible
                                   Man is, Doctor.

              CUT TO:

F-6   INT. SITTING ROOM
       CLOSEUP...DR. CRANLEY

              Dr. Cranley lowers his
              head, but makes no reply.
              CUT TO:

F-7   INT. SITTING ROOM
       MED. TWO SHOT...

              On the Chief of Police and
              Dr. Cranley - The Chief goes
              on - sharply and decisively.

                              CHIEF OF POLICE
                                   You realize you are conceal-
                                   ing a murderer? You realize
                                   that your silence may be re-
                                   sponsible for other murders?

              A Sergeant whispers a
              word to the Chief of
              Police - who nods, and
              addresses Dr. Cranley
              again.
              CUT TO:

F-8   INT. SITTING ROOM
       CLOSE SHOT ON...

              The Chief of Police.

                              CHIEF OF POLICE
                                   I understand you have another
                                   assistant, besides Dr. Kemp.
                                   A Dr. Griffin. Where is Dr.
                                   Griffin?

              CAMERA PANS TO Dr.
              Cranley.
                              DR. CRANLEY (in a low voice)
                                   He's - gone away.
              CUT TO:

F-9 INT. SITTING ROOM
   FULL SHOT...

    There is silence - sudden-
    ly broken by Kemp's loud,
    trembling voice.

        KEMP
      It is Griffin! What's the
      good of concealing it! It's
      Griffin - and he's threaten-
      ed to murder me! He may be
      here now, beside us! - or in
      the garden - looking in that
      window - or - or in a corner
      of my bedroom waiting for me!-
      waiting to kill me! - and you
      just sit there! - doing noth-
      ing!

    The scene darkens, and
    ....DISSOLVES TO:

F-10 INT. POLICE STATION
   FULL SHOT....

    The Chief Detective is
    sitting at the table.
    Inspector Lane comes in
    and salutes.

        INSPECTOR LANE
      We've doubled the search
      party ten miles round Kemp's
      house. There's nothing to
      report, sir. The policeman's
      trousers were found in a
      ditch, a mile away, that's
      all. We found naked foot-
      prints in the dust - they go
      into a field and disappear.

    There is silence. The
    Detective lies back in
    his chair; he looks tired
    and ill.

        CHIEF DETECTIVE
      It's beaten me. I'll give ten
      thousand dollars for a prac-
      tical idea. He's roaming
      the country at will - a mad-
      man!

    DISSOLVE TO:

F-11 EXT. WOODS
   LONG SHOT...

    A search party - beating
    through a wood.
    CUT TO:

F-12 EXT. WOODS
   MED. SHOT...

    One man separated from the
    rest, suddenly throws up his
    hands and gives a cry. He
    struggles with an unseen
    opponent who has him by the
    throat. He is dragged through

    (continued)

F-12   (CONTINUED)

the undergrowth, CAMERA
PANNING WITH HIM - and
disappears with a cry of
terror into a deep chalk
pit.
CUT TO:

F-13   EXT. WOODS
        FULL SHOT...

Men come running vaguely and
helplessly to the brink.
Another man is given a vio-
lent push by the unseen hands
and follows his companion into
the depths below. One of the
search party yells out.
                          ONE OF SEARCH PARTY
                          Stand away! - keep back!

The men get back.
CUT TO:

F-14   INT. SIGNAL'S BOX
        FULL SHOT...

A signalman's box on a railroad. The signalman is quietly working his signals, smoking
his pipe, when the door opens.
He looks up surprised. A heavy
lamp rises from the table and
crashes down on his head. He
falls unconscious.
QUICK CUT TO:

F-15   A FLASH...OF...

A signal lever is seen to be
drawn back.
QUICK CUT TO:

F-16   FLASH OF...LONG SHOT...

A train roaring by.
QUICK CUT TO:

F-17   FLASH OF...LONG SHOT...

Another train coming in the
opposite direction.
QUICK CUT TO:

F-18   RAILROAD

The trains rushing to their
destruction - a terrible crash -
bursting flames - (Miniature or
newsreel)
CUT TO:

152

F-19   INT. BANK
        LONG SHOT...

            The clerks busily at work -
            customers standing at the
            rails - people moving to and
            fro. CAMERA DOLLEYS UP TO a
            Bank Clerk attending a cus-
            tomer - examining a check.
            The drawer beside him slowly
            opens, comes right out of its
            recess and floats in the air.
            CAMERA PULLS BACK - the clerk
            gazes in amazement. The drawer
            floats away - through the door
            leading into the public area,
            and out of the main entrance.
            CUT TO:

F-20   INT. BANK
        MED. SHOT ON...

            The people as they gather in
            astonished groups and gaze
            after the drawer.
            CUT TO:

F-21   EXT. BANK
        FULL SHOT...

            The drawer hangs in the air a
            few feet above the pavement.
            Suddenly handfuls of notes rise
            out of it and fly amongst the
            crowd - handfuls of coins follow
            it - the people have rushed out
            of the bank. A voice rings out
            of the air.

                            INVISIBLE MAN
                        There you are! A present
                        from the Invisible Man! -
                        Presents for everybody!

            There is a shout of
            laughter from the empti-
            ness above the drawer,
            and mad confusion in the
            street. Some people turn
            and run - others fight and
            scramble for the money.
            CUT TO:

F-22   EXT. BANK...STREET
        MED. CLOSE ON...

            A policeman makes towards the
            floating drawer. It gives a
            jerk, and shoots a shower of
            money in his fafe. The empty
            drawer comes down with a crash
            upon his head and stuns him.
            DISSOLVE TO:

F-23   INT. OFFICE AT POLICE
        STATION...FULL SHOT...

       The Chief Detective - in his
       office. The room is filled
       with reporters with open
       notebooks. He is address-
       ing them.

                           CHIEF DETECTIVE
                        I tell you in confidence that
                        twenty men of the search
                        parties have been killed -
                        and a hundred in the train
                        disaster. But I appeal to
                        you, gentlemen, to keep all
                        the news of these disasters
                        from your papers.

       CUT TO:

F-24   INT. OFFICE
        PAN SHOT OF...

       The reporters notebooks
       rapidly writing.
       CUT TO:

F-25   INT. OFFICE
        MED. CLOSE ON GROUP...

       of reporters.

                         CHIEF DETECTIVE (continues)
                        The public are naturally in
                        a very nervous condition -
                        all manner of rumors are
                        flying around. The Invisible
                        Man has been reported in a
                        hundred different places. I
                        appeal to you to help us keep
                        the public calm.

       CUT TO:

F-26   INT. OFFICE
        CLOSE SHOT ON...

       One of the reporters.

                         REPORTER
                        Can you tell us what plans
                        you've got for capturing him?

       CUT TO:

F-27   INT. OFFICE
        TWO SHOT ON...

       Chief Detective and a
       reporter.

                         CHIEF DETECTIVE
                        A hundred thousand men are
                        searching - and watching.

                        REPORTER
                        But have you any special
                        secret means of getting him?

       (continued)

F-27   (CONTINUED)

                                        CHIEF DETECTIVE
                                            The police have offered twen-
                                            ty thousand dollars for the
                                            first effective means.

                                        REPORTER
                                            Why not bloodhounds?

                                        CHIEF DETECTIVE
                                            The bloodhounds have lost the
                                            scent.

                                        REPORTER
                                            Why not put wet tar on all
                                            the roads? - then chase the
                                            black soles of his feet?

                CUT TO:

F-28   INT. OFFICE
        CLOSE SHOT ON...

        The Chief Detective.

                                        CHIEF DETECTIVE
                                            Because he's not a fool. He
                                            keeps to the open country.
                                                (he pauses - and goes on
                                                    impressively)
                                            We've got one hope, gentle-
                                            men, - but I dare not say a
                                            word of it here. He may be
                                            standing there with you, lis-
                                            tening. I can only say that
                                            we expect to catch him - at
                                            ten o'clock tonight. If you
                                            come here at midnight I may
                                            have good news.

                DISSOLVE TO:

F-29   INT. KEMP'S SITTING ROOM
        FULL SHOT - HIGH CAMERA (NIGHT)

        The Chief Detective is stand-
        ing there, with several Police
        Officers. Dr. Cranley and
        Kemp are also present.
                                        CHIEF DETECTIVE
                                            Everything depends upon the
                                            way we carry out my plan.
                                            I'll tell you directly we've
                                            made certain he's not in this
                                            room.
                CUT TO:

F-30   INT. SITTING ROOM
        MEDIUM SHOT...

        The Chief Detective turns
        to two detectives who are
        holding a large net.
                                        CHIEF DETECTIVE
                                            Draw that net right across
                                            the room. Stand back, gentle-
                                            men, close against the wall.

        (continued)

F-30   (CONTINUED)

    CAMERA PANS WITH the two
    detectives as they take
    their stand in opposite
    corners upon the far side
    of the room. They raise
    the net as high as possible -
    and keeping close to the wall,
    bring the net straight across
    the room, passing so close to
    the men against the wall that
    no invisible body could slip
    by.
    CUT TO:

F-31   INT. SITTING ROOM
    MED. CLOSE SHOT...

    The operation finished, the
    Detective turns with a slight
    laugh.

                    CHIEF DETECTIVE
                    Well, we're safe in here at
                    last! Keep an eye on the
                    windows.

    He leans forward - all
    crowd round him as the
    CAMERA MOVES IN CLOSER
    GETTING SCREEN FULL of
    heads close together in
    conspiracy. He lowers
    his voice, and speaks
    tensely and clearly.

                    CHIEF DETECTIVE
                    Now listen carefully. We've
                    got a chance tonight that'll
                    never come again. He's threat-
                    ened to murder Dr. Kemp at
                    ten o'clock. For what we
                    know of him he'll do his ut-
                    most to carry that out. He
                    is certain to be watching
                    near this house for some
                    time beforehand. At half
                    past nine, Dr. Kemp, with
                    a bodyguard of police will
                    leave this house and walk
                    down to the Police Station.
                    It's a natural thing for Dr.
                    Kemp to seek protection. The
                    Invisible Man is certain to
                    be near - he is certain to
                    see what is happening.

    CUT TO:

F-32   INT. SITTING ROOM
    CLOSE TWO SHOT...

    Kemp and the Chief
    Detective.

                    KEMP (in a trembling voice)
                    You mean - you're going to
                    use me as a bait?

                  CHIEF DETECTIVE
                    Yes.

    (continued)

F-32   (CONTINUED)

                                     KEMP
                                        I can't.

                                 CHIEF DETECTIVE
                                        You must. You're perfectly
                                        safe.

Kemp gives a hard, dry
laugh...as we...
CUT TO:

F-33   INT. SITTING ROOM
      MEDIUM SHOT ON...

The group listening
to Kemp.

                                        KEMP
                                        Safe! He's not human! - he
                                        can pass through anything -
                                        prison walls - everything!

                                 CHIEF DETECTIVE
                                        Don't be a fool!

                                   KEMP
                                        I tell you - I can't sit
                                        there in the station - wait-
                                        ing! - He'll kill you! - kill
                                        you all - then take the keys
                                        and come to me!

The Detective is silent
for a moment. He con-
siders Kemp thoughtfully.
CUT TO:

F-34   INT. SITTING ROOM
      CLOSEUP OF...

The Chief Detective.

                                CHIEF DETECTIVE
                                        Very well, then. If you're
                                        afraid of staying in the
                                        Police Station you can leave
                                        it - directly you are inside.
                                        There's a secret way out thru
                                        the Inspector's private house.
                                        We'll disguise you as a police-
                                        man. You can go out with
                                        other uniformed men and drive
                                        away. Even if he sees you go
                                        he won't recognize you - he'll
                                        most probably be in front -
                                        waiting to break in at ten
                                        o'clock.

            CUT TO:

F-35   INT. SITTING ROOM
      CLOSEUP ON...KEMP

                              KEMP
                                    What happens to me then?

            CUT TO:

F-36   INT. SITTING ROOM
          TWO SHOT ON...

        The Chief Detective and
        Kemp.

                    CHIEF DETECTIVE
                    I'll have you driven back to
                    this house - quietly - by the
                    back lanes. Get in your car
                    and drive away, miles away -
                    and stay in the country till
                    you hear we've got him. You
                    needn't fear. We shall get
                    him this time. I shall lay
                    traps that even an invisible
                    man can't pass.
                      (he looks at his watch)
                    You've got an hour to get
                    ready. I shall send a dozen
                    policemen at half past nine.

        DISSOLVE TO:

F-37   EXT. COURTYARD OF PRISON
          LONG SHOT...(NIGHT)

        The Chief Detective, surround-
        ed by uniformed men, is de-
        monstrating his plan. A
        large white sheet is nailed
        to one of the walls; before
        it stands a paint spraying
        machine - the type used for
        cellulosing cars. He presses
        a button - a spray of black
        paint covers the sheet ex-
        cept for the corners.

                    CHIEF DETECTIVE
                    You see it covers a wide
                    range - even at close quarts.
                    I've got twenty of these
                    machines - a good man to
                    each. One splash of this
                    on his skin - and you've
                    got something to follow at
                    last.

        CUT TO:

F-38   EXT. COURTYARD
          CLOSER GROUP SHOT...

                  A SERGEANT
                    Why not paint the top of the
                    wall?

                  CHIEF DETECTIVE
                    Because he would smell it.
                    I've got a better plan. I'm
                    laying a thin layer of loose
                    earth along the top. The
                    slightest touch will disturb
                    it....and we've got something
                    to follow at last.

        DISSOLVE TO:

F-39   INT. FLORA'S BEDROOM
         FULL SHOT...(NIGHT)

         She is seated in her dress-
         ing gown. Dr. Cranley is
         by her side. It is clear
         that the terrible events of
         the day have brought her to
         the verge of collapse.
         CAMERA ON DOLLEY MOVES IN
         CLOSER as Dr. Cranley leans
         over her and speaks kindly.
                            DR. CRANLEY
                     Try and sleep now, my dear.
                     There's nothing you can do.
                     We must just pray that the
                     police can take him without
                     harming him.

         He leans over her, and
         kisses her, then quietly
         leaves the room. She sits
         wearily in her chair. Be-
         fore her on a little table,
         stands a photograph. She
         draws it towards her - gazes
         at it - (but we do not see
         the face). Her head falls
         between her hands. Her
         shoulders tremble as she
         tries to stifle the con-
         vulsive agony within her.
         DISSOLVE TO:

F-40   EXT. KEMP'S HOUSE
         FULL SHOT...(NIGHT)

         The front door of Kemp's house.
         A squad of uniformed men are
         waiting. Kemp emerges - takes
         his place in their centre, and
         the little group moves out into
         the moonlit lane. CAMERA PANS
         WITH THEM - The last policeman
         closes the gate behind him.
         CUT TO:

F-41   CLOSE SHOT ON...
         GATE

         The gate stands closed for a
         moment - then the latch clicks
         up; the gate opens and closes
         as the Invisible Man steps out
         to follow Kemp and his bodyguard.
         CUT TO:

F-42   EXT. POLICE STATION
         LONG SHOT...

         CAMERA PANS with the group going
         down the street and entering the
         police station. It is a forbidding,
         prison-like building, standing iso-
         lated from other habitation. A stone
         wall, about six feet high, surrounds
         all sides.
         CUT TO:

F-43   INT. COURTYARD
        FULL SHOT...(NIGHT)

        The Chief Detective is in the
        courtyard as the party enters -
        in a solid block to prevent all
        possibility of an invisible body
        slipping through beside them.
        Policemen are stationed round
        the walls, each with a spraying
        machine beside him. The Chief
        Detective is standing by.
                              CHIEF DETECTIVE (in a low voice)
                                   All right? Go straight
                                   ahead!

        Kemp and his bodyguard
        enter the station. The
        door closes behind them.
        DISSOLVE TO:

F-44   INT. POLICE STATION
        MEDIUM SHOT...(NIGHT)

        Kemp is feverishly buttoning
        a police greatcoat up to his
        chin. Several uniformed men
        stand by.
        CUT TO:

F-45   EXT. BACK OF STATION
        MED. LONG SHOT...(NIGHT)

        The secret, back entrance to
        the Station. It is simply the
        door to the Inspector's house.
        A car draws up. A Sergeant and
        a policeman get out - go up to
        the door, knock and gain ad-
        mittance.
        CUT TO:

F-46   PASSAGE INSIDE THE HOUSE
        MED. SHOT...

        Kemp stands waiting. The
        Inspector curtly says:
                              INSPECTOR
                                   Come on.
        Kemp swiftly leaves the
        house with the Inspector.
        CUT TO:

F-47   EXT. BACK OF STATION
        MED. LONG SHOT...

        Kemp and Inspector comes out
        of the house and enter the car,
        which drives off into the night.
        CUT TO:

160

F-48   EXT. COURTYARD
        FULL SHOT...

        The guards tensely on the
        alert. The Chief Detective
        looks at his watch.

                            CHIEF DETECTIVE (softly)
                                Twenty minutes to ten.
                                Keep your eyes open now,
                                boys.

        There is a shot of various
        policemen standing by their
        strange weapons - their eyes
        fixed on the wall.
        CUT TO:

F-49   EXT. COURTYARD
        MED. TWO SHOT...

        One policeman suddenly grows
        excited - he whispers to the
        Chief Detective who is passing.

                            POLICEMAN
                                Here! Quick, sir!

        The Detective crosses
        to the man.

                                I heard footsteps outside -
                                soft footsteps, like naked
                                feet!

        CUT TO:

F-50   EXT. COURTYARD
        CLOSEUP OF...

        The two heads - as the
        Chief Detective and the
        policeman stand tensely
        listening and watching.
        CUT TO:

F-51   EXT LAND (NIGHT)
        MED LONG SHOT ON...

- the police car - drawing up
  in a dark narrow lane behind
  Kemp's house.

F-52   INT CAR. CLOSE TWO SHOT

Kemp leans forward to the
driver.

                      DRIVER
                 Where are you going to?

                    KEMP
                 Up in the mountains - a
                 hundred miles away!
                 This'll do - drop me here!

The car halts. Kemp
quickly gets out and makes
off through the darkness.
DISSOLVE TO:

F-53   INT KEMP'S GARAGE
        FULL SHOT ON...

Kemp climbing into his car
in his garage.

F-54   EXT COURTYARD. MED TWO SHOT

The Chief Detective is anxiously
looking at his watch. The Sergeant is standing beside him.
Both are obviously in a state
of great nervous tension.

                  CHIEF DETECTIVE
                 It only wants ten minutes
                 to ten. He's bound to do
                 something in a minute.

CAMERA PANS to show the
guards in their positions round
the walls; it pauses by the
heavily barred front gate.

F-55   EXT COURTYARD. CLOSE SHOT

The Chief Detective and the
Sergeant.

                  SERGEANT
                 Those certainly were steps
                 outside - like naked feet.
                    (he pauses)
                 D'you suppose he'll try
                 getting in through the
                 house?

                  CHIEF DETECTIVE
                 Every door and window's
                 barred - with a couple of
                 guards on each. He'll try
                 the wall right enough -

CUT BACK TO:

162

F-56   EXT COURTYARD. CLOSEUP ON..

     one of the guards - anxiously
     listening.

F-57   OUTSIDE PRISON WALLS
     MED CLOSE ON...

     a white cat, strolling round
     outside the prison walls.
     QUICK CUT TO:

F-58   EXT COURTYARD. CLOSEUP ON..

     the guard, who has heard a
     faint sound, and is acutely
     on the alert.

F-59   OUTSIDE PRISON WALL
     MED SHOT ON..

     The cat, jumping up from
     the outside, onto the wall.

F-60   EXT COURTYARD. MED CLOSE SHOT

     opposite side of wall. A little
     shower of loose earth is dis-
     turbed as the cat's paws alight
     on it. The guard gives a shout
     of excitement and lets fly with
     his spray of black paint.

F-61   EXT COURTYARD. FULL SHOT

     Shouts of warning - the Chief
     Detective runs excitedly about.

                      CHIEF DETECTIVE
                         Keep to your stations!
                         Watch the wall there!

     CAMERA MOVES to a fat,
     goggle-eyed policeman,
     shouting to the Chief
     Detective.

                    POLICEMAN
                         He's over the wall! - I
                         felt breathing! - Down my
                         neck!

F-62   EXT COURTYARD. MED SHOT

       The cat - now a completely
       black one - galloping madly
       off in the moonlight.

F-63   EXT ROAD IN MOUNTAINS..
         FULL SHOT ON...

       Kemp - alone in his car, crouch-
       ing over his driving wheel, tear-
       ing furiously through the night.
       He is up in the mountains now -
       we can see the forbidding moonlit
       crests and the ominous ravines
       beside the road. The car flies
       through a little wayside village.
       The Church clock is slowly strik-
       ing ten.

F-64   INT CAR. MED CLOSE ON...

       Kemp - listens and throws back
       his head in exultation.

                   KEMP
                Ten o'clock - at ten
                o'clock he wanted to murder
                me!

       He laughs loudly and
       triumphantly, bends to
       the wheel and flies on
       through the night - a grim
       smile of victory on his face -
       up and up the winding mountain
       road - into the desolation.
       Slowly CAMERA PANS from his set
       profile and concentrates upon
       the empty back seat of the car.
       CAMERA REMAINS FIXED upon the
       bare seat for a few seconds -
       until a calm voice comes from
       the emptiness; the voice of the
       Invisible Man.

               INVISIBLE MAN
                I think this'll do nicely,
                Kemp. We'll stop here.

F-65   INT CAR. TWO SHOT

       Kemp is too astonished and
       horrified to utter a sound.

               INVISIBLE MAN
                It's ten o'clock. I came
                with you to keep my promise.

       The car has come to a
       halt.

F-66   INT CAR. CLOSEUP ON

        Kemp, suddenly finds his voice -
        hoarse and unreal though it
        sounds.

                            KEMP
                        No - it's all a mistake,
                        Griffin! I swear I never
                        told the police! I want
                        to help you - let me be
                        your partner!

        The voice of the Invisible
        Man comes calmly and relent-
        lessly..

                            INVISIBLE MAN
                        I've had a cold and uncom-
                        fortable journey - just to
                        keep my promise at ten
                        o'clock.

F-67   INT CAR. MED SHOT

        The Invisible Man pauses, then
        continues, Kemp listening in
        terror.

                            INVISIBLE MAN
                        ...I went into the Police
                        Station with you, Kemp.
                        I stood by while you chang-
                        ed into that coat. - I rode
                        on the running board of
                        the car that took you home
                        again --

        Kemp makes a sudden dive for
        the door - a thick scarf that
        he is wearing suddenly jerks
        back and nearly throttles him.

F-68   INT CAR. CLOSEUP ON

        Kemp - strangling. His head
        is pulled back over the driving
        seat - he gives a strangled cry.
        There follows a fierce struggle -
        Kemp snarling and groaning like
        a beast at bay. But he is powerless
        against his stronger opponent -
        hopelessly out-pointed by his op-
        ponent's dreadful advantage.

F-69   EXT ROAD. MED SHOT

        Kemp is dragged by invisible hands
        from the car to the grass verge
        of the road - his hands are lashed
        behind him by a piece of rope -
        his feet are bound together.

165

F-70   EXT ROAD. CLOSE SHOT ON

          Invisible hands tying Kemp's
          hands and binding his feet.

F-71   EXT ROAD. MED SHOT ON KEMP

          Powerless and impotent he rises
          from the ground - hovers in a
          sitting position and sails slowly
          back into the car - into the front
          seat beside the driver. In a moment
          the car starts up, the steering
          wheel moves.

F-72   INT CAR. CLOSE SHOT ON

          The gear handle slips into
          connection - the accelerator -
          and the brake.

F-73   EXT MOUNTAIN ROAD. LONG SHOT

          The car moves off apparently by
          itself - climbing up the mountain
          road.

F-74   INT CAR. MED CLOSE KEMP

          His eyes roll around in agony
          to the empty seat beside him. Once
          more the voice comes - from the
          emptiness above the wheel.

                                        INVISIBLE MAN
                                        I hope your car's
                                        insured, Kemp. I'm
                                        afraid there's going
                                        to be a nasty accident
                                        in a minute.

F-75   EXT MOUNTAIN ROAD. FULL SHOT

          The car has climbed to a great
          height upon the winding mountain
          road. Slowly it pulls up and
          steers into a little piece of
          slightly sloping ground - the kind
          of clear space used by picnicers
          to get the magnificent view beneath
          them. A little flimsy white rail-
          ing marks the further end of the
          space - beyond that the mountain
          steepens into the dreadful, boulder-
          strewn descent of the ravine.

                                        INVISIBLE MAN
                                        ---a very nasty accident.

F-76   INT CAR. MED CLOSE ON

       Kemp - as he cries out in
       terror..

                       KEMP
                         Griffin! - I'll do any-
                         thing! - everything you ask
                         me!

                    INVISIBLE MAN
                       You will? - that's fine.
                       Just sit where you are.

F-77   EXT MOUNTAIN ROAD
          MED SHOT

       Kemp, sitting in the car,
       terrified.

                  INVISIBLE MAN
                       I'll get out and take the
                       hand brake off, and give
                       you a little shove to help
                       you on. You'll run gently
                       down - and through the
                       railings. Then you'll have
                       a big thrill for a hundred
                       yards or so - till you hit
                       a boulder. Then you'll do
                       a somersault and probably
                       break your arms - then a
                       grand finish up with a
                       broken neck.

       There is a moment of
       silence. The driver's
       door opens and closes.

F-78   INT CAR. CLOSE SHOT ON

       Kemp - frantic with fear.
       The voice comes again from
       outside.

                  INVISIBLE MAN
                       Well, goodbye, Kemp. I
                       always said you were a
                       dirty little coward. You're
                       a dirty, sneaking little
                       rat as well. Goodbye.

       Kemp's terrified eyes are
       on the hand brake - the catch
       rises and the lever moves for-
       ward - slowly the car begins
       to move as we... CUT TO:

F-79   EXT MOUNTAIN ROAD. MED LONG SHOT

       The car quickens its pace as
       strong, invisible hands assist
       it from the behind. It comes to
       the railings.

F-80   MED SHOT

    As the car breaks through
and breaks the railings and
begins its terrible descent
into the ravine.

F-81   EXT RAVINE. FULL SHOT

    of the falling car.

F-82   MED SHOT. OF THE RAILINGS

    The railings are broken. We
hear the low, maniacal laughter
of the Invisible Man as if he
were standing by the railings
watching the car go to its destruction.

F-83   BOTTOM OF RAVINE. LONG SHOT

    A shot of the shapeless, blazing
wreck at the bottom of the ravine.
Off stage we hear again the low,
maniacal laughter of the Invisible
Man.

    FADE OUT

END OF SEQUENCE "F"

SEQUENCE "G"

FADE IN:

G-1   INT. CONFERENCE ROOM
      DOLLEY SHOT. DAY

    At general Police Headquarters.
A sternly furnished, lofty apartment with a long table down the
center. A conference is in pro-
gress. The Chief of Police is
at the head of the table; seated
round are the senior Detectives
and Officers concerned in the man-
hunt. The Chief of Police is
summarizing the case. CAMERA STARTS
ON MED. CLOSE on the Chief of Police
and PULL BACK to a FULL SHOT showing the stupid, formal arrangement.

                      CHIEF OF POLICE
           A thousand replies have
           come to my appeal for sug-
           gesting ways of catching
           the Invisible Man. Some
           are clever - some are
           stupid - all are impos-
           sible. Most of them sug-
           gest laying tar, or other
           substances that would
           stick to his feet. Some
           suggest getting together
           all the blind people in
           the country - to track him
           with their acute instinct-
           ive senses. That's no
           good. Crowds of searchers
           are a waste of time - he
           can slip through with
           absolute ease.

G-2   INT. CONFERENCE ROOM
      CLOSE SHOT ON..

    A very stupid, sleepy-
looking Police Officer.

                 POLICE OFFICER
           But he's got to sleep.
           They might catch him
           asleep.

    CUT TO:

G-3   INT. CONFERENCE ROOM
      CLOSE SHOT ON..

    Another one of the Police
Officers.

              2ND POLICE OFFICER
           He's got to eat and drink.

    CUT TO:

nn   G-4   INT. CONFERENCE ROOM
                 MEDIUM SHOT..

              The Chief of Police is sitting
              at the head of the table - the
              others in their respective
              places.

                                              CHIEF OF POLICE
                                          A cafe was robbed last
                                          night in Manton - but
                                          it's no proof. There are
                                          robberies every night -
                                          by ordinary burglars -

              As the Chief of Police is
              speaking, the picture
              DISSOLVES TO:

        G-5   EXT. FIELDS..LONG SHOT..

              showing an old barn, stand-
              ing isolated upon some flat,
              bare fields.
              CUT TO:

        G-6   CLOSE SHOTON...THE DOOR

              The door of the barn opens
              with a rusty grating sound -
              and gently closes.
              CUT TO:

        G-7   INT. BARN...DAY...MED LONG SHOT

              A remarkable old place: a few
              farming implements along the
              walls - a pile of straw in one
              of the corners - CAMERA PANS
              over to the straw and we see
              evidences of feet disturbing hay,
              etc. Slowly the straw is pulled
              back: it forms itself into all
              kinds of weird heaps as the
              Invisible Man prepares for him-
              self a resting place. Then some
              of the straw forms itself into a
              little mound. The Invisible Man
              has pulled it over his tired
              body. The straw becomes still.
              All we hear is a long drawn sigh -
              and weary, rhythmic breathing.
              CUT BACK TO:

        G-8   INT. CONFERENCE ROOM
                 MED SHOT..HIGH CAMERA   .

              The Chief of Police is summing
              up the Conference.

                                              CHIEF OF POLICE
                                          There's only one thing to
                                          do. We must wait until
                                          we hear of him again.

                                              POLICE OFFICER
                                          You mean - another murder?

        CONTINUED

                                    170

G-8   CONTINUED

                                    CHIEF OF POLICE
                                         If necessary we must wait
                                         for another murder.
                                         Directly the news comes
                                         we must race every man we
                                         have - by lorry and car
                                         and cycle and aeroplane -
                                         five hundred police and
                                         ten thousand soldiers
                                         will surround the area -
                                         not one deep but five
                                         deep - and close in until
                                         we take him. I've with-
                                         drawn all the search
                                         parties: they are standing
                                         by - waiting for the
                                         signal.

         DISSOLVE TO:

G-9   EXT. BARN...LONG SHOT..DAY

         The barn in the bare fields.
         The sky is overcast. Snow
         is lightly floating down in
         the still sky. An old farmer
         comes slowly along with a rake
         over his shoulder.
         CUT TO:

G-10   EXT. BARN
         CLOSER SHOT...ON

         The old farmer as he goes up
         to the door - opens it and
         goes in.

G-11   INT. BARN...MED SHOT ON...

         He leans his rake against the
         wall and picks up a little straw
         to clean his hands. As he
         wipes them, a faint sound at-
         tracts his attention. He pauses
         to listen.
         CUT TO:

G-12   INT. BARN...MED CLOSE SHOT..

         On the straw - there comes the
         heavy, rhythimic breathing of a
         sleeping man - now and then a
         faint snore.
         CUT TO:

G-13   INT. BARN...MED PAN SHOT...

         The old farmer looks surprised,
         and glances round, expecting to
         find a tramp. He looks still more
         surprised when he sees nobody.
         CAMERA PANS as he approaches the
         sound of the snoring and sees the
         strangely piled heap of straw which
         covers the Invisible Man.
         CUT TO:

G-14   INT. BARN...CLOSE SHOT ON...

          The old farmer as he listens
          again. There is no mistaking
          the position of the heavy
          breathing - or the faint rise
          and fall of the straw that
          accompanies it.
          CUT TO:

G-15   INT. BARN...MED LONG SHOT...

          He very stealthily examines the
          straw - and his jaw drops in
          astonishment when the straw moves
          more definitely as the Invisible
          Man stirs in his sleep, and gives
          a deeper snore. The farmer backs
          very stealthily away. He gets to
          the door, slips out, and runs off
          as fast as he can through the
          snow. THE CAMERA PANS with him
          and we see him running away.

          The snow is falling more heavily
          now. It is beginning to whiten
          the ground.
          CUT TO:

G-16   INT. CONFERENCE ROOM...LONG SHOT

          The Committee are rising from
          the table.
                              CHIEF OF POLICE
                         Go back to your stations
                         now - and stand by for
                         orders.

          As the men turn from the
          table, one of them looks
          towards the window and
          sees the snow. The significance
          of it flashes to his mind.
          He turns excitedly to the
          Chief of Police and points
          to the window.

                              DETECTIVE
                         Look there! - We wanted
                         help! There it is!

          The Chief looks out
          upon the street. Already
          it is powdered white. He
          turns to the waiting man
          and they all go to the
          window.
          CUT TO:

G-17   INT. CONFERENCE ROOM...MED
          SHOT ON...

          The group at the window looking
          out into the street at the snow.

                              CHIEF OF POLICE
                         It's now or never. Snow
                         won't lie long this time
                         of year. It may be gone
                         in a few hours.

CONTINUED

172

nn   G-17   CONTINUED

CHIEF OF POLICE (contd)
            (he turns briskly to
            his lieutenant)
Norton! Find out if the
snow's general over the
country - get a broadcast
message out! He can't
stay out in this bitter
cold - he'll seek shelter--
every barn and building
must be searched - every
field and wood and road
must be watched for bare
foot-prints - quick! Get
ahead!

As the men start to
leave the window we ...
CUT TO:

G-18   EXT. VILLAGE STREET
        EXTREME LONG SHOT...DAY

The old farmer, lumbering as
quickly as he can down the
street of a small village.
The snow is falling heavily.
He reaches the local Police
Station and runs in.
CUT TO:

G-19   INT. POLICE STATION...MED.
        SHOT...DAY

A Police Officer looks up in
astonishment at the excited,
panting old farmer.
CUT TO:

G-20   INT. POLICE STATION...TWO SHOT...

                        FARMER   (between gasps for
                                   breath)
                        Excuse me, sir - there's
                        breathing in my barn.

                        POLICEMAN
                        What d'you mean? - breath-
                        ing in your barn?

                        FARMER
                        The - Invisible - Man!

The Policeman sits up,
as the Farmer continues:
                        -Sure as I stand here!
                            (he gasps)
                        Went to put my rake away-
                        and there he was - asleep
                        in the straw! - snoring,
                        sir!

The Policeman eyes the
Farmer thoughtfully.

                        POLICEMAN
                        Where is the barn?

                        FARMER
                        The one down in Five-acre
                        Field! - 'bout a mile from
                        'ere - on the main road!

        CONTINUED

173

The Policeman picks up
his telephone.

                                POLICEMAN
                           Give me Headquarters -
                           quickly!

CUT TO:

G-21   INT. CHIEF DETECTIVE'S OFFICE..
        MED SHOT...DAY

        Chief of Police - speaking to
        the Chief Detective in his office:
        other officers standing eagerly
        round - all together like sheep.

                                CHIEF OF POLICE
                           The farmer may have im-
                           agined it! - but we can't
                           leave anything to chance.
                           Surround the barn - it's
                           no good trying to take
                           him inside - force him
                           out into the snow! - take
                           a pile of wood and some
                           gasoline - and set fire to
                           it.

CUT TO:

G-22   EXT. POLICE STATION...
        MED LONG SHOT...DAY

        The policemen running out -
        all in rows.
        QUICK CUT TO:

G-23   EXT. ROAD...FULL LONG SHOT

        Lorries full of soldiers swing
        out of some barracks and roar
        off down a road.
        QUICK CUT TO:

G-24   EXT. ROAD...FULL SHOT...

        Mobile Police on fast cycles -
        moving quickly down a straight
        road.
        QUICK CUT TO:

G-25   EXT. POLICE STATION...FULL SHOT

        The Chief of Police - and the
        Chief Detective with his Staff -
        coming out of Headquarters and
        quickly climbing into a large
        car.
        DISSOLVE TO:

G-26   EXT. FIELD...FULL SHOT...

        The Police car is drawn up - a
        Chauffeur at the wheel. The
        Chief of police sitting in car.

        The barn can be seen - half a
        mile away, across the fields.
        The snow is still falling, but
        somewhat lighter now. The ground
        CONTINUED

is covered about half an
inch deep. The roof of the
barn is as white as the ground
surrounding it, but the dark,
rough timbered walls stand
starkly in their isolation.
CUT TO:

G-27   MED CLOSE ON

The old Farmer and the Chief
of Police.

> FARMER   (pointing)
> That's it, sir! He's in
> there! - under a pile of
> straw!

> CHIEF OF POLICE
> Are there any windows he
> can watch from?

> FARMER
> No, sir, there's only the
> door.

The Chief of Police stands
for a moment, looking at the
barn: his keen eyes take in
the surrounding country.
CUT TO:

G-28   INT. BARN...FULL SHOT...DAY

The straw lies as it was when
the Farmer left it. The peaceful
breathing of the sleeping man comes,
as before, from the dim corner
of his refuge. CAMERA DOLLEYS UP
TO CLOSE SHOT on the Invisible Man.
CUT BACK TO:

G-29   EXT. ROAD...FULL SHOT...

The Chief of Police and the Farmer
are standing up in the car. The Chief
of Police, completing his survey.
He turns to the Farmer.

> CHIEF OF POLICE
> Thank you. There's a re-
> ward of one thousand
> pounds waiting for you if
> we're successful.

The CAMERA MOVES to the
Farmer's dazed face, then
follows the Chief of Police
down the lane to where it
branches from the main
thoroughfare. A line of
lorries, filled with soldiers,
stands waiting. The Military
Officer in charge of the party
is standing beside the leading
lorry, and comes eagerly to the
Chief of Police.
CUT TO:

an   G-30   MED SHOT ON...GROUP

                                        CHIEF OF POLICE (indicating the
                                                    barn)
                                        That's the place. We're
                                        lucky to have the open
                                        country. Take your men
                                        over to that line of trees
                                        and cover the country
                                        from the road to the top
                                        of the hill.

        The Military Officer
        salutes, and swings
        himself onto the seat
        beside the driver of the
        leading lorry. The lorries
        move off down the road.
        CUT TO:

G-31   EXT. FIELD...FULL SHOT...

        The Chief of Police, Chief
        Detective and other important
        officials, standing together
        beside a fence. The barn lies
        below them - a few hundred yards
        away.

                                        CHIEF DETECTIVE
                                        There's no time to lose.
                                        We can't wait till he
                                        comes out to search for
                                        food. We must fire the
                                        barn at once and drive
                                        him out into the snow.

        He turns. The CAMERA PANS
        to a line of policemen stand-
        ing nearby. Each has a pile
        of dry wood stacked under his
        arm. The Detective gives his
        orders.

                                        CHIEF DETECTIVE
                                        Keep in a single file - we
                                        don't want a lot of your
                                        footprints round the hut -
                                        we want the snow left for
                                        his feet alone.

        CUT TO:

G-32   EXT. FIELD...MED SHOT

        He nods abruptly to the men,
        who make off stealthily - in
        single file - about five of
        them in all. The last carries
        a can of paraffin.
        CUT TO:

G-33   EXT. BARN...LONG SHOT...

        The men - their approach softened
        by the snow, reach the wall, and
        stack the wood against its side.
        CUT TO:

G-34   EXT. FIELD...MED.SHOT...

        Quick shot of a line of soldiers,
        standing waiting behind the trees.
        CUT TO:

nn   G-35   EXT. ROAD...MED SHOT...

         Policemen, lining the hedge
         alongside the road.
      - CUT TO:

      G-36   EXT. LANE...MED CLOSE SHOT ON...

         The old Farmer - stolidly watch-
         ing in the bye lane.
         CUT BACK TO:

      G-37   EXT. BARN...MED SHOT...

          The men beside the hut. The
         fuel is laid. The man with the
         can of paraffin comes forward
         and empties its contents over
         the wood and upon the wall of
         the hut.

      G-38   EXT. BARN...CLOSER SHOT...

         One man strikes a match and
         applies it to the wood. There
         is a sheet of flame - the men back
         away from its heat and retire the
         way they came.
         CUT TO:

      G-39   EXT. FIELD...MED SHOT....

         The Chief Detective, standing with
         his staff - binoculars to his eyes.
         CUT TO:

      G-40   A BINOCULAR VIEW...CLOSE UP...

          Of the door of the burning hut.
         The door remains closed.
         CUT TO:

      G-41   INT. BARN...FULL SHOT...

         The interior of the hut. Smoke
         begins to wreath the ceiling
         and creep round the pile of straw -
         suddenly the straw heaves, and a
         way is broken between it.
         CUT BACK TO:

      G-42   EXT. FIELD...MED SHOT...CLOSE

         The Chief Detective - standing
         rigidly with the glasses to his
         eyes - THE CAMERA MOVES FORWARD
         getting medium shot of the barn.
         Although the snow has naturally
         melted upon the ground to the side
         where the fire is blazing, it still
         lies thickly up to the door of the
         barn on the opposite side. The snow
         has ceased to fall now: the air is
         bright and clear. Suddenly the door
         is flung open. Nothing happens
         for a moment. It is as if the In-
         visible Man has thrown the door
         open and now stands looking out from
         the threshold - dismayed at the sight
         CONTINUED

of the thick snow in front of
him. But the fire has now got
the barn firmly in its ravenous
grip - a swirl of dark smoke
eddies from the thatch above the
door.
CUT TO:

G-43   EXT. BARN...MED CLOSE SHOT...

Slow, furtive footsteps appear in
the snow as the Invisible Man is
forced to advance across the bitter,
desolate field.
CUT TO:

G-44   EXT. FIELD...TWO SHOT...

The Chief Detective, who has
lowered the binoculars and is
excitedly holding the arm of the
Sergeant beside him

                    CHIEF DETECTIVE
                He's out! Look!

He hands the binoculars
to the Sergeant, who scans
the scene fascinated.
CUT TO:

G-45   SHOT OF...

The blazing barn through the
binoculars. The Chief Detective's
voice comes over the picture.

                    CHIEF DETECTIVE
                The fire's got hold all
                right - he'll never get
                back now.

CUT TO:

G-46   EXT. BARN...MED SHOT...

PAN SHOT of the trail of footsteps advancing from the hut -
the Invisible Man has not yet
seen the hidden watchers around
him.
CUT TO:

G-47   EXT. FIELD...MED SHOT...

The Chief Detective and his
group. He turns to the
Sergeant.

                    CHIEF DETECTIVE
                Give the signal to
                advance.

The Sergeant raises his
revolver and fires into the
air. The sound echoes over
the silent meadows.
CUT TO:

nn   G-48   EXT. FIELD...LONG SHOT...

            HIGH CAMERA. The soldiers,
            leaving the shelter of the
            trees advancing in close line.
            CUT TO:

   G-49   EXT. LANE...LONG SHOT...

            HIGH CAMERA. The police, rising
            from the hedgerows of the lane.
            CUT TO:

   G-50   EXT. FIELD...LONG SHOT...

            The Chief Detective, advancing
            with his staff - a line of
            police behind them.

   G-51   EXT. BARN...MED SHOT...

            The footprints in the snow. The
            trail has stopped dead, upon the
            sound of the revolver. The In-
            visible Man is standing quite
            still: we feel that he is gazing
            round - taking in the scene around
            him - the waves of men - inexorably
            closing upon him from every side.
            Behind him the blazing barn sends a
            pall of dark smoke into the sky.

            THE CAMERA HOLDS the smooth sur-
            face of the snow - the trail of
            footsteps ending in two prints side
            by side, where the Invisible Man
            stands waiting.
            CUT TO:

   G-52   EXT. FIELD...LONGER SHOT...

            Suddenly they move forward again -
            turn abruptly to the left and widen
            as the Invisible Man runs - straight
            towards the line commanded by the
            Chief Detective. There are medleyed,
            excited shouts.
            CUT TO:

   G-53   EXT. FIELD...MED CLOSE ON...

                            CHIEF DETECTIVE
                     Look out - there he goes.

            CUT TO:

   G-54   EXT. FIELD...MED LONG SHOT...

            The Chief Detective, the Sergeant
            beside him. They watch, fascinated
            as the deep, clear footprints come
            towards them.
            CUT TO:

nn   G-55   EXT. FIELD...CLOSE SHOT ON..

The Chief Detective raises his
revolver - takes careful aim
and fires into the emptiness
above the advancing steps.
CUT TO:

G-56   EXT. FIELD...MED SHOT...LONG

The steps halt - there is a
moment of stillness - and then
the snow-white space is churned
by the falling body. Slowly -
fascinated the Chief Detective
comes forward and kneels beside
the roughened dented surface.
His hands steal forward -
searching - feeling over the
invisible, wounded body. Other
men come forward and stand
silently around. Someone says:

                    "Is he dead?"

CUT TO:

G-57   EXT. FIELD...MED CLOSE ON...

The Detective makes no reply.

FADE OUT

FADE IN:

H-1   A SMALL WAITING ROOM
       IN A HOSPITAL - FULL SHOT.

    Two policemen stand on guard
    to either side of a door that
    leads into a private ward.

    The Chief Detective is slowly
    pacing the room. Dr. Cranley
    stands waiting by the windows.
    Presently the door from the
    private ward is softly opened,
    and a white-coated Doctor enters.
    The Chief Detective quickly turns.

                  DOCTOR   (to Chief Detective)
                  I don't think your guard
                  will beneeded any longer.
                  (there is a moment
                  of silence before
                  the Doctor speaks
                  again)

                  He's very near the end.
                  (he turns to the old
                  Doctor)
                  Are you Dr. Cranley?

             DR. CRANLEY
                  Yes. I had a message - to
                  come immediately.

             DOCTOR
                  Towards dawn this morning
                  he grew quiet. He called
                  the name of a girl. I
                  understand - your daughter,
                  Dr. Cranley.

             DR. CRANLEY (with a slight nod)
                  She's waiting below.
                  (he pauses)
                  Is there - any chance?

    CUT TO:

H-2   INT. WAITING ROOM
       CLOSE TWO SHOT...

    The Doctor shakes his
    head.

             DOCTOR
                  The bullet passed through
                  both lungs. It's impossible
                  to treat the wound. Do
                  you think your daughter -
                  could bear to go to him?
                  I'm afraid the end may be
                  - rather terrible. The
                  effect of the drugs will
                  die with him; his body
                  will become visible as
                  life goes.

    (CONTINUED)

H-2   (CONTINUED)

       Dr. Cranley faces the
       Doctor in silence for
       a moment, then turns
       to the door.

                        DR. CRANLEY
                I'll bring her now.

       DISSOLVE SLOWLY TO:

H-3   INT. HOSPITAL ROOM.
       FULL SHOT...

       Where the Invisible
       Man lies dying. A small
       plainly furnished private
       ward. A nurse moves away
       as the Doctor comes for-
       ward and looks down at
       the empty bed. The
       clothes are tucked
       round as they would cover
       the body of a still, pros-
       trate form. They rise and
       fall very slightly to the
       shallow breathing of the
       dying.man. A weak, urgent
       voice comes up to the
       waiting Doctor.

                        INVISIBLE MAN
                - is - Flora there?

       The Doctor bends down a
       little.

                     DOCTOR
                She is coming - now.

       CUT TO:

H-4   INT. HOSPITAL ROOM
       MEDIUM SHOT...

       The door opns, and
       Dr. Cranley enters. He
       stands aside to make way
       for the girl, who crosses
       quietly to the bed. The
       Doctor draws up a chair
       and motions to the girl
       to approach. He withdraws
       to a far corner of the room
       with Dr. Cranley, and the
       two men stand waiting in
       silence. The girl sits be-
       side the bed.

       CUT TO:

H-5   INT. HOSPITAL ROOM
       CLOSE SHOT OF...

       The pillows. There is no
       sound until the tired,
       weak voice rises from
       the empty pillows.

       (CONTINUED)

H-5   (CONTINUED)

                              INVISIBLE MAN
                         I - knew you would -
                         come to me, Flora.

        CUT TO:

H-6   INT. HOSPITAL ROOM
        CLOSE SHOT ON....

        Flora - she raises
        her hand and gently
        feels along the side
        of the bed until she
        grasps the hand of the
        dying man. He speaks again -
        scarcely above a whisper.

                              INVISIBLE MAN
                         I wanted to come back to
                         you - my darling, I failed.
                         I meddled in things that
                         man - must leave alone...

        His last words die
        away.

        CUT TO:

H-7   INT. HOSPITAL ROOM
        MED. CLOSE ON FLORA

        The girl sits with his
        invisible hand in hers -
        she is helpless to do
        more than comfort him
        in this little way. At
        last she speaks, alarmed
        at his silence.

                              FLORA
                         - Jack! -

        CUT TO:

H-8   INT. HOSPITAL ROOM
        MED. FULL...

        The clothes around the
        body no longer rise and
        fall with the faint breath-
        ing. Without moving her
        hand, she turns to her
        father and calls -

        CUT TO:

H-9   INT. HOSPITAL ROOM
        CLOSE UP ON..FLORA.

        Calling to her father
        in a low, urgent voice:

                              FLORA
                         Father - come quickly!

        CUT TO:

H-10   INT. HOSPITAL ROOM
          MEDIUM SHOT...

Dr. Cranley and the
hospital Doctor
turning and approach-
ing the bed.

CUT TO:

H-11   INT. HOSPITAL ROOM
          MED. CLOSE ON.....

The bed - the dented
pillow - and tucked in
clothes. Very slowly -
from the emptiness -
begins to gather a thin
grey mist. Gradually
it takes form - a human
head and shoulders -
as transparent as glass -
that slowly gathers a
thin opaqueness, that
deepens and hardens into
shadows and substance -
until at last there lies
upon the pillows a human
face. A strong, handsome
face - dark and very
peaceful in death.

THE PICTURE FADES.

THE END

***

CARL LAEMMLE *presents*

H.G.WELLS'

FANTASTIC CREATION

THE INVISIBLE MAN

with GLORIA STUART, CLAUDE RAINS
W.M. HARRIGAN, DUDLEY DIGGES, UNA O'CONNOR
HENRY TRAVERS, FORRESTER HARVEY
Screen play by R.C. SHERRIFF *Directed by* JAMES WHALE *who directed* "Frankenstein" *Produced by* CARL LAEMMLE, Jr.
A UNIVERSAL PICTURE

Scene from "The INVISIBLE MAN" UNIVERSAL PRODUCTION

Cut "L"

Universal Worked Two Years To Make "Invisible Man" Visible

(Current Feature)

TO be or not to be: that WAS the question!"

And technical experts, cameramen, and electricians at Universal City wagged their heads—for two long years!

The reason was the perplexing production problems which Universal faced, and finally solved, in transferring H. G. Wells' fantastic story, "The Invisible Man" now at the.............Theatre, to the screen.

In directing Boris Karloff in the memorable "Frankenstein," Director James Whale chose to keep the terrifying Monster silent throughout the picture. But in directing "The Invisible Man," Whale was forced to reverse the rule that weird screen characters should be seen and not heard, and make his audience feel the presence of a menacing creature without seeing him.

How could a man actively participating in a well lighted photographic scene be made invisible? How could he become a menace—a dramatic figure, when he was not visible to either the actors in the scene with him or the audience?

Photograph invisibility?

Studio experts, cameramen and electricians were outspoken in their protests. After all, there were some things outside the pale of possibility even in a picture studio.

Nevertheless it had to be done. There was the story, marking time in vaults. It had been bought and paid for. And the price was a pretty penny.

So for two whole years Universal studio technicians knit their brows and drove their ingenuity to the breaking point. But the total results were nothing to speak about.

"Show the presence of The Invisible Man by spirit wires moving books, chairs and what not. Show him by suspending a coat, trousers, or hat on wire," were the most persistent offerings. But that was too obvious. It might have been done a few years ago, but today—never!

However, studio ingenuity would not go down to defeat. The problem was finally solved. The picture was made.

How?

There are studio secrets that are never told. They are, perhaps, guarded as stock in trade. This much, however, is known.

Director Whale, Cameraman Charles Edeson, and Jack Pierce, Universal make-up expert discovered, after months of ceaseless experiment and the employment of the well-known trial and error system, the tremendous possibilities offered with the use of small mirrors, arranged in much the same manner as magicians employ in creating optical illusions. Perhaps an idea was borrowed from Mr. Thurston or the late Harry Houdini. At any rate the idea worked, and "the invisible man" stalks through the picture, a moving force, without form or feature. With this complicated process it was even made possible for Claude Rains, who plays the title role, to be seen as he fades from his real self into the shadow that is the man, invisible. He is seen disrobing, and his clothes fall from his form. Nothing but invisibility remains.

"This much you can say," says Director Whale with a twinkle in his eye, The Invisible Man is NOT wrapped in cellophane!"

With the exception of Gloria Stuart, who has the feminine lead, the cast of "The Invisible Man" is all-English. Dudley Digges, Henry Travers, Una O'Connor, William Harrigan and Merle Tottenham—all of them hail from the British Isles.

Cream of British Theatrical Talent Appears in "The Invisible Man"

(Current Feature)

THE cream of Britain's histrionic crop together with the most currently outstanding actors in Hollywood lend realism to the fantastic H. G. Wells drama, "The Invisible Man," which is playing this week to crowded houses at the.............Theatre.

Faced with the problem of translating the English author's startling novel into screen entertainment, James Whale, who directed "Frankenstein," "Journey's End" and other exceedingly tense screen dramas, spent over six months assembling the protagonists in this picture which has already caused the most talk and excitement of any film in recent years.

Claude Rains, who makes his screen debut in the uncanny character of the super scientist, was brought from triumphs in New York with the Theatre Guild to portray the most unusual and difficult part of Wells' tale. Fresh from successes in "The Man Who Reclaimed his Head' and "Too True to Be Good," Rains brought to the film a rich background of stage experience in London and New York.

William Harrigan was selected for the intensely dramatic role of "Dr. Kemp" because of his sensational rise to fame in powerful roles of "Criminal at Large" and "Moon in the Yellow River." Gloria Stuart's remarkable impression during her meteoric screen career won her the feminine lead with the difficult assignment of playing the sweetheart of an unseen man.

Henry Travers, veteran of London stage triumphs who recently scored with John Barrymore and Diana Wynward in "Reunion in Vienna," and Dudley Digges, a New York stage favorite via London, lend further distinction to the cast of "The Invisible Man," while entrusted with the semi-humorous character parts which make this picture outstanding in this respect as well as its bizarre effects, are Una O'Connor, beloved maid of "Cavalcade" and premier Irish screen star, Forrester Harvey, inimitable "cockney" actor and Merle Tottenham, also from the British Isles.

The locale of the weird play is in England which influenced Whale to select genuine English artists for the major cast assignments. "The Invisible Man" tells an amazing screen story of a scientist who succeeds in making himself invisible and then sets about to rule the world with his unholy power.

R. C. Sherriff, talented playwright of "Jorney's End" fame, prepared Wells' novel for screening.

H. G. Wells' Favorite Story Now at ....Theatre

(Current Story)

H. G. Wells, the great British writer whose brain conceived the sensational story of "The Invisible Man," Universal's startling film which is thrilling theatregoers this week at the ....Theatre, is known as "the author who never wrote anything but a best seller."

Wells' list of literary triumphs includes "War of the World," "The Sleeper Awakes," "Food of the Gods," "A Modern Utopia," "Ann Veronica," "Tono Bungay," "Men Like Gods" and the famous "Outline of History."

His "The Invisible Man," from which R. C. Sherriff prepared the screenplay for the strangely fascinating picture, is one of his own favorite stories, and intrigued him with its possibilities as it intrigues those who are thronging to see its screen version.

Claude Rains, William Harrigan, Gloria Stuart, Dudley Digges, Una O'Connor, Henry Travers and an unusually large cast of brilliant stage and screen players portray the strange Wells characters in "The Invisible Man," which James Whale directed with exceptional finesse.

Scene from "The INVISIBLE MAN" UNIVERSAL PRODUCTION

Cut "M"

Current Notes

Claude Rains pulls a chestnut out of the fire when he cracks that the theme song for Universal's "The Invisible Man" should be "I Ain't Got No Body." "The Invisible Man" is the current attraction at the ....Theatre.

* * *

Gloria Stuart, who was discovered a little over a year ago by Carl Laemmle, Jr., at the Pasadena Community Playhouse, has in that time played leads in a dozen pictures. She is playing this week at the ....Theatre in Universal's "The Invisible Man," by H. G. Wells.

* * *

It took Duddley Digges 29 years to become an American citizen, but the feat was finally accomplished during the recent filming of Universal's "The Invisible Man," in which he plays a featured role at the.............Theatre this week. The Irish-American actor, who came to this country for the first time with a troupe of Irish players sent to the World's Fair in St. Louis in 1904, liked the country and took out papers at that time, but he has moved around so much they were never completed until he recently "settled" in Hollywood.

* * *

Una O'Connor, whose delightful role of the inn proprietress in Universal's "The Invisible Man" at the ....Theatre this week is adding another palm to her motion picture record, once played before British royalty at the Court in Shakespeare's "Macbeth." She was a witch, but has had more kindly roles since then in "Cavalcade" and many other films.

* * *

Although William Harrigan is well terrorized by the invisible menace of Universal's sensational "The Invisible Man" at the.............Theatre this week, in real life the actor is a World War Hero. Harrigan was a captain in the 77th Division. It was his outfit which rescued the famous "Lost Battalion." Claude Rains, Gloria Stuart, Dudley Digges, Henry Travers and Una O'Connor are other featured cast members. James Whale directed this H. G. Wells' sensational novel.

Scene from "The INVISIBLE MAN" UNIVERSAL PRODUCTION

Cut "N"

The Man Who Rescued "The Lost Battalion"

Strange Contrasts Mark the Career of William Harrigan, Featured Player of H. G. Wells' "The Invisible Man"

(Current Feature)

REAL and make-believe!

The man who rescued the Lost Batallion, the nephew of Lillian Russell! Theatrical heritage of 273 unbroken years—That's William Harrigan.

The greatest theatrical heritage of any actor in Hollywood belongs to William Harrigan, who is appearing at the.............Theatre, in H. G. Wells' "The Invisible Man," in support of Claude Rains.

Harrigan's professional ancestry reaches back 273 years in history beyond the French pantomimists, the Ravels, on his mother's side; while his father's part of the family boasts progenitors who entertained British royalty. The noted Braham family of Germany are included in the ancestory, and one member first staged the Gilbert and Sullivan operas in this country. Another first sang "God Save the King" in England at a public gathering. Generation by generation from one to five members of his direct line have been famous before the footlights without an interruption for almost three centuries.

Harrigan's father, Edward Harrigan, of Harrigan and Hart fame, was an important factor in the growth of the New York stage. He wrote over 50 successful plays and staged one of his own plays a year for 29 successive years, building four theatres as the city grew. "Old Lavender" is perhaps the best known of the Harrigan-Hart productions which are still remembered by Manhattan's "old timers," and the songs which characterized them, such as "When Poverty's Tears Ebb and Flow" were written by his mother's father David Braham.

Lillian Russell was Harrigan's aunt, and his whole family tree is literally bending down with talent's rich fruit. He himself made his stage debut at the age of five, and deserted Princeton to go with his father at 19.

A distinguished stage record on Broadway including "The Acquittal," "Polly Preferred," "The Dove," "The Great God Brown," "Moon in the Yellow River" and "Criminal at Large" has preceded his entry into motion pictures.

Besides distinction in theatricals, the actor is regarded as one of the nation's outstanding war heroes, being the captain in command of the Third Battalion of the 307th Infantry which rescued the famous "Lost Battalion" during the Argonne Forest engagement, the most romantic episode of the A. E. F.'s service record.

Reunion of Theatre Guild Stars Takes Place in "The Invisible Man"

(Current Story)

"THE Invisible Man,' the H. G. Wells weird story which is now playing at the.............Theatre, brings together three of the Theatre Guild's most prominent players, now become screen stars, and the Universal City sound stage where the Wells classic was being filmed was the scene recently of a most agreeable reunion of the three troupers,—Claude Rains, Dudley Digges and Henry Travers.

Rains, who is making his screen debut in "The Invisible Man," came to Universal City direct from New York and many years of stage triumphs. Included among these were "The Man Who Reclaimed His Head," "The Constant Nymph," "And So to Bed," "Volpone," "Marco Millions," "Karl and Anna," "The Apple Cart," "Miracle at Verdun," "He," "The Moon in the Yellow River," and most recently "The Good Earth." While with the Theatre Guild, he appeared in many of their productions with Dudley Digges and the two became close friends. Digges was signed by Universal at the same time as Rains, but had to complete his role in "Emperor Jones" before joining Rains at Universal City for his role in "The Invisible Man."

Henry Travers completes the trio and is another of that famous acting institute to translate his talents from stage to screen. His work in the film version of "Reunion in Vienna" was delightful. In "The Invisible Man" he has one of the most important roles.

Review

H. G. WELLS' imagination, Jame's Whale's direction and expert acting on the part of a large cast of distinguished stage and screen actors make Universal's "The Invisible Man," which opened last night at the.............Theatre, the most striking picture seen in years.

How Universal managed to put this extraordinary story on celluloid remains one of the mysteries of Hollywood, because throughout all of the exciting reels, things happen so incredible that one is prone to shake his head and blink his eyes to look again. Naturally, with such a wonderful idea and theme, beyond ordinary proportions was expected, but nothing so astounding as this uncanny film.

It's all about a super scientist who manages to make himself invisible by means of an obscure drug and then, half crazed by its effect, sets about to make the world realize his unlimited power. He does so in a graphic, startling manner, and strangely enough, there isn't a moment when the audience is not aware of the unseen man's presence on the screen, when he is meant to be there. Of course, being invisible, he is not actually seen, but how he is felt!

His wild course is so cleverly shown on the screen that it would be downright treason to describe it. And his fate is worked out in such a spectacular manner that memories of "The Invisible Man" are bound to linger long with those so fortunate to see it. Somehow the treatment given this weird tale by R. C. Sherriff, who is credited with the screenplay, makes the picture entirely reasonable and not fantastic in the least, and the expert characterizations lent by Claude Rains in his picture debut, William Harrigan, Gloria Stuart, Dudley Digges, Henry Travers, Una O'Connor and Forrester Harvey, enhance this effect of entirely logical occurrences, although the menace of the unseen is present always.

Undoubtedly "The Invisible Man" is crowded with genuine entertainment besides being a definitely new departure, a brand new idea and a spectacular photographic achievement. You can't help but enjoy it, and we'll guarantee you such an evening of thrills as you've never had before. See it as soon as you can!

"THE INVISIBLE MAN"

Advance Publicity

Scene from "The INVISIBLE MAN" UNIVERSAL PRODUCTION

Cut "A"

At A Glance

Title .... "THE INVISIBLE MAN"
Brand .... Universal Production
Star .... CLAUDE RAINS
Featured Players ... Gloria Stuart and William Harrigan
From the Novel by ... H. G. WELLS
Screenplay by .... R. C. Sherriff
Directed by .... JAMES WHALE
Photographed by .... Arthur Edeson
Time .... The Present
Place .... England

The Cast

The Invisible One ...... Claude Rains
Flora Cranley .... Gloria Stuart
Doctor Kemp .... William Harrigan
Doctor Cranley .... Henry Travers
Mrs. Hall .... Una O'Connor
Mr. Hall .... Forrester Harvey
Chief of Police ...... Holmes Herbert
Jaffers .... E. E. Clive
Chief of Detectives ... Dudley Digges
Inspector Bird .... Harry Stubbs
Inspector Lane .... Donald Stuart
Milly .... Merle Tottenham

GLORIA STUART and WILLIAM HARRIGAN in "The INVISIBLE MAN" UNIVERSAL PRODUCTION

Cut "B"

The Story

Latest Screen Sensation Coming

For The Program

Amazing Film

Goal of man to achieve invisibility reached in unique Feature coming here today.

Advance Notes

Leading Personalities

CLAUDE RAINS
Cut "C"

Cut "E"

WILLIAM HARRIGAN
Cut "D"

DUDLEY DIGGES
Cut "F"

Advance Notes

HENRY TRAVERS
Cut "G"

Screened Behind Closed Doors

"The Invisible Man," Year's Most Unusual Film, Comes to the .... Theatre to Amaze .... ers.

187

Feature Stories | "THE INVISIBLE MAN" | *Scene Cuts and Mats*

WILLIAM HARRIGAN and GLORIA STUART in "The INVISIBLE MAN" UNIVERSAL PRODUCTION

Cut "H"

Now Comes the Climax of Grotesquerie

(Advance Feature)

"THE INVISIBLE MAN" has arrived to join the weird procession of characters who have beaten a fantastic path across the pages of screen history.

"The Invisible man," moreover, threatens to become the most effective of all the blood chilling creatures created by Hollywood for hair raising and spine tingling purposes. Coming to the.........Theatre on ...., the unseen character who vanishes into the ether to upset the rhythm of the universe proves beyond doubt his right to a prominent position in the ranks of the grotesque.

"The Invisible Man" recalls the host of macabre creatures beginning with the contorted dwarf "Quasimodo" of "The Hunchback of Notre Dame," a silent spectacle of some ten years ago. The ugly creature who dwelt in the ancient cathedral was much more of a human character than the ghoul-like "Phantom of the Opera" who followed him at Universal. Perhaps no early screen character inspired as much horror as the "Phantom" in his unholy love for pretty Mary Philbin. Both the "Hunchback" and "Phantom" sets remain standing on the back of lots of Universal studios, as silent reminders of the screen ghosts of yesterday.

It remained for Bela Lugosi, the sinister Hungarian actor, to revive weird characterizations for the modern talking screen with his strange "Count Dracula," the vampire menace whose success in Universal's "Dracula" presaged "Frankenstein." Lugosi's character was preceded by "The Man Who Laughs" a grotesque creature created by Conrad Veidt, another Teuton, but "Dracula" and its singular appeal to the theatregoing public very probably accounted for the filming of "Frankenstein" which set an all-time record for unholy screen beings. Strangely enough, the macabre monster was not created originally by the movies, but by Mary Wollstonecroft Shelley, the wife of the great English poet. Only the movies brought to actual visibility, and shadow form the hulking resurrection assembled from the graves of the dead.

Undoubtedly "Frankenstein" remains the most remembered of motion picture "nightmares," although "Dr. Jekyll," or if you prefer, "Mr. Hyde," of "Dr. Jekyll and Mr. Hyde," deserves more than casual mention. A person of intended evil, when transformed into his lower self, the dual-personality gentleman succeeded in working his audiences up into a state of frenzy. Likewise, "The Mummy," thousands of years old, and a cadaver who walked, talked and invoked mystic spells of the ancient Egyptian gods was a follow-up achievement for Karloff almost as effective as the Monster role which rocketed him to stardom.

But "The Invisible Man" tops these chilly creatures by performing his sinister deeds under the always scary cloak of invisibility. Just as the dark is fear compelling because of the unseen things which might lurk in its inky blackness, a man who can blend his bodily substance and outline into the air, such as "Jack Griffin," the mad super scientist of the H. G. Wells tale, possesses more than human power. It is this power and its graphic effect on the other characters of the screen play which provides "The Invisible Man" with its stunning strangeness. Not in many months has a film caused such a startling sensation as this speculative screen treatise on invisibility, a subject, by the way, which has intrigued man for countless ages.

It is interesting to note that while Hollywood has provided the theatres with these frightening characters, Europe actually conceived them. Victor Hugo, Robert Louis Stevenson, Bram Stoker, Mary Shelley and now H. G. Wells very probably never had Hollywood faintly in mind when they imagined their strange tales.

Claude Rains, a New York Theatre Guild star, plays the unseen protagonist of "The Invisible Man" and already his work in this evidently difficult role has won the praise of the nation's critics. Gloria Stuart, William Harrigan, Dudley Digges, Henry Travers and Una O'Connor head the large and brilliant cast which James Whale *assembled to give life to the Universal* production. Whale directed "Frankenstein."

The Vogue of Gloria Stuart

Amazing Popularity Achieved by Universal Player After Only A Year in Films

(Current Feature)

THE most sought after young lady in Hollywood is a beautiful blonde who has been there only a little over a year!

She is Gloria Stuart, who started off on her screen career with a battle between two studios for her contract and has been keeping producers busy seeking her talents ever since. The ideal American type, Miss Stuart plays with amazing ease the role of a young English girl in H. G. Wells' sensational tale, "The Invisible Man" which Universal has screened and which is now playing at the.........Theatre.

As a matter of fact, although Universal first signed the actress on the well known dotted line, and have seen to it that she has had parts suited to her talents ever since, her first role was at the request of Warner Brothers for "Street of Women" with Kay Francis. The Universal pictures, "The Old Dark House," "Airmail" and "The All American" rocketed the statuesque blonde to great favor with theatregoers and soon the requests for "loan outs" were flooding the offices at Universal City.

Lionel Barrymore wanted her—and finally got her—to play with him in RKO's "Sweepings." Fox clamored for her services to play opposite Raoul Roulien in "It's Great To Be Alive," Paramount presuaded Universal to spare her for the lead opposite James Dunn in "The Girl in 419." Almost daily requests pour in for this talented actress who was first discovered only 18 months ago on the stage of the Pasadena Community Playhouse.

Acting ability alone doesn't account for the unceasing calls for Gloria Stuart, although undoubtedly it is the major factor. There are few actresses on the screen with the graceful charm and air of fine breeding which makes her distinctive—few such thoroughly classic types of beauty, and few such genuine artists. For Gloria Stuart is a deep student of the drama, and has acted in three of the most famous "little theatres" on the Pacific Coast.

In "The Invisible Man" she plays the role of an erratic scientist's sweetheart, who tries to win him back from the invisible world, where his experiments have taken him.

James Whale Demands Perfection

(Advance Feature)

THAT "genius is the rare capacity for taking infinite pains" possibly accounts for the unusual success which James Whale has enjoyed as one of the most distinguished of motion picture directors.

The man who is credited with the startling effectiveness of Universal's sensational production of H. G. Wells' "The Invisible Man," opening a long awaited featured engagement ....at the......... Theatre, has a creed of thoroughness in the production of pictures approached by few cinema masters.

To Whale, who first rocketed to screen recognition with his production of "Journey's End," and later proved his right to eminence with "Waterloo Bridge," "Frankenstein," "The Old Dark House" and "The Kiss Before the Mirror," every picture is a complete study, and a matter of perfection or nothing.

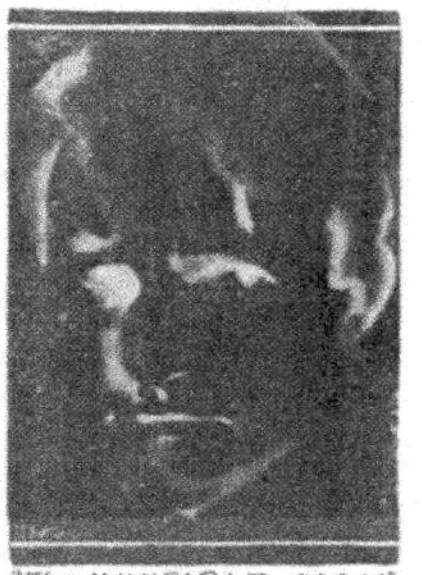

"The INVISIBLE MAN" UNIVERSAL PRODUCTION

Cut "I"

Respected by all those who have acted under him, Whale is a hard taskmaster on the motion picture set. Rehearsals do not cease until timing, dialogue and the mood of the scene are just right no matter how much time or effort is necessary. The British director, who earnestly believes that motion pictures differ from stage plays only in the manner of their pictorial presentation, is a stickler for dramatic excellence, obtained by thorough familiarity with the play and its action.

In screening "The Invisible Man," Whale worked with a theme and locale which was just made for his unusual talents. The tense suspense which is said to characterize the bizarre H. G. Wells story of a mad scientist who made himself invisible and then set about to rule the world with this invincible power, is the type of drama that he has scored in before, and the setting in England, whose people he knows so well, allowed him to devise many authentic and picturesque effects in creating the images which bring the drama to life on the *screen.*

"The Invisible Man," which has created a veritable furore wherever it has been shown, because of its speculative theme and uncanny unseen star, is enacted by a cast of distinguished actors including Claude Rains, William Harrigan, Gloria Stuart, Dudley Digges, Una *O'Connor, Henry Travers* and Forrester Harvey.

Tremendous Possibilities Suggested By Invisibility Idea

(Current Feature)

IT'S quite a trick to find an invisible man. Those who think there's nothing to it should try it some time, or go to the......... Theatre this week where Universal's sensational picturization of H. G. Wells' "Invisible Man," is playing and see what a job can be made out of tracking down a fellow you can't even see.

It wasn't an easy matter to find an invisible man who was at times visible, for that matter. Especially when all the forces of Universal studios were marshalled to prevent even a sly peek at the strangest character of the screen.

However, Claude Rains was apprehended in the visible state and cornered in the magic make-up room at Universal where some of the screen's most uncanny characters, including the grotesque hunchback of "The Hunchback of Notre Dame," the monster of "Frankenstein" and the desiccated relic of "The Mummy" were created. He was not invisible but totally obscured by strange penetrable glasses—accessories to conceal his invisibility, and which when removed would leave nothing.

"Just how does it feel to be an invisible man?"

The uncanny head turned in reply, and there must have been a smile for the wrappings creased ever so faintly.

"Well, it's really my first offense," replied Claude Rains, "but I don't know why I never thought of it before. It's really a marvelous idea. I rather fancy the idea of invisibility, and I may see what can be done about it when this picture is completed. Since I came on this studio lot fresh from the turmoil of New York, life has become one grand sweet song. No one can see me, but I can see everyone. No one can bother me, but I can bother everyone. It's an advantage, you will admit—and I am becoming more and more convinced that as a permanent state it wouldn't be so bad.

"For instance, just imagine how consoling it would be to realize that no matter how crooked your nose, how bowed your legs or how cowlicked your hair, no one could see it. Inferiority complexes, inhibitions, Freudian complexes of all sorts would immediately vanish, and the world would be just about like it was before Pandora tipped over the fatal box. Creditors, could they find you? No. Salesmen, peddlers, unwelcome admirers, nuisances of all sorts—completely baffled. Think of the peace.

"I rather imagine Col. Lindbergh would like to have a treatment for invisibility every now and then—I even know of a few actors who could use a little. You can't stare at a person you can't see. It gives you a tremendous edge on the world."

So the invisible man had a sense of humor! It was rather astounding, especially when such an unholy looking person sat before me submitting to the ministrations of the makeup artist. The odd feeling crept up that this uncanny face might be making a grin, a grin at the person to whom he now talked, and it created a slightly uncomfortable feeling. He was right, an invisible man would have a tremendous edge on the rest of the world. It was time to go. The makeup man had completed his task and a messenger informed Claude Rains that James Whale wanted him on the set for a scene with William Harrigan and Gloria Stuart. It was an important scene where the unseen scientist arrives for a tryst with his visible sweetheart, in the presence of her other visible lover.

The odd interview was over.

"Well, I'll be seeing you!"

"Oh, no you won't!" reminded Claude Rains, the invisible man.

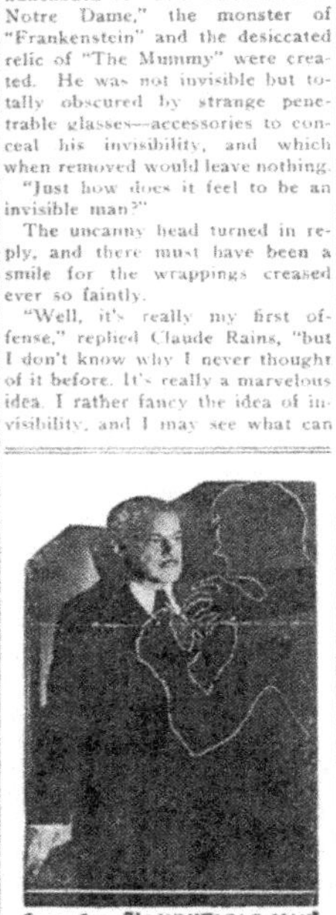

Scene from "The INVISIBLE MAN" UNIVERSAL PRODUCTION

Cut "J"

Scene from "The INVISIBLE MAN" UNIVERSAL PRODUCTION

Cut "K"

Making A Man Invisible

Black Magic, Camouflage and Other Houdinisms Scorned by Clever Director and Cameraman

(Advance Feature)

NOW that Universal has completed the filming of "The Invisible Man," coming ....to the.................Theatre, a studio spokesman—there are always several—explained why a period of more than two years was permitted to elapse between the purchase of the H. G. Wells story and its transfer to the screen.

The problem was how to photograph invisibility. The idea of an invisible man is all very well in a book, but motion-picture characters have to be shown. The technicians were consulted, as is the invariable rule. For once they could do little more than shake their heads, Camera men snorted at the notion and the individuals responsible for the purchase of the story wore a path in the carpet leading to the executive desk.

"Show the presence of the invisible man by spirit wires, moving books, chairs and other articles. Show him by suspending a coat, trousers and hat on a wire. Have a cloud of steam, or mist, or a shroud of something pass before the camera."

There were a few of the suggestions, but the verdict was "too obvious." It might have been done a few years ago, but not today. And so, for two years the problem was discussed while the precious story accumulated a few layers of dust in the vaults, or closets, or filing cabinets, or wherever it is that stories are kept.

But the invisible man has been photographed and the credit must go to James Whale, the director; Charles Edeson, the photographer, and Jack Pierce, the studio makeup experts. After long experiment, they discovered the possibilities of small mirrors, arranged as the magicians employ them in creating optical illusions. The mirrors were tried and the problem was no more.

Claude Rains, who is the picture's invisible man, will be seen walking along, completely dressed and with a hat perched jauntily on what would be a head, if any head were there. On his deathbed his head and shoulders will be visible, but the rest of his body will be merely a dent in the covers. In another scene he will be shown disrobing and, as his clothes fall away, nothing but invisibility will remain.

There will even be some episodes where he will be totally invisible, both to his fellow-players and his audience. On first thought it would seem that this would be more difficult to photograph than the scenes where only part of him is invisible. The naive question was put to Universal's oracle, who replied:

"Oh, no. Whenever he was totally invisible, the scenes were made without him. Mr. Rains simply had a day off."

Then, with a chuckle, the spokesman drew a few mirrors from his pocket and faded away.

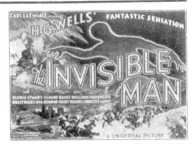

SHOWMANSHIP!

MADE BY THE MEN
WHO MADE "FRANKENSTEIN"
AS BIG A MYSTERY-THRILLER AS
"FRANKENSTEIN" WAS A SHOCKER!

"THE INVIS

With — CLAUDE RAINS · WILLIAM HARRIGAN ·
DIRECTED BY JAMES WHALE

FROM THE NO

WORLD TERRORIZED BY MAD SCIENTIST! $50,00

INVISIBLE DRIVER BALLYHOO

LOOKOUT FOR
"THE INVISIBLE MAN"
YOU CAN SEE HIM
ONLY AT THE
RIALTO THEATRE

Start working on this "driverless" stunt a couple of weeks ahead to give your local auto mechanic time to fix up the car. The type of automobile model shown in the illustration is best for the purpose. The mechanic simply extends the hood, puts the windshield further back, and provides a fake dashboard. In the space thus gained, an operator can be concealed. By raising the fake hood a few inches above the other, the driver can get an ample view of the street. Placard the car as shown.

If it is possible to get a radio-operated car locally, by all means use it. A few such automobiles are available round the country. In either case, it is suggested that you work with local auto agencies in arranging the stunt as it is an equally sensational stunt for the car manufacturer entering into it. You may be able to promote the whole ballyhoo in this way.

DAY AND NIGHT BALLYHOO

Here's a sidewalk ballyhoo stunt that will be a flash day or night. Rig up a costume for your man as indicated by the sketch—build the shoulders extra high to conceal his head. Build a fake head out of a wire framework and cover this with gauze bandages. Inside the framework, have a red bulb operated by a flashlight battery. The ballyhoo man can turn this off and on, making the head glow in an eerie manner. If you put this man in evening clothes, you can also have him illuminate his shirt-front with the title of the picture, using a stencil and concealed light for the purpose.

SET OF TEASER SNIPES

You'll want to sell your title far in advance and here is a cracker-jack way to do it! Use the set of three snipes shown below on this picture—it deserves a big advance—and this is how to get it cheaply! Ten days in advance, get out these curiously-provoking snipes—then follow up with your regular billing campaign. The snipes are available at your local Universal Exchange. The size is 13" x 25". Imposing space is provided at the bottom of each. The price is low: ONLY 18c. A SET.

H.G. WELLS' FANTASTIC SENSATION
"THE INVISIBLE MAN" IS COMING!

LOCK YOUR DOORS!
BOLT YOUR WINDOWS!
PULL DOWN YOUR SHADES!
"THE INVISIBLE MAN" IS HEADED THIS WAY!

$50,000.00 REWARD!
offered for the capture of
"THE INVISIBLE MAN"
CATCH HIM IF YOU CAN!

MANY "INVISIBLE" TIE-UPS

Look around locally for tie-ups you can make on the "invisible" angle. Many types of merchandise can be tied up with some such general line as: Quality is invisible—but you get only the best when you shop at Blank's. In addition there are so many things which have a direct hookup with the "invisible" angle. For example: Invisible Hair Nets, Invisible Mending, Invisible Suspenders, Invisible Hair Lotion, Built-in Invisible Quality, etc. Get all these tied up with your showing of "The Invisible Man."

STREET STENCIL

LOOKOUT FOR "THE INVISIBLE MAN"

The street stencil is especially appropriate for "The Invisible Man" since it is through his footprints in the snow that he is traced. Put a trail of these footprints all over town. A stencil as illustrated. Size 15" x 24". PRICE $1.00. Order direct from
J. TORCH, 145 West 14th St., N. Y. C.

USE A VENTRILOQUIST

Either an amateur or professional ventriloquist can be hired during the showing of "The Invisible Man" to create extra word-of-mouth advertising about the picture. His job would be to walk about town and throw his voice into houses, empty automobiles, doorways, etc. He can say something to the effect: Beware! Beware! I am "The Invisible Man"—You cannot see me unless you go to the Rialto Theatre to-day!

TRY A SCRIM STUNT

A scrim can be used in your shadow-box or any dark spot in the theatre for a fine effect. On the scrim itself paint—Watch for "The Invisible Man"—Here (playdates). Behind the scrim have a head cut-out of the character from one of the posters. Use a dimmer behind the scrim. As it slowly lights up, the cut-out becomes visible; as it slowly goes out, the figure disappears!

WEIRDLY-LIT TRANSPARENT HEAD WILL DRAW ALL EYES!

Make your front suggest the many angles of this thriller—its fantastic character and terrific entertainment value! The sketch suggests how this can be done! On your marquee, a cut-out of the 24-sheet will strike the keynote. On either side of your lobby, the 3-sheet art will carry out a startling effect. For the box-office, use a display of stills showing other weird characters in screen history and top it off with catchlines saying that "The Invisible Man" surpasses them all. For this purpose, use pictures of "Dracula"—"The Mummy"—"Quasimodo"—"The Phantom" and "Frankenstein!" Over the box-office, build up a "face" of "The Invisible Man." Do this by winding light gauze bandages around a wire framework. Add a pair of dark glasses for extra effect. Within the wire have hooked up various colored electric lights worked with a dimmer so that red, green and blue light alternately shines through the bandages. These bandages should be of a proper transparency for the purpose and the light should not be too strong—use frosted bulbs. Surround the "face" with a blue and green neon tube and the title as indicated. Lit will give an eerie effect. Spot rough-lettered hanging signs under the marquee. Fix up shelves out front for a display of chemical retorts, mortar and pestle, test-tubes, etc. Also use an electrical spark-gap and similar equipment to attract attention and for it atmospheric suggestion.

The sidewalks of the lobby can be decorated with a panorama scene showing "The Invisible Man" stalking over the city while crowds flee in terror. Also use the teaser snipes or a sign carrying similar copy.

SIX-SHEET

THREE-SHEET

At Left:
Suggestions
for Two
Poster
Cut-outs.
Also note
"24" over
Marquee!

INVISIBLE MAN ANSWERS QUESTIONS IN LOBBY

Place a huge chair in the lobby with weird green and red spot lights playing on it—a rope in front to keep people at a distance—and sign reading as shown on sketch. The question and answer gag is worked, of course, with a two-way radio connection. Someone concealed in the Manager's Office or Ticket Booth, who can see the inquirers, can answer their questions.

ASK HIM the Question HE will Answer YOU
See HG WELLS' fantastic sensation
The INVISIBLE MAN

RADIO FAN'S CONTEST

Tie-up your local radio station on a unique stunt to be called "The Invisible Man" Contest. This is to be based on the voices of the invisible men who announce and entertain over the air—listeners are to be asked how many of them they can identify only by their voices. The radio station can arrange a program on which a number of well known personalities will appear—they will identify themselves by number but their names will not be announced. The fans submitting the best guesses as to the identities of these invisible men will receive passes to see "The Invisible Man."

FILL IN THE FACE OF "THE INVISIBLE MAN"

A sure-fire stunt that never fails to produce results is the drawing contest. Plant the mat reproduced here with your local paper and ask readers to fill in the face of "The Invisible Man." (This is Exploitation Service Mat 1M No. 1, available in 1 or 2 col. size from your local exchange.) The contest is so simple that almost anyone can draw a face and enter the competition. Of course, the face sketched is to be the imaginative conception of the contestant. Your local paper should publish publicity about the picture to exploit the contest and also reproduce some of the best drawings submitted. Art merchandise promoted from local stores and passes to "The Invisible Man" can be prizes. Make up cards carrying groups of sketches submitted for exhibition in various store windows.

Name
Address

LUMINOUS PAINT

The idea of using phosphorescent paint as a stunt on this picture will occur to many showmen. If you wish to use it, pick a weird-looking head of "The Invisible Man" like the one reproduced on the 1-sheet and outline with luminous paint. Use this on the back wall of your theatre or in any other dark spot around the house. Have a strong light regulated by a slow flasher directed at the picture. When the light is on, only the vague outlines of the face will be seen. When the light is off, the face only will be seen glowing with an eerie luminosity.

This same idea can be used as an advance plug from your stage by painting a black drop in the manner indicated above.

MAGIC MI

CONCEAL A M

You can easily have made a mirror which permits someone concealed behind it to look through but does not permit anyone in the similar visibility. Merely an optical illusion with a large glass, coating it with leaf, silver leaf or quicksilver, and painting in black. When this is done it will be possible to conceal a man behind the mirror as described and have him notify your patrons by describing and talking to them whenever they approach the glass. It is best that this be done with a microphone hookup somewhere behind the mirror is not. Caption the looking glass accordingly.

If you do not want to use the man behind the mirror, use a cut-out of one of the posters with a flash so it will be seen whenever the light is on.

APPARIT

The magic stunt of making for the use of a series of mirrors in your lobby or in a prominent gician who will work this out

INVISIBLE INK

There are many invisible ink trick throw-aways for this picture are rubbed, others when they are moistened in water.

If your local printers cannot touch with C. M. DEVITAL, Room 900, who can prepare at a cost of $20 per thousand.

FOUR GOO

The title of this attractive contest. Here are several:

1. HOW WOULD YO
Give your newspaper ible Man" is coming to the ing character cannot be see who has stumbled on a great terror. The police offer a How would YOU act about Man?" In the story, some his presence is suspected—What would you suggest? awarded for the best answers.

2. What Would You Do the local paper ask its read or interesting answers and

3. "The Invisible Man" charity work, behind mass meets activities but shuns p of such men they know. YO going out and doing so who

4. You supposedly send and offer $1000 For Identif ence and simple but great the paper offers $1000 to the shoulder and says I'm invisible, this is, of course, to land space locally. The

SEE INSID
FOR BIG
HANGER,
OTHER

INVISIBLE MAN"

INS · WILLIAM HARRIGAN · GLORIA STUART · DUDLEY DIGGES · UNA O'CONNOR

FROM THE NOVEL BY H. G. WELLS   SCREENPLAY BY R. C. SHERRIFF

CIENTIST! $50,000 REWARD FOR HIS CAPTURE!

ANSPARENT
ALL EYES !

...es in this thriller—its fan...
...vidow! The sketch suggests...
...cutout of the 24-sheet will...
...lobby, the 3-sheet art will...
...mirce, in a display of still...
...frames and for it off with...
...he brilliance item all. For this...
..."Quasimodo—
...to the box-office, build up a...
...winding light-dance bandage...
...fully changes for extra effect...
...colored electric lights worked...
...the light alternately shine...
...until in a proper transport...
...for dramatic use frosted...
...red over neon tube and the...
...ect. Spot complicated hung...
...lays translucent material to...
...here, etc. Also has an electrical...
...of attention and for it atmo...

...ted with a panorama scene...
...of the city which crowds then...
...very carrying similar copy.

At Left:
Suggestions
for Two
Poster
Cut-outs.
Also note
"24" over
Marquee !

...LL
...ISIBLE MAN

SHEET

INVISIBLE MAN

H. G. WELLS' FANTASTIC SENSATION
"THE INVISIBLE MAN"
YEAR'S BIG MYSTERY THRILLER

ANSWERS
LOBBY

The INVISIBLE MAN

See
The
Invisible
Man
on the
Screen
next
Week

...LL
ISIBLE MAN

MAGIC MIRROR STUNTS

CONCEAL A MAN BEHIND MIRROR

You can easily have made up for you a "mirror" which permits someone concealed behind it to look through but does not permit anyone in front of it similar visibility. Merely an ordinary reflection will be seen. This is done by taking a large glass, coating it with gold leaf, silver leaf or quicksilver, then backing it with another glass, instead of painting it black. When this is done, it will be possible to conceal a man behind the mirror as described and he can mystify your patrons by describing them and talking to them whenever they pass the glass. It is best that this be done with a microphone hookup so his presence behind the mirror is not suspected. Caption the looking glass as indicated. If you do not want to use a man behind the mirror, use a cutout head from one of the posters with a flasher light—it will be seen whenever the light goes on.

The
INVISIBLE
MAN
is looking
at you

LISTEN TO WHAT HE
HAS TO SAY

APPARITION STUNT

The magic stunt of making a man appear and disappear in a mirror (by the use of a series of mirrors), can be worked to good advantage in your lobby or in a prominent store window. Consult a local magician who will work this out for you.

INVISIBLE INK THROWAWAYS

There are many invisible inks that can be put to good use on throwaways rubbed, others when they are heated, and some when they are moistened in water.

If your local printers cannot prepare this material for you get in touch with C. M. DEVITALIS, 505 Fifth Avenue, New York City, Room 900, who can prepare such throwaways on a sheet, size 7x9, at a cost of $20 per thousand.

FOUR GOOD CONTESTS

The title of this attraction makes it a natural for newspaper contests. Here are several suggestions for contest titles and usage:

1. HOW WOULD YOU CATCH "THE INVISIBLE MAN?" Give your newspaper copy along the following line: "The Invisible Man" is coming to the Rialto Theatre and in this picture the leading character cannot be seen—he is actually invisible, a mad scientist who has stumbled on a great secret and tries to create a reign of terror. The police offer gigantic rewards for his capture, $50,000. How would YOU go about trapping and catching "The Invisible Man?" In the story, someone suggests throwing ink on him when his presence is suspected—what fantastic plans are brought forward. What would you suggest? Prizes to see "The Invisible Man" will be voted for the best answers to this problem.

2. What Would You Do If You Were "The Invisible Man?" Have the local paper ask its readers this question. It permits of a variety of interesting answers and should get a big response.

3. "The Invisible Man" Who Is He? In business or politics, in charity work, behind many big people is an invisible man who directs activities but stays publicly. Ask readers of the paper to write in who's who they know. Or the gag—a newspaper feature, a reporter going out and digging up the material himself.

4. You suppposedly send out an "invisible" man to roam the streets and offer $1000 for identifying "The Invisible Man." This is a gag stunt and sounds but great stuff for the columnists. The idea is that the paper offers $1000 to anyone who can slap "The Invisible Man" on the shoulder and say: "You are 'The Invisible Man.'" Since he is invisible this is, of course, impossible. A humorous stunt and it ought to land space locally. The money? Easy that you say "invisible."

FACE OF
E MAN"

PAINT

...there phosphorescent
...paint on the picture will
...no luminescent. It your story
...tells a weird-looking dead
...looking Man" like the one
...on the 3-sheet and outline
...his paint. Use this on the
...er or theatre, or in any
...gem around the house.
...ting light regulated by a
...placed at the picture.
...off it on, only the title
...gene outlines of the Invis-
...ible Man, the head is off,
...en will be seen glowing
...he luminescent.

...idea can be used as an
...will be announced on page 1
... also shown in the manu...

SEE INSIDE BACK COVER
FOR BIG ROTO HERALD,
HANGER, STREAMER AND
OTHER ACCESSORIES

H. G. WELLS BOOK TIE-UP

GROSSET & DUNLAP 75c PHOTOPLAY EDITION

H. G. Wells is today one of the world's most famous authors, and his works hold a selling books. Libraries, both public and private, book stores, book departments— all should be easy to tie-up with this picture on the basis of the reputation of its author. The list of his books would be too long to give here, but the tie-up can be arranged with any which are in stock and special emphasis put on the fact that his greatest thriller "The Invisible Man" is now published in a special photoplay edition for 75c and can be seen as a picture. A few of the titles for which H. G. Wells is famous may be helpful: "Tono Bungay," "Mr. Britling Sees It Through," "Kipps," "The Sleeper Awakes," "Food of the Gods," "A Modern Utopia," "The First Men In The Moon" and "The Outline of History."

Use one of the single-column ad cuts to print up a bookmark which can be distributed by bookdealers. List the works mentioned above and the dealers name on one side and bill the picture and your theatre on the reverse. For further information, communicate direct with publishers of "The Invisible Man."

GROSSET & DUNLAP, 1140 Broadway, New York City

PLANT THIS IN NEWSPAPER

CAN YOU FIND "THE INVISIBLE MAN?"
DARKEN IN DOTTED SECTIONS

From this mass, now make illustrated at right in your local newspaper! It is not a picture. It is not necessary to cut the pieces apart. Just tell readers to take a pencil and black in the little dotted sections. When they are all blacked in, "The Invisible Man" will appear. A great feature for a children's page or magazine section! Exploitation Service Mat (M) No. 2 is available in 2-col. width (order from your exchange).

ROCKING CHAIR STUNT

This stunt because of its spookiness, will get lots of interest and attention. It consists simply of a rocking chair placed in one corner of your lobby where a concealed wire can be connected to it, merely leading to an oscillating fan motor which will put the chair slowly in the appearance of rocking mysteriously. A book can be suspended over the chair at the height where it would be held for reading—the pages wires being used for the purpose. Use a weird light over the display and sign around it reading: BEWARE! HE'S HERE! YOU CANNOT SEE HIM! HE'S INVISIBLE! THE INVISIBLE MAN—FOR THE THRILL OF YOUR LIFE—SEE HIM ON THE SCREEN! H. G. WELLS' FANTASTIC SENSATION.

If you want to elaborate on this stunt, you can have a table in a dark corner, with the dishes dancing around, pulled on wires, or you can use a magnet underneath, move ideas and have small articles rolling around on a table.

FANTASTIC MYSTERY AND SUPER-THRILLS SOLD IN THESE STARTLING, COLORFUL POSTERS!

B-I-G!
HERE'S
YOUR
GIANT
ACTION
PACKED
24
SHEET!

24 SHEET—VIOLET AND PALE GREEN BACKGROUND—BLUE AND RED EXPLO-SION—GREEN VISION—BLACK AND WHITE TITLE—YELLOW OUTLINE—PINK FOREGROUND—FIGURES IN BLUE AND BLACK.

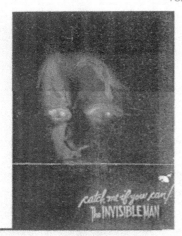

ONE SHEET "A"

ONE SHEET "B"

SIX SHEET

THREE SHEET "C"

SELL IT LIKE A ROAD SHOW!

IMPRINT SPACE

WINDOW CARD

THREE SHEET "D"

192

About the Author

Gregory William Mank won acclaim in 1981 for his first book, *It's Alive! The Classic Cinema Saga of Frankenstein*. Subsequently he authored the published books: *The Hollywood Hissables*; *Karloff and Lugosi: The Story of a Haunting Collaboration*; *Hollywood Cauldron*; *Hollywood's Maddest Doctors*; *Women in Horror Films, 1930s*; *Women in Horror Films, 1940s;* and *Bela Lugosi and Boris Karloff: The Expanded Story of a Haunting Collaboration,* for which he won a Rondo Award for Best Book of 2009, as well as a Rondo for Writer of the Year. He has written the production histories for 12 of the previous MagicImage books, is co-author of *Dwight Frye's Last Laugh* (with James T. Coughlin and Dwight D. Frye) and *Hollywood's Hellfire Club* (with Charles Heard and Bill Nelson), and has written many magazine articles. He wrote and recorded the audio commentaries for the DVD releases of *Abbott and Costello Meet Frankenstein*, *Dr. Jekyll and Mr. Hyde*, *Cat People*, *The Curse of the Cat People*, *The Mask of Fu Manchu*, *Chandu the Magician*, *The Mayor of Hell*, *The Walking Dead*, and *Island of Lost Souls*. He has appeared on the TV shows *E! Mysteries and Scandals*, *Entertainment Tonight*, and *Rivals*, and on many documentaries on film history. A graduate of Johns Hopkins University and Mount Saint Mary's College, MD, he also has enjoyed a career in education and in theatre. His upcoming book is *The Very Witching Time of Night: Twists and Tangents in Classic Horror*. Greg lives with his wife Barbara in Delta, Pennsylvania. Visit his website, www.gregorymank.com.

"I've Just Heard The Invisible Man!"
Music and Monsters in Universal's Early Horror Period
By Randall D. Larson

During the early years of Universal Pictures' monster movies, as the studio first introduced the creatures which would become icons of the studio's classic monster pantheon in years to come, the use of music was a tentative component of Hollywood cinema. Musical accompaniment had been a large part of the silent films of the 1920s, initially to mask the sound of noisy film projectors but later, especially in films like Universal's own PHANTOM OF THE OPERA (1925) and in German expressionist films like NOSFERATU (1922) and METROPOLIS (1927), broadly orchestrated scores were composed to accompany and augment the drama depicted on the screen – and the horrors. As early as Edison's 1910 version of FRANKENSTEIN, filmmakers realized the value of music in heightening an audience's emotional reaction to the misshapen and misanthropic creatures who silently went bump in the night on their movie screens.

But by the time sound came into the movies, dramatic film music nearly met an early grave. Whereas in silent films, music was used to avoid the complete absence of sound, filmmakers in the blossoming 1930s' era of talking films felt that music needed a source – a radio, a café band, a piano player – shown on seen to justify its presence, and that the focus should be on the novelty of sound effects and spoken dialog to enthrall audiences.

Universal's inaugural fearsome foursome of movie monsters – 1931's DRACULA and FRANKENSTEIN, 1932's THE MUMMY, and 1933's THE INVISIBLE MAN (the fifth and sixth members of the studio's classic predatory pack would come along in the following decades with 1941'sTHE WOLF MAN and 1954's CREATURE FROM THE BLACK LAGOON) – contained little music. Of this formative quartet, the first two captured music only to announce their startings and celebrate their closings. DRACULA made use of the mysterious and exotic strains of Tchaikovsky's ballet Swan Lake (opening scene) under its beginning credits (as did 1932's THE MUMMY and MURDERS IN THE RUE MORGUE), while Universal's music director David Broekman engaged composer Bernhard Kaun to create the electrifying footsteps-like monster chords that thundered beneath the opening titles of FRANKENSTEIN (the first example of original music composition in a universal sound horror film).

No other music is used for dramatic effect in either film (perhaps reflective of the theatrical stage versions of the classic tales that both pictures were adapted from).

With Kaun's inspired and influential monster music relegated only to the first minute of FRANKENSTEIN, Karl Freud's THE MUMMY contained some 10 minutes of original music composed by James Dietrich, supplemented by another ten minutes of library music culled from earlier Universal films. While THE MUMMY (which was also Universal's wholly original monster movie) showed what music could offer these films (1933's DESTINATION UNKNOWN also had a relatively lengthy score, composed by W. Franke Harling, but it mostly consisted of paraphrases of Liszt and Wagner), fully functional dramatic film scores were still a few years away. It would take the large-scaled scores of Franz Waxman for THE BRIDE OF FRANKENSTEIN and Karl Hajos for THE WEREWOLF OF LONDON (both 1935) – along with Max Steiner's pivotal score for 1933's KING KONG over at RKO – to really establish the value of music as an important component of filmic storytelling.

Directed by FRANKENSTEIN's James Whale, THE INVISIBLE MAN followed fashion, containing a brief 90-seconds of main title music but an extended underscore during its finale. The music was original material composed for the film by Heinz Roemheld, a former concert pianist and conductor who had impressed Universal's president Carl Laemmle with his musical accompaniment to showings of Lon Chaney's PHANTOM OF THE OPERA in 1925. Laemlle brought Roemheld in as a staff composer in 1929; the following year Roemheld succeeded David Broekman as head of the studio's music department. He was let go in 1931 and spent two years seeking a living as a piano instructor and hotel mezzanine pianist in Washington D.C. before returning to Hollywood in 1933 and being rehired by Universal to score THE INVISIBLE MAN.

Despite the expressive example set by Dietrich and Freund in THE MUMMY and its overall 20-minutes of music, Whale's THE INVISIBLE MAN contains a sparse but effective eight minutes of original music. The first cue is heard following the introductory Universal Studios "airplane passing globe" logo, a thundering soundscape is introduced with blaring brass and crashing cymbal as the first few title cards float past the viewer onto the screen. A portentous five-note motif is introduced, three stridently ascending notes, following by a flourishing descent/ascent in the final two notes that serve to punctuate the preceding melody. Significantly, the motif contains a tritone, a harmonic and melodic dissonance signified by a musical interval or gap between two notes played in succession or simultaneously; in early musical history the tritone has been branded as "The Devil's Interval" by medieval musicians who found its tonality "evil," and thus its use in horror films such as this one has been especially favored.

The five-note motif is repeated from the brass over a flurry of vibrato strings as the music continues. When the film's title appears on screen, the music is joined by the sound effects of a snowy windstorm, which anticipates the opening scene showing Jack Griffin, head thoroughly bandaged, trudging through a road likewise masked, by snow, during a blizzard. In addition to the five-note motif, another distinct musical motif (heard between the title card and the cast and crew credits) captures a slightly whimsical sensibility. A syncopated rhythm is evident within the music, capturing something of the sense of a tango, as the Invisible Man stealthily makes his way through the snow towards the lighted inn.

As film music historian William H. Rosar has noted in his essay "Music for the Monsters," published in the final issue of The Quarterly Journal of the Library of Congress (Fall, 1983), "Roemheld sought to capture the atmosphere of falling snow in his music with orchestral effects such as woodwind runs suggesting snow flurries..." Rosar added that, during the film's opening credits, "the music seems so orchestrated and timed as to blend and synchronize with a superimposed image of snow blowing and the periodic sound of a snow blizzard."

The opening music lasts a scant minute and a half, resolving with a solo violin decrescendo that segues into a piano heard from within "The Lion's Head" Inn – Griffin's destination. The music playing from the piano is a jaunty version of the old Scottish song "Annie Laurie." Whale finds room for a site gag when the man "playing" the piano turns to the crowd to accept their applause only to have the next song begin without him playing – revealing it to be a player piano (that second song is John Philip Sousa's 1888 "Ben Bolt" march).

In addition to background source music such as this, Whale's INVISIBLE MAN, like Tod Browning's DRACULA before it, incorporates sporadic moments of source music that serve a simultaneous functional purpose to heighten drama. For example, the early sequence where the invisible Griffin steals in and confronts his former colleague Kemp in the latter's study is given a tense air via source music heard from Kemp's radio. The tune being played is the sentimental favorite, "Hearts and Flowers." As Rudy Behlmer has explained in his DVD commentary track, the piece is performed in an old-fashioned-like manner on what sounds like an upright piano. "Presumably, this is an inside joke put in by a music editor some years later to replace the music used for the initial release of the film, that music being 'La Rosita,' a 1923 composition that became a semi-standard," Behlmer said. "The substitution probably stemmed from a music clearance situation."

There are moments in Roemheld's music that seem to echo the not always subtle element of humor within the film. "It has a rather satirical quality – an impish mock-serious character – perhaps reflecting these elements in the film as well as Roemheld's own proclivity for musical humor," Rosar pointed out.

THE INVISIBLE MAN is bookended by a pair of snow sequences, both heralded by music. In contrast with the brevity of the main title music, the film's finale and end credits contain a comparatively lengthy amount of music that accompanies another snowstorm, in which the falling snow betrays Griffin's invisibility and results in his being shot by police. In these concluding sequences, Roemheld's music is heard almost continuously for nearly seven minutes, beginning after the death of Kemp as the scene shifts (at 1:04:14) to a planning meeting at police headquarters through the reappearance of the visible Griffin and his demise in the hospital bed (ending at 1:11:22). These scenes are actually comprised of 21 individual cues, most lasting just over a minute, but overlapped in the picture to form a continual composition. Variations of Roemheld's two primary motifs as well as a number of incidental orchestral figures underline the activities of police when Griffin is discovered trapped in a barn.

"Roemheld's development of these two motifs is ingenious and effective; quasi-Wagnerian horn lines are interwoven with sparse, impressionistic woodwind and pizzicato string effects, constantly punctuated with Debussyan major ninth chords, which he used like musical exclamation points," explained Rosar. "At certain spots the music accompanying the Invisible Man's stealthy movements or presence seems to allude, tongue in cheek, to old fashioned villain music used in silent films."

When Griffin is smoked out of the burning barn in which he is hiding, his footsteps appear in the snow, musically accompanied by a series of descending arpeggios from a bassoon, which is overcome by the sound of a gunshot, and then the imprint of Griffin's body collapses the fresh snow as he falls, shot by a policeman. The downward footsteps of the bassoon seem to suggest Griffin's final march toward imminent oblivion – a morose musical "Dead Man Walking" dirge – punctuated by a sudden discord of vibrato strings and moaning horns, as sympathetic intonations of solo piano and violin humanize the event as even the police reflect sorrow at what they have had to do.

After a sequence of incidental violin figures as Griffin says goodbye to his girl, Flora, as he lies dying in the hospital bed, a series of string figures of increasing urgency and velocity attend to his visual reappearance (for the first time in the film), culminating in a final statement of the main five-note theme, which repeats and then resolves with a humble flourish as the camera pulls away from the dead Griffin, now a Visible Man, and the picture fades to black. The concluding music is reprised briefly as the Universal logo reappears and the cast list scrolls up and then fades out.

The film's use of music throughout its final seven minutes is particularly effective in both providing progressive musical energy for the story's resolution as well as reinforcing the use of thematic motifs to signify, in the leitmotif manner of Richard Wagner, specific characters or attributes in the film's story. Roemheld's primary five-note motif suggests Griffin's menace and growing madness under his chemical change into the Invisible Man, while the secondary, almost satirical motif, suggest the film's often whimsical presentation. The jaunty character of the latter motif also seems to portend Griffin's hysterical laughter as he reveals himself to the people in the inn and then parades invisibly down the snowy street, mischievously terrorizing the populace as he flees.

Roemheld's music from THE INVISIBLE MAN found a happy home in later Universal movies. Recycling music from earlier films (housed in a studio music library in the interim) was a common practice at all the studios during the 1930s (as it would in the succeeding two decades), and thus the music from THE INVISIBLE MAN is heard in later Universal films. Roemheld supplemented Karl Hajos' original score to THE WEREWOLF OF LONDON with about 13 minutes of library music, culled from THE INVISIBLE MAN and 1934's THE BLACK CAT, and Roemheld's INVISIBLE MAN music became the signature musical motto used throughout Universal's FLASH GORDON and BUCK ROGERS serials during the 1930s. In an online essay on the FLASH GORDON serials, write Tom Aldridge noted that Roemheld's INVISIBLE MAN theme "accompanies every chapter foreword in FLASH GORDON'S TRIP TO MARS and the majority of them in BUCK ROGERS, and also is typically interjected as a rocket ship or stratosled takes off."

Roemheld went on to contribute music to hundreds of films during his three-decade Hollywood career. He's credited with more than 600 films, although most of these consisted of re-used library music and uncredited staff music contributions. He died in 1985. Roemheld never received the kind of recognition that other influential composers of the era did, but his original work in early-talking-era films such as the Universal monster films is extremely significant in these seminal, evolving years motion picture music. Roemheld shared an Academy Award with Ray Heindorf for YANKEE DOODLE DANDY (1942), the music of which was largely adapted from the work of its biographical subject, George M. Cohan.

Long-time films music journalist Randall D. Larson currently writes a film music column for buysoundtrax. com and is the author of more than a hundred soundtrack album commentaries and several books on film music, including *Musique Fantastique: 100 Years of Science Fiction, Fantasy & Horror Film Music* (www.musiquefantastique.com).

CPSIA information can be obtained
at www.ICGtesting.com
Printed in the USA
BVHW010943160619

550991BV00012B/14/P